Darkness By Cursed

A Hexcraft Collection

PATRICK THOMAS

PADWOLF PUBLISHING INC.
WWW.PADWOLF.COM
www.facebook.com/Padwolf

WWW.PATTHOMAS.NET
WWW.MURPHYS-LORE.COM
www.facebook.com/PatrickThomasAuthor

BY DARKNESS CURSED
a Hexcraft™ collection
© 2017 Patrick Thomas

A MOTHER'S TEARS and HARSH CHORDS were originally published in the limited edition HEXCRAFT: CURSE THE NIGHT

CHANNELING XIPE TOTEC was originally published in
TV GODS edited by Jeff Young

THE HAND THAT ROCKS THE GRAVE was originally published in
EMPTY GRAVES

VAMPYRE UNDER GLASS was originally published in NIGHTCAPS

DARKLY REFLECTED was originally published in
Hellfire Lounge # 4: Reflections of Evil edited by R. Allen Leider

Book edited by John L. French

Cover Art by Patrick Thomas and Roy Mauritsen

Cover Design by Roy Mauritsen

Hex, Plasma, Bulfinche's Pub, Murphy's Lore, Hell's Detective, Terrorbelle, Graveyard Angel, and all related characters are © & TM Patrick Thomas

10-digit ISBN 1-890096-71-7, 13 digit ISBN 978-1-890096-71-7
Printed in the USA
First Printing

"What will you do if I turn you down, Alice?" I asked.

"How did you know my name?" she asked, showing signs of worry for the first time.

"I know things. Well?"

"You can't turn me down. I have you in the pentagram, I know your true name. You have to do what I say or else you are going to be trapped in there. Forever."

"I see," I said, with the slightest hint of humor. "Actually, the proper term is a pentacle. Would you really do that to me?"

She thought about if for a minute, trying to act Dirty Harry tough. Alice didn't have it in her. She shook her head no.

"Good," I said, "Because you do not know my true name, only my taken name," Everyone has at least three types of names. The ones you are given, the ones you take and the one true name that defines your essence. A true name gives power over that individual. Very few people even know their own true name. I never bothered to learn mine because, if I know it, sooner or later someone else is bound to get it from me. It is a classic blunder. Safer all around to live in ignorant bliss. "This type of pentacle only works on demons, spirits, and gods. It has no effect on people," I said as I stepped out of the chalk outline. It almost gave her a heart attack.

"Oh, my God!" she shouted, backing away from me in abject terror.

"You should be more careful. If you had summoned a demon, you wouldn't have held it. The wax from your candles washed away your chalk lines in two places. You would have been carried off to one of the circles of Hell by now," I lectured. "Don't worry. I won't hurt you. Why don't you sit down?"

Alice took my suggestion. I sat as best I could without revealing my inner self, so to speak.

"Will you help me?" she pleaded.

"Yes," I said. It was what I did, after all. Most of the powers that be looked at humanity as commodities, not people. I was one of the few who could stand up to the powers and walk away. Besides, I was a sucker for the little guy.

"Do you know anything about vampyres?"

OTHER BOOKS BY PATRICK THOMAS

THE MURPHY'S LORE™ SERIES
TALES FROM BULFINCHE'S PUB
FOOLS' DAY: *A Tale From Bulfinche's Pub*
THROUGH THE DRINKING GLASS: *Tales From Bulfinche's Pub*
SHADOW OF THE WOLF: *A Tale From Bulfinche's Pub*
REDEMPTION ROAD
BARTENDER OF THE GODS: *Tales From Bulfinche's Pub*

THE MURPHY'S LORE AFTER HOURS™ UNIVERSE
NIGHTCAPS - *AFTER HOURS Vol. 1*
EMPTY GRAVES - *AFTER HOURS Vol. 2*
FAIRY WITH A GUN: *The Collected Terrorbelle™*
FAIRY RIDES THE LIGHTNING: *a Terrorbelle™ novel*
DEAD TO RITES: *The DMA Casefiles of Agent Karver™*
LORE & DYSORDER: *The Hell's Detective™ Mysteries*
BY DARKNESS CURSED: *a Hexcraft™ collection*
BY INVOCATION ONLY: *a Hexcraft™ novel*
GREATEST HITS: *a Soul For Hire™ collection*

MURPHY'S LORE STARTENDERS™
STARTENDERS
CONSTELLATION PRIZE

MURPHY'S LORE AFTER HOURS Books by Patrick Thomas & John L. French
RITES OF PASSAGE: *A DMA Casefile of Agent Karver and Detective Bianca Jones*
BULLETS & BRIMSTONE a Mystic Investigators™ book
featuring Hell's Detective & Bianca Jones
FROM THE SHADOWS a Mystic Investigators™ book
featuring The Nightmare, Nemesis & The Pink Reaper™

Other Mystic Investigators™ books
MYSTIC INVESTIGATORS
ONCE MORE UPON A TIME *by Patrick Thomas & Diane Raetz*

OTHER BOOKS
AS THE GEARS TURN: Takes of Steamworld
NEW BLOOD edited by Diane Raetz & Patrick Thomas

DEAR CTHULHU™ Series
HAVE A DARK DAY
GOOD ADVICE FOR BAD PEOPLE
CTHULHU KNOWS BEST
WHAT WOULD CTHULHU DO?

THE JACK GARDNER MYSTERIES
THE ASSASSINS' BALL

For Diane
who inspired Hex's curse

Contents

A MOTHER'S TEARS

It had been a long night and the sun couldn't rise soon enough to suit me. Physically exhausted, not even a scalding shower was able to revitalize me completely. At least the soap and water was succeeding in getting the blood off. Luckily, none of it was mine. Most of the crimson did not even belong to the people whose veins it came spurting out of. Damn blood junkies.

Getting a few hours of sleep was all I could think about. In my quest for slumber, I completely forgot to reset my wards. That kind of sloppy gets you dead in my business. I only realized my lapse when I heard my name whispered on the ether winds.

"Crap," I said. I had two choices. I could reset the ward, probably too late to do me any good, or I could grab a towel. I went for the towel and wrapped it around my waist as I heard my name the second time. The voice was that of a stranger, a woman. Her summoning had major amounts of raw emotion behind it, but not much skill. Whoever she was, her timing was horrible. I resigned myself to my fate as I heard my name the third and final time. My body slid across time and space.

Disorientation always takes hold after a body slide. It's one of the reasons why it's so dangerous. The slider is usually helpless for minutes after arrival. I was better than most. I got my bearings in a few seconds.

I stood in the center of a poorly drawn pentacle, a candle burning on each of its five corners. A woman sat in front of me with her legs crossed and her bloodshot eyes wide in awe.

"Why do people always call when you're in the shower?" I asked, with a smile. Water ran off my body onto her floor.

"Oh, my God. I don't believe it. It really worked," she exclaimed, jumping to her feet.

"Congratulations," I said. "There are easier ways to get a date. Bars, personal ads, dating apps."

"What are you talking about?" she asked, confused.

"Obviously, you've heard of my sexual prowess and wanted to try me out for yourself. Sorry to say, I'm not that easy. You have to at least buy me dinner first. Maybe a show."

"Wait. You're Mr. Hex, aren't you?"

"The one and only. In the flesh, quite literally," I answered. "How can I be of assistance this morning?" She took my sarcasm as a real invitation.

"I need your help. My son is dead," she blurted as tears streamed down her face. Mixing with mascara it made dirty tracks on her cheeks. At least I had an explanation for the bloodshot eyes and the power behind the summoning. A mother's tears work a powerful magic.

"I'm sorry for your loss. Unfortunately, bringing the dead back to life is beyond what I can do," I said, trying to figure out a way to get soap out of my eyes without giving the lady a free show. My solution worked as I turned my back to her, bent and wiped my eyes on the end of the towel.

"You don't understand. David was killed by a group of vampyres," she said, waiting for a reaction. I was obviously not the first person she'd told, but apparently, I was the only who did not think she was a lunatic. Encouraged by my calm reaction, she went on.

"It happened last night. He was out playing on the street, it had gotten dark. I leaned out the window, over the fire escape to yell for him to come home for dinner. I saw four people grab David and drag him into an alley near the corner. I screamed and ran as fast as I could, but I was too late." Fury halted the flow of tears. "Monsters stood over my baby, their red eyes glaring up at me. They ran at my screams. I picked up David and held him until an ambulance arrived. The EMT's pried his dead body out of my hands. All I could think was those bastards killed my baby. I told the police what I saw, but they thought I was nuts. They can't explain how David was killed or why the blood was drained from his body, but they refuse to even look for the vampyres. They're blaming it on a gang."

"They have to believe what allows them to keep their sanity," I said, failing miserably in an attempt to comfort her.

"Today I made arrangements for David to be buried. On the way home from the funeral parlor I passed a fortune teller's shop. Something compelled me to walk in. I told the woman what happened. She told me about you and that sometimes you help people, then explained how I could summon you."

My own fault for setting up the summoning spell. True summoning only works on gods, demons, and the like. Humans need a little more preparation to enable themselves to be summoned. When my wards are up, I feel the call, but go only when and where I want to.

"What do you want me to do?" I asked, wanting to help.

"I want you to find the vampyres that did this and I want you to kill them. I want the bastards that killed my son dead. The murdering scum should not be allowed to live. I want to make sure they never do this to another mother's child."

"What will you do if I turn you down, Alice?" I asked.

"How did you know my name?" she asked, showing signs of worry for the first time.

"I know things. Well?"

"You can't turn me down. I have you in the pentagram, I know your true name. You have to do what I say or else you are going to be trapped in there. Forever."

"I see," I said, with the slightest hint of humor. "Actually, the proper term is a pentacle. Would you really do that to me?"

She thought about if for a minute, trying to act Dirty Harry tough. Alice didn't have it in her. She shook her head no.

"Good," I said, "Because you do not know my true name, only my taken name," Everyone has at least three types of names. The ones you are given, the ones you take and the one true name that defines your essence. A true name gives power over that individual. Very few people even know their own true name. I never bothered to learn mine because, if I know it, sooner or later someone else is bound to get it from me. It is a classic blunder. Safer all around to live in ignorant bliss. "This type of pentacle only works on demons, spirits, and gods. It has no effect on people," I said as I stepped out of the chalk outline. It almost gave her a heart attack.

"Oh, my God!" she shouted, backing away from me in abject terror.

"You should be more careful. If you had summoned a demon, you wouldn't have held it. The wax from your candles washed away your chalk lines in two places. You would have been carried off to one of the circles of Hell by now," I lectured. "Don't worry. I won't hurt you. Why don't you sit down?"

Alice took my suggestion. I sat as best I could without revealing my inner self, so to speak.

"Will you help me?" she pleaded.

"Yes," I said. It was what I did, after all. Most of the powers that be looked at humanity as commodities, not people. I was one of the few who could stand up to the powers and walk away. Besides, I was a sucker for the little guy.

"Do you know anything about vampyres?"

I nodded yes. I knew quite a bit. Blood war had erupted between some vampyre bloodlines. It was hardly the first and there was no way it would be the last. Almost seven years of relative peace in New York City had been tossed aside in a moment of anger. The innocent and the guilty alike were paying the price. Alice would be paying the rest of her life.

We discussed more details of Eric's death. I asked for a picture of him and some clothes.

"Why?" she asked. "Can't you just teleport yourself back to where you started?"

"I could, but the act of doing that would alert too many people to where I live and I like to keep that as anonymous as possible."

Alice was a single mom; her husband having run off years before. She was a small woman and had no men's clothes. The only thing we found that fit me were a pair of pink sweatpants and an oversized T-shirt with a giant sunflower on it. It was going to be a fun walk home. Luckily, I was still in Manhattan.

"Hex, I just want to thank you for agreeing to help me out. I'm sorry about the way I got you here," she said.

"Don't be. I was tired and I got sloppy. I should have reset my wards before I got into the shower. I will do what I can to find your son's killers."

"Can I pay you?"

"No, not in money. But there may come a time when I need your help. You will have to help me then, no questions asked."

"Okay," Alice agreed.

I left in my pink sweats and sunflower shirt, amazed at how many people noticed me and got a chuckle from my attire. These self-same people – as well as most of the rest of the population of New York City – weren't even aware of the life and death battles that raged around them. In all five boroughs, there were less than a thousand vampyres. Compared to the ten million plus human population, it was a minuscule number. Small enough to allow most people the illusion that the blood suckers were creatures of myth and movie. The odds of running into a vampyre are upwards of one in ten thousand. The odds of being attacked were much higher. Knowing those odds would do nothing to help Alice's grief, so I didn't share them.

As far as odds go, my entire life went against them. In the last two weeks alone, I had run into seventeen of the blood junkies. Fourteen of them would never run or feed again. The other three numbered among my friends and would live to see another moonrise. One of the trio – Layla – and I went way back. She knew me when I was a kid and I knew her when she was still human. People change, but sometimes the important parts remain the same.

Layla ran a club down in the Village called Plasma. It was a hangout for the undead element, as well as a bunch of pale black clad vampyre wannabes. The Goth and emo folk loved the place. The wannabes were desperately trying to touch the real thing, despite the danger. I didn't know whether to pity or protect them. Layla just wanted their money. To that extent, she insisted Plasma remain a neutral territory. The problem was, she didn't always have the juice to back it up. That's where I came in. Layla asked for my help. I have juice up the wazzo. A few of my exploits have become urban legends, yet I remain almost unknown in most circles. I like it that way. Among the more mystically inclined, I am a full-blown legend, considered perhaps the most dangerous man on Earth and beyond. Don't believe everything you hear about me, but enough is true to kept the opposition on its toes.

Most vampyres try to avoid me. When times were rough, Layla employed me as a bouncer for just that reason. Vampyres hate mages, especially ones they can't figure out how to kill. Usually my reputation is enough to keep the peace. Lately, I've had to re-earn it. Last week, I managed to tick off the head of one of the bloodlines. He had procured ten new born babies for the main course at a party he was throwing. The thing that limits me is a curse that only lets me intervene when asked. If no one asks me, I can't butt in using magic unless they are stupid enough to attack me. Luckily, one of the baby's siblings asked. I saved all ten infants and basically ruined his party. In retaliation, he sent thirteen of his best blood suckers after me. At sunrise, I was the only one left standing. The bloodline boss was dead before darkrise.

Sadly, I haven't had much chance to rest since, which was why I was running on E. Another side effect of the curse is spell-weaving wipes me out and causes me serious pain. The more powerful the magic, the worse the pain.

After I made it back to my apartment, I changed into some more suitable clothing, then headed out for the funeral home where David was laid out. I didn't bother to ask permission to examine the body. It would have just complicated things.

The method of death was gruesome. The cops weren't totally off base. It was a gang kill, just not your typical gang. Each of the vampyres had bit off one of his fingers or toes and sucked out his lifeblood through the amputated digit. It was the bloodsucker equivalent of drinking an ice cream soda with two straws. Their idea of romantic. Judging by the imprints from the teeth there were two male and two female vampyres. It is easily for the trained eye to tell the difference. The fangs on she-vampyres are more curved than their male counterparts.

Seeing a child in that state was not something that I wanted to do, but I found out what I needed to know. Not only did I know the number and sex of the vampyres, I knew the bloodline. David had been attacked by Upyr. Contrary to popular belief, there is not just one kind of vampyre, there are several. Each has its own strengths and weaknesses. The Upyr are a particularly blood thirsty lot. The bloodline originated in Russia a few centuries back and tends to prey on children before moving on to their parents. Alice was in some danger. Not all vampyres disintegrate on contact with sunlight. The Upyr could wander about in daylight as long as they avoided bright light, especially after feeding. The light just limited their powers to that of a weak human.

I made a few phone calls and arranged to have Alice spend some time on holy ground with a friend of mine down in the Bowery. Vampyres can go on holy ground, but it's a painful experience, not one they're going to try in the daylight hours.

Exhausted as I was, I tried to track the lot of them. On a better day with more sleep, I might have found them. The closest I came was finding their lair, which was in a sewer underneath Chambers Street. When I got there, nobody was home. The only thing I could do was go home and get some rest.

I woke two hours before sunset and, considering what happened last time, decided to skip a shower. I dropped by Plasma and let Layla know that I would be gone for part of the evening. She was upset, but understood. I told her my problem and she called over Barber. Barber was the head bouncer at Plasma. He stood six foot six, as black as night, and as wide as two normal men, made of almost solid muscle. Barber had virtually no neck. Back in the days when he was brought over to the side of the undead, most vampyres still used the neck. I often kidded him about where his sire must have had to bite him.

Barber was the baddest vampyre around; even the bloodline heads gave him a wide berth. A group of Upyr had spent part of the previous evening trying to impress Barber and had failed miserably. When they told him what they did to the child, he was not amused. He was a father before he was converted. Furthermore, they told him their planned exploits for that night. Barber shared them with me.

The scum were going to hit a nursing home around ten o'clock. It seemed like a perfect time. The residents would be asleep and the nursing staff would be tired with only an hour left in their shift. The Upyr would probably be able to get in and out without anyone noticing, at least until sun up.

I needed to be inside the nursing home before they got there. Getting in wasn't much of a problem, security was lax. I simply walked in the door with a bouquet of flowers in my hand, as if I was visiting one of the residents. I chose a woman named Mabel.

She was sitting in the common area and after a few minutes of observation, I could tell that she had Alzheimer's. Life was slowly eating away at her memories. She remembered only a fraction of her ninety-two years. Mabel was thrilled to see me, even more thrilled to see the flowers. She insisted on taking my arm in hers and leading me around the small grounds of the nursing home. We talked, or rather she did. In her mind, it was the fifties and she going on about how wonderful an invention television was. Then we talked about her family, of which she was very proud.

At first, she thought I was her son Richard, but eventually she realized I wasn't.

"What's your name?" Mabel asked, holding onto my arm for support. Her breath smelled faintly of butterscotch.

"Hex, ma'am."

"Hex? What kind of a name is that? Certainly not a proper Christian name for such a nice young man."

"My full name is Mr. Hex."

"Well, I guess that sounds a little better. I just don't know about you kids today. Back when I was a little girl, everyone was named after somebody in the Bible. Today people name their children after snacks and anything else that strikes their fancy. It's a different world."

She led me back to her room, where we talked some more. I started putting newspapers down on the floor. Mabel didn't act as if this was a strange thing to do. In fact, she took the paper from me and starting helping lay down newsprint.

"We used to do this when we got a new puppy. It helps to housebreak them. Am I going to be getting a puppy?" Mabel asked, hopeful.

"No, I don't think so," I answered with a smile.

"That's too bad, Arthur always loved dogs."

"Who's Arthur?" I asked.

"Arthur is my husband. We were married for forty-one years." Mabel pointed to a black and white wedding picture on her dresser before picking it up and handing it to me. They were a handsome couple.

"What happened to Arthur?" I asked. Mabel stiffened up at my question. Apparently not all of her memories had left her. It seemed that this was one she would have been better off without.

"Arthur and I were walking home one night from visiting my daughter's house. A gang of boys mugged us. They told Arthur and me to give them all our money. Arthur hated to do that because he had worked so hard for so many years to get the money, but he did it. Then they tried to take my wedding ring. Arthur went crazy, he wouldn't let them do it. He fought with them, three big boys and one had a knife. That one stabbed Arthur right in the heart, but he got two hearts for the price of one. I still have my wedding ring, but I don't have my Arthur," she said softly with a faraway look in her eyes. At that moment, Mabel seemed very tired and looked every day of her ninety-two years. Bowing to gravity, she sat down on the bed.

"I was so afraid for years after that. My kids had all moved away and with Arthur gone there was nobody to protect me. To tell the truth, I'm still frightened because I still don't have anyone to protect me and help me. I wish I did. Would you?"

Her asking was as good as magic words. "I'll protect you, Mabel."

Mabel looked up at me, her ancient eyes holding the simple innocence of a child. "Hex, you promise?"

"I promise," I said. I don't give promises lightly. "Mabel, I have another present for you."

"More flowers?" she asked looking up with a smile like that of a child on Christmas morning. It was a sweet smile.

"No, not more flowers," I said. Instead I put my index and middle fingers on both of her temples and closed my eyes for a brief moment. *"Remember,"* I intoned.

"Arthur!" she exclaimed as she slowly collapsed onto the bed. I lifted the covers up to her shoulders as her face convulsed in joy. Mabel was reliving her memories of Arthur, starting with when she first met him. Her memories were so vivid she could actually believe she was there once again and for this brief moment the Alzheimer's wouldn't be able to steal her life. It was well worth the twinge of pain and minor flashbacks the spell caused me.

I finished my preparations for the Upyr then turned the lights off. I sat waiting in the dark. It was almost ten o'clock. The wait wasn't long. At five after ten, one of the bloodsuckers climbed in Mable's window. Many vampyres have a problem entering people's homes uninvited, but the nursing home was set up so that it was a public facility. Those rules did not apply here. This vampyre was male, about five foot seven and he didn't notice me as he stood over the foot of Mable's bed.

"Well, Grandma, you can call me the big bad wolf," whispered the Upyr.

"I guess you can call me the woodsman," I said. "If you leave now and stop killing innocents, I'll let you live."

The vampyre spun as if he had been struck and launched himself at me in an attack. He was clumsy. I sidestepped while throwing a punch at his jaw. I put a little magic behind it. My fist connected with a satisfying crack and I actually knocked one of his fangs out. He landed on all fours on the floor, staring straight at the tooth.

"I'm going to kill you." he promised, as he leapt to his feet.

"We all have to have a dream I suppose," I said, as I stepped into the pale shaft of moonlight that came through the window. He saw my face and the symbol I wore on my navy T-shirt. It was a crescent moon with bandages.

"Hex," he said disdainfully as he recognized the shirt. As I said, I have a bit of a street rep. This blood junkie didn't seem scared. I must be slipping in my old age or maybe I needed tough guy lessons. The Upyr launched another attack, deciding to give silence a try. This one was better planned than the last. He caught me on the side of my head with a punch that had me seeing stars. He spun and came back at me so I sidestepped again, grabbed his head and brought it down to meet my knee, which had been on its way up, fortified with a spell to give it a little extra oomph. The blow managed to knock out his other fang. He looked at it laying on the floor, then at me.

"What do you want with me?" He whistled though the gaps in his teeth when he spoke.

I smiled.

The vampyre leapt upon Mabel's bed, waking her with a start.

"Arthur!" she screamed. "The muggers... no not again!"

The vampyre made a grab for her throat. I blocked it and knocked him to the floor. Mabel was still screaming. The blood sucker and I wrestled. I'm good, but the vamp was stronger. He managed to get a couple of good kidney shots in. He tried to bite me with his remaining teeth and got a head butt for his trouble. As we grappled, we both managed to make it to our feet.

"You don't have a chance. You don't even have a stake," the vampyre said as he tried to bite my hand which was holding his arm. He came away with most of my sleeve, but no skin or sinew. I needed to end this soon or he was going to get lucky and I was going to get hurt or worst. That would hardly be a good way to keep my promise to Mabel.

"I don't need a stake to deal with the likes of you," I said. Besides killing Upyr with a stake is tricky business. With most vampyres, you just try and ram it in. Almost impossible without enhanced strength or a sledgehammer. With the Upyr you get one shot, the second shot jars the stake loose. Then they reanimate and come after you with the stake sticking out of their chest. Not a pretty sight. Curse and consequences be damned, it was magic time.

"*Fry,*" I ordered. The vampyre went even paler as his hair started to smoke, followed by the skin all over his body. It was burned away like melting plastic. He screamed as flames from within him roared to consume his flesh. A moment later there was nothing but a pile of ashes, large bones, and gristle which conveniently landed on the newspapers I had placed down earlier. Mabel was still frightened, but had stopped screaming. Thanks to the side effects of my curse, I had to endure my body overheating. Still it was probably no worse for me than it had been for Mabel back when she'd gone through menopause, that is as long as she got her hot flashes while she was in the sauna.

"It's okay. Mabel," I said, as I got her to lay back in the bed and tucked the covers up over her.

"You protected me," said Mabel sleepily. "Thank you."

"You're welcome," I said. I moved the bed out from the wall and took a piece of chalk out from my pocket and drew a circle around her bed. The lines I drew no vampyre would be able to cross and live. I had done the same thing earlier to all the other beds in the nursing home, as well as the nursing station. Then I had put a sleep spell on the nurses and the staff so that they wouldn't be aware of what happened. I had to overdose on caffeine to counter the curse's side effects from that one.

The other Upyr had undoubtedly learned of my preparations, judging by the howls of anger that filled the halls.

I sat down in a wheelchair and put a borrowed shawl over my head. I then wheeled myself out the door and down the corridor. I made sure the wheelchair squeaked so I would be found easily.

The three remaining Upyr were on me, charging like a pack of mad dogs. They flanked me with the easy confidence of hunters who had never met prey that could fight back. Like fishing with dynamite.

"Finally, unprotected meat," groaned the remaining male. He was even shorter than his compatriot, barely five four. The two women were of super-model height. They even looked like super models, if you overlooked the fangs. Part of that was glamour. Each was easily six feet tall. Part of that was high heels. One was blond, the other a redhead. They had looks to die for and I had no doubt that many men had.

"Leave and stop killing people. This is your only warning," I said.

"That's awful nice of you, but we'll pass, but we'd like to invite you for dinner, old man," said the blond, massaging my shoulders, while she licked my shawl covered ear. Her tongue was cold and her breath sank of decay.

"I'll take good care of you," giggled the redhead, as she rubbed my chest. "Just let me suck on your finger."

"If you want to go out in style, it doesn't have to be your finger," promised the blond, as she went down on her knees in front of me, running her fingers across my inner thigh. Her whisper was laced with a laugh so dark, that despite myself, I was chilled to the bone.

"So, what will it be, old man? You choose. Finger or weasel?" the male asked, putting his face in mine. I had learned my lesson dealing with the first one. If I was going one on three, I was going in with spells blazing. I snapped up my head, throwing off the shawl and grabbed his throat.

"I think I'll give you the finger," I said, flipping him off. "*Incinerate.*"

He went up in flames even quicker than the first. Sadly, the effort made me sweat profusely and there were no newspapers for the remains to fall on. I hoped the smoldering parts wouldn't burn and stain the tile. Didn't need any busybodies trying to figure out what happened.

The women didn't know what was happening, only that it was time to run away. They were smart and went in two directions. I stood slowly, trying to get a lock on each of them. I didn't want to lose either and I felt like I was going to pass out from a fever. I stopped to splash my face and head with cold water.

The redhead left the building, so I went after her first. Upyr cannot fly for more than a few yards and they couldn't transform into a mist. She had however morphed into a red wolf and was running all out. She ran smack into a small-time drug deal and ripped out part of one of the participant's neck. In her haste, she had left only a flesh wound. The dealer would survive, mainly because she didn't have time to feed. She ran down a dead-end alley. As she turned to retrace her canine steps, I blocked her path.

She tried growling in an attempt to intimidate me. I wasn't impressed. My spirit guide was a wolf and I had seen him and his pack do worse to my mailman.

"Give it up," I suggested.

"Will you let me live if I do?"

"No. You ignored my warning, so this is on you. I will give you a choice. You can die as a woman or a wolf."

"I have a better idea. How about you die instead?" the red she wolf growled, as she launched herself into the air toward my throat. I ducked, but she was good and got a piece of my trench coat's collar, slamming me into a wall in the process. The shock knocked the breath out of me.

I turned as she was leaping again. This time she shredded my other sleeve and I barely got the red she-wolf in a head lock before she started gnawing on flesh. She pulled back using all four paws and snapping with her jaws. In seconds, she'd be loose and I wouldn't be able to stop her a third time, so I let her go. Of course, I added a little force in the direction she was pulling and slammed her into a wall. During the second it took her to recover, I nailed her with another word of power.

"*Nova.*"

This time it only lasted a second. The wolf body lit up like a magnesium flare and there weren't even any ashes left to mark her passing, which was good. I was still going to have to get rid of the other two vamps' remains. I was drenched with the resulting perspiration the curse feedback caused. The sweat stains on my t-shirt where never going to come out.

Despite the risk, I body slid to just outside the nursing home. I got my bearings in under three seconds. A personal record. In six more, I had a lock on the blond. She hadn't left the building.

I found her in the basement, cowering in a fetal position next to the boiler. She didn't even try to run.

"Would it help if I said I'm sorry?" she asked in a little girl voice.

"Wouldn't help your victims."

"I could be your sex slave," the blond offered on her knees, flashing me her beautiful vampyre flesh and licking her lips with the promise of earthly pleasures.

"Hardly a tempting offer. I have no desire to become a eunuch." Upyr women have a tendency to swallow after they've bitten it off.

"Can't blame a girl for trying. Will it hurt?"

"Yes."

"Hold me until the end?" she asked. It was a last-ditch effort to get me close enough to attack. I enjoy a challenge.

"Sure," I said, pulling her close. As her mouth got close to my neck, I heard the hiss and felt her hot breath atop my jugular.

"Sucker," she cackled.

"Yes, you are," I said as I yanked back on her blond locks, snapping her neck before she got close enough to give me a hickey. I tossed her on the floor. Her eyes were still open and aware of everything that was happening, but she was unable to speak or move. Even with a vamp's healing factor a spinal cord injury would take days to heal. The blond only had minutes.

Outside, the first rosy rays of sunlight announced the dawn. I decided to save on magic and dragged the blond outside in the nursing home's courtyard and set her down in direct sunlight. In less than a minute she was smoldering and eventually burst into flames. My pal Murphy would have made a crack about me turning her into a vamp-pyre.

The whole while she screamed with her eyes since her paralyzed body couldn't manage a real one. I watched until her accusing eyes had turned to ash. I retrieved the ashy remains of the males and laid them in the morning light, which reduced the few pieces that remained to dust. Before I left, I sprinkled the ashes with a mixture of salt and garlic suspended in holy water. None of them appeared to have the power level to reanimate their own ashes, and I had never heard of an Upyr doing it, but I hadn't survived this long by taking chances. I scattered the ashes between three different dumpsters and a sewer grate.

I stopped in to say goodbye to Mabel. She was in a half sleep state and I promised I would visit her. I keep my promises.

Then I headed to Plasma and finished the night shift. Thankfully the evening was mostly uneventful. I even managed to take a frigid shower to help me cool down and get a few hours sleep before I put on my black suit and went to David's funeral. It was a mob scene. All of the kids from his school and most of their families came, as well as dozens of well-wishers who had heard about the tragedy on the news.

On the way to the Calgary Cemetery in Queens, I rode with Alice in the black limo. She wore a simple black dress.

"I took care of it. They will never hurt another mother's child."

"Thank you, Hex."

"I wish I could do more."

"You did plenty. I just have one question. Since David was killed by vampyres, does that mean he will become a vampyre?"

"Don't worry. I will take care of that too."

Normally, there are two ways a vamp victim turns. One is by drinking or otherwise ingesting vampyre blood or exposure of the vampyre blood to an open wound. The other is to die after multiple exposures to a vamp feeding, usually the same vampyre over a series of days. In David's case, he was exposed to the essence of four vampyres at once. It would probably be enough to turn him.

Later that night I was back in that cemetery, this time with a shovel. I wasn't alone.

"Put some effort into it," suggested Layla. "Use your knees, not your back."

"If you're such a grave digging expert, why don't you climb down here and give me a hand?"

"It would ruin my manicure and get my clothes filthy. I have an image to uphold you know," she quipped. She would help, but Layla was acting as a lookout, in case anyone stumbled by. What we were doing would be very difficult to explain.

As the hole got deeper, I began to hear scratching and screaming from inside the coffin.

"Relax," I said. "I'll have you out of there in a minute."

Once I cleared the dirt off the lid, Layla jumped down and helped me pull it open. Inside was a hysterically screaming and crying little boy.

"They're trying to kill me!" David screamed. He was having a flashback to when he was killed.

Layla gathered him up into her arms and calmed him down.

"It is okay, David. Everything is going to be okay," Layla promised as she stroked his hair. This was the Layla I had first come to know and love. She had been my social worker and counselor when I was a kid back when people thought I was crazy because of all the things I could see that they couldn't. She got me through some rough times. It was that part of her nature that even the curse of blood could not conquer completely. It was the reason I had let her live.

In moments, the kid was calmed down.

"My name is Layla and this is Mr. Hex."

"Hi," I said. David waved back, not yet willing to let go of his grip around Layla's neck.

"The people who attacked you were vampyres and they did kill you. But you're okay now," explained Layla.

"You mean I'm a vampyre like Dracula?" asked David, a little excited by the idea.

"Kind of."

"Will I have to kill people and drink their blood?" asked David, upset. Layla smiled. That was the reaction she was hoping for. It meant there was hope for him and we would not have to put him down like a mad dog in the street.

"You will have to drink blood, but there are other ways of getting it besides killing."

"We have to go see my Mommy. She must think I'm dead."

"I've talked to your Mommy and I can tell you she loves you very much. She does think you're dead and that is the way it's going to have to stay," I said.

"Why?" asked David, heartbreak in his eyes. He loved his mother every bit as much as she did him.

"It is safer this way," explained Layla. "Right now, you are stronger than your mother. What happens if you were hungry and you got angry at her? You might try to hurt her and drink her blood."

"I would never hurt Mommy," David protested.

"No, not on purpose, but you're a vampyre. You have a very bad temper now, whether you realize it or not. If you get angry or hungry you will do things you wouldn't normally do. You wouldn't be able to undo them. So, if you hurt your mother, she would stay hurt. You wouldn't want that, would you David?" asked Layla.

"No," David admitted sadly. "But that means I'll be all alone."

"You're not alone. You'll live with me. I will teach you how to be a vampyre that can survive among humans without killing them," said Layla. "And Hex here is your friend. He killed the nasty vampyres that did this to you."

"Really?" asked David. I nodded. "Cool. Thanks. Hey, my middle fingers are missing! And my big toes hurt!"

"The vampyres that killed you bit them off. Don't worry. They'll grow back once we get some blood into you. We have to get going," said Layla.

"Isn't Hex coming with us?" asked David.

"Nope. He has a job to do first. But he will be by my club later."

"You own a nightclub, too?"

"Yes."

"Wow. Bye, Hex," said David, putting out his hand for me to shake. I obliged.

"Bye, David. See you later." I said as I picked up my shovel to fill the grave back in. "Later, Layla."

Layla made her goodbyes, but couldn't resist a parting shot. "Remember, lift with the knees."

VAMPYRE UNDER GLASS

I'll admit freely that I'm really a dog person, but there was something about the tomcat that caught my attention. Maybe it was his odd brown color, but more than likely it was the way his feline shape coalesced from a cloud of mist.

Mind you, I was hidden behind a dumpster, doing my best to hold on until the aspirin kicked in to get rid of my curseover. It's a lot like a hangover, but instead of being caused by alcohol, I get it from using magic. It takes different forms depending on what I do, but it all stems from a curse which gives me pain for any use of magic. It's something I try to keep under wraps, otherwise the bad guys wouldn't be afraid of me and I'd be much closer to dead. So, in the interest of maintaining my rep, I was laying down in that alley and leaning against the wall when the cat appeared.

As if becoming solid wasn't impressive enough, the large tomcat walked over to me, put his front paws on my chest, and looked me in the eyes.

"Please help me," he whispered.

This was unusual, even for me, but he had said the magic words. Another effect of the curse prevents me from using magic to interfere in any situation that doesn't directly involve me unless asked.

"What do you need?" I asked.

Before he could answer, a voice from above shouted, "I found him." When I looked up, I saw another large tomcat perched on a fire escape. This one was black, and his eyes were glowing red. Both cats had especially pronounced incisors.

The cat on my chest turned back into smoke, unfortunately at the same time I was taking a deep breath. An instant later I retched up everything in my stomach. The smoke rose up above the fire escape and again became a cat. The brown tom dropped on top of the black one, claws and jaws flashing, fighting with all he had. The talking black cat was soon hurt and bleeding. Too bad for brownie that his opponent wasn't alone.

A man in a brown trench coat with a bit of a belly came into the alley. The guy had long, scraggly hair and a beard to match. In his right hand was a containment bottle. They were used to imprison spirits and other things immaterial, such as, I was guessing, a certain transforming cat.

"*Get in the bottle*," intoned the mage, his words part of the spell. I read his umbra. The guy was a trapper, a type of mage whose powers lean toward imprisonment. Handy to have around if you are trying to capture a demon or jinn or the like. Nasty if you are on the receiving end.

The brown cat hissed and extended the middle finger of his paw and the claw popped up. Then he dropped from the fire escape onto the bearded mage's head and proceeded to scratch the hell out of his face. The man fought back, grabbing him behind his neck, and then pressing a ceremonial looking blade to the tomcat's throat.

I stood unsteadily. "Put the knife down and step away from the cat. There's easier ways to get your favorite Chinese food dish. This is your only warning."

"Take care of him," the bearded mage said. I was hurting enough from the curse-over that I forgot about the black cat, who also could take the form of a vomit-inducing cloud.

I was sick a second time, falling to my knees until I was heaving dry. The black cat then took the shape of a man. When he stood over me in a dark shadow and smiled, I saw the fangs. Great. Another breed of vampyre and one I knew nothing about. I thought I knew all the breeds in New York. You learn something new every day. I just wished for once that what I learned about wasn't trying to kill me.

The mage pushed the blade into the brown cat's throat, so the cat turned into a mist to escape the blade. The trapper opened the bottle and it sucked the mist in until the vamp was gone.

I readied a hand spell. Spells by gesture hurt me more than spoken ones, but I wasn't convinced I could speak without vomit interrupting me. Bad thing to interrupt a spell, and a gesture spell would probably knock me unconscious at this point, but it would be worse to do nothing and let this guy kill me.

As I made ready to fry both of them, the mage spoke. "Norman, leave the homeless man alone and come and get your reward."

I must have been looking bad if he thought I was homeless, but the vamp obeyed and turned his back to me. The vamp leapt into the air, transforming into his black cat form and landing in the bearded mage's outstretched arms. The mage kissed him on the mouth, and the cat licked the man's lips. Looks like they were close. The mage then pricked an index finger with the knife and offered the digit to the cat. The vamp feline started lapping it up, then began to suck on it like he was nursing. I caught a stray thought that he had taught a god how to do this, to use his blood to control others, but couldn't get any more details.

I could feel the pain of the vamp they had trapped in the containment bottle. I had to help him, but when I tried to stand, my knees buckled and I threw up some more. They were walking out of the alley, so I did the only thing I could think of. I snapped a picture with my cell phone.

"*Help*," I sent mentally. A moment later, two of my roommates were with me, a spirit wolf and a spirit coyote. I knew they would stand watch over me, so I let myself pass out behind the dumpster.

I woke up before sunset, but not by much. I had been left alone, which may in part be due to Mordi and Sly's innate ability to be invisible to the mortal eye unless they willed otherwise. They extended that to hide me. With one on either side, I was functionally invisible.

I got home, showered, and changed. The rest of my horde of roommates fussed over me. I tend to take in strays, but that may be because, in a lot of ways, I'm a stray too. My other two spirit wolves licked my face. Jeeves, a golem who I rescued from slavery, insists on acting the part of my butler, despite my telling him he doesn't have to. He considers it his rent. By the time I got into the shower, he had a fresh pair of jeans and my blue bandaged crescent moon t-shirt laid out and ready for me. Bollywog is a pixie whom I saved from a vengeful queen of the fairies. She buzzed around like a hummingbird and I had to insist she not watch over me in the shower. For her, it's a giant peep show.

When I got out, Jeeves had supper ready—soup, iced tea, and brownies. For someone with no taste buds, Jeeves is a great cook. He is also big into the internet and computers. The golem had already printed me ten copies of the picture from my phone.

Now I just had to find the bearded mage and the two vamps. My first stop was Plasma. I figured somebody at the vamp club would have a clue as to the type of vamp I was dealing with, and maybe even know where to find this particular one.

It was a bit after sunset, but well before opening. This time of night was a vamp's morning.

I knocked on the door. Barber opened it, his massive body dwarfing the frame. "Hello, Hex." The bouncer opened the door, and I went in. "What do you need this time?"

"What makes you think I need something?" I asked.

"You're not working tonight. And Layla didn't mention she was expecting you."

I shrugged as Barber shut and locked the door behind me. I showed him the picture. Barber looked at it without saying a word. He wasn't sharing anything without a reason. I decided to give him one.

"The guy with the beard is a trapper. He took a vamp prisoner, but I'm not familiar with the breed."

Barber chuckled. "About time you admitted ignorance about something. You figure Layla or I might know more?"

"Pretty much. They can turn into cats which can go out in sunlight. They can also become a cloud or mist that makes people violently ill. The black cat is working with the trapper."

"Who's the one in the bottle?" asked Barber.

"Jake Rathburne." Up until Barber asked his name, I didn't realize I knew it. Being a cursed magi is like that. Sometimes the magic works under the curse's radar and gives me info I'm not consciously aware of triggering. "He's fighting his entrapment. He won't obey the bearded man, and the trapper hasn't been able to break him. I think he may decide to take the bottle and throw it away. It was already done decades ago." The magic again. "He just let him out to see if Jake's spirit had been broken. It hadn't. I have to rescue him."

Barber nodded. "They're bajang. That breed gets used as familiars sometimes. Until a couple of nights ago, I hadn't seen one since disco was big." Barber's been around more than a couple centuries. "The black cat is named Norman."

"That's what the guy in the beard called him."

"Heard talk behind the velvet rope that he was back in New York with a mage."

"Any idea where?" I asked.

"Layla'd know. She's getting ready for a meeting tomorrow night that Norman set up with some people who wanted to make her a business proposition."

We went into the back office, the one no patrons were allowed in. Incense burned a pleasant lavender scent. Most vamps have a heightened sense of smell, which is not always a good thing. Incense helped drown some of the more unpleasant scents. Barber rapped on the door.

"Come in," she said. Layla saw me, smiled, and stood to hug me. "What do you need, Hex?"

"Am I that transparent?" I asked.

"At times," she said, motioning me to sit.

I explained the problem. Layla mulled over giving me the information versus what it might cost in business. She made the right decision. She always does.

"I'm supposed to meet with some Stormer high-ups. They claim they've figured a way to juice up animal blood so it's more potent that the human variety. It could be worth a fortune and save lots of human lives. They want to test market it here. If it goes well, I get the exclusive distributorship for the tri-state area, they get my endorsement for the rest of the country," said Layla.

"That's troubling. Paddy Moran banned the Stormers from New York City." The nationwide gang's Manhattan chapter made the mistake of hurting his adopted kids. Paddy flipped out and tore down a building, then basically exiled them.

"I didn't know that. Moran is one of the last people I'd want to alienate." Layla's fang chewed on her lips. The owner of Bulfinche's Pub not only sat on the biggest concentration of raw power on the continent, but he was a billionaire. Paddy would put everything into saving a single person, but he'd also tear down anyone he thought deserved it. Unlike me, he didn't always give one warning. Plus, he had Greek gods on his payroll.

"I will not do anything against Moran," Barber said. Paddy had once been a conductor on the Underground Railroad, using Faerie as an in-between track route. Barber's human family had been among those the leprechaun saved. Paddy tends to inspire loyalty that lasts a very long time. Plus, Barber used to bounce at Bulfinche's Pub during Prohibition.

"What should I do?" Layla asked.

"Maybe talk to Paddy. If their product is everything they say it is, it could save lives, both human and vampyre. That's something he could get behind. I doubt he'll let the Stormers back in, but he might allow the deliveries," I said.

"I better call him," said Layla.

"Good idea. Now, where can I find Norman?"

"The Stormers are in Jersey City." Layla gave me the address. "But Hex, these guys are serious gangbangers with weapons and at least one vampyre. Even you aren't going alone, are you?"

Layla knew about the curse.

"I'll take Barber if he'll come." The black vamp nodded that he would.

"Fine, but you're leaving me without any muscle bouncing tonight," said Layla. She had a team, but the others were regular-strength vamps, nowhere near Barber's class of power. "If you take him with you, I need a replacement."

I thought about it a moment. My first thought was Hercules, the god-hero of legend. He bounces at Bulfinche's Pub these days, but that might expose Layla to problems if she hadn't contacted Paddy about the Stormers first. I needed someone with enough muscle to keep order and who wouldn't be intimidated by bloodsuckers. Two people jumped to mind.

"What if I could get Nemesis or Terrorbelle?" I suggested.

"You could get the enforcer for the Council of Thrones to watch the door at my bar? That would be more intimidating than even you, Hex," said Layla. "Failing that, Terrorbelle would do nicely."

I tried not to be too offended. More people in New York knew who I was, but those who were acquainted with both of us tend to be more afraid of her. The lady is known as a god-killer, after all. She was a good friend, despite the fact that I had once dated her mother. I like older women, and Nyx predates this universe's emergence. And Nemesis and I owed each other favors.

It was worth a call. I had her direct line. "Nemesis, it's Hex. I was wondering if you or Terrorbelle would do me a favor." I told her what I needed.

"Terrorbelle will do it. What time do you need her?" I told her, mentioned the dress code, and asked her to thank T-Belle for me.

Barber and I made a quick side trip to an Army surplus store a few blocks away, then headed to the PATH. I could have body slid or otherwise teleported us to Jersey City, but I was already hurting from yesterday. Besides, the trapper would probably feel the power surge and the element of surprise would be lost so we took the train. There are times people who don't know me will unconsciously or otherwise move to avoid me in a crowded subway. There was nothing subtle about people avoiding Barber. He was more massive than a linebacker and didn't much go out for smiling. Other than me, there was nobody within a seven-foot radius of the vamp. In a crowded train car in New York or Jersey, that is highly unusual.

Once we were in Jersey City, it didn't take long to find where the Stormers were. They tended to take over a business through any means available to them. They used some of them as meeting places. They weren't as big as the Crips or the Bloods, but it wasn't for lack of trying. They even had a business portfolio, and there was actual talk at one point of them offering an IPO, but nobody could make the legalities work.

This time, they had taken over a tax business to facilitate

identity theft and had trained, well-dressed gang members doing the returns during business hours. We were definitely visiting after hours. I could sense Jake and his bottle had been inside recently. The other vamp too, but not the trapper. I also sensed the faded presence of a minor god, but I couldn't get a handle on which one, not even which pantheon. Probably the one the trapper was teaching blood games to.

We tried subtle first. I knocked on the door and kept knocking until someone responded.

A teen dressed in shirt and tie answered in a surly tone. "We're closed. Please come back tomorrow."

I wasn't expecting polite.

"We're here to see a man about a cat. He's the one in the bottle with the waggily tail," I said.

The Stormer glared at me and slammed the door. Normally, I would have stuck my foot in to block it, but normally I didn't have Barber.

"That was rather rude," I said.

"Very," Barber agreed.

I tried knocking again but was ignored. Well, not exactly. Everyone inside was grabbing guns.

"This doesn't seem to be working. I must be knocking wrong. Would you mind giving it a try?" I asked.

Barber, the original strong and silent type, simply nodded and hit the door once with his hand. It splintered into tiny shards. Barber didn't bend or turn as he went through the door, making a wider opening in the process.

I waited outside while the gangbangers emptied about two clips each at Barber. He's the only vamp I've ever met who is actually bulletproof as opposed to fast healing. Barber's a first-generation vamp, having ticked off the son of Adam himself. Barber doesn't have a breed named after him because, as far as I know, he's never turned anyone.

"Anyone who fires another shot will piss me off," Barber said. He lifted a desk and crushed it accordion style to accentuate his point. Guns hit the floor as fast as gravity could slam them down.

I walked in. The entire office was covered in bullet holes, glass was shattered, and sheetrock was turned to powder.

"Love what you've done with the place. Very gangsta chic," I said.

"We know who the big guy is. Who the hell are you?" demanded a gangbanger in a suit. He actually wore a nametag that said his name was Gary.

"Well, Gary, the name is Hex," I said. "Mr. Hex to you."

"I've heard of you. Now leave. The two of you are trespassing on private property. Get out before I call the cops," said Gary.

"Yeah, right, because concerned citizens always open fire with automatic weapons first, then call the police. I'm sure Jersey City PD will love just how many bullets are in these walls. Do you actually think they won't assume there is a dead body because of all the shots? I imagine they'll be going over the entire building with a fine tooth forensic comb. They find one drop of blood and they will be DNA testing it to every unsolved murder and missing person case in the tri-state area. I wonder if they'd find any blood?"

I had meant it as a rhetorical question, but Barber sniffed the air. "They will."

"Then what do you want? I thought the Stormers were going to be working with Plasma to move some choice hemo," said Gary.

"That was before we found out that you were banned from the city by Padraic Moran," Barber said. Gary looked sheepish and I got a vision from his past. "Not that any of you necessarily were involved." Barber was being diplomatic, in hopes of not blowing the blood deal for Layla.

"Gary here was, although he went by Turk at the time. Very into ballet, apparently," I said. Paddy and the rest had dressed Turk up in a pink tutu before they tore down his building. There were some chuckles from Stormers who caught my reference. Turk glared at me, murder in his eyes. "So, he knew and didn't care. Either very brave or very stupid. Guess which one I'm betting on?"

"What do you want?" asked Gary.

"Norman and the vampyre in the bottle," I said.

Gary narrowed his eyes when he glared at me. "Why?"

"Because he's being held prisoner against his will," I said.

"That's it?"

"That's it," I said.

"I tell you where to find him and you walk away?" asked the tax preparer formerly known as Turk.

"If you mean will I tear this building down on top of your head—not unless you lie to me or otherwise screw me over," I said.

Turk looked at Barber. "Could he do that?"

Barber nodded.

Gary the Turk wrote down an address and handed it to me. "They're there."

"Thank you. Was that so hard?"

Turk's parting words were impressively vulgar.

"If you think we're still doing business with Plasma, you've got another think coming," yelled Turk to our backs.

Barber turned and walked to within three inches of Turk, who cowered into the wall. "That is too bad. I was going to approach Mr. Moran and try to broker his blessing on this deal. Since there is no deal, I will simply tell him that Stormers were in New York."

"I'll call and tell Daks you're coming," said Turk. Daks must be the trapper's name. Barber shrugged, pulled out his cell phone, and did just what he said. So did Turk.

When Barber hung up, he smiled. "I'd advise you to vacate the building."

"They're in Manhattan. Even without traffic, it'll be a half-hour before—"

Which is when Hercules came through the roof like a cannonball, his lion-skin trench coat wrapped around him. When I say cannonball, I meant both the metal ball and the type people do off a diving board. It was especially impressive when you realize we were in a five-story building. Hermes had obviously dropped him from *way* up.

The Stormers went for their guns on the floor, but they had already vanished courtesy of Hermes.

Paddy walked in the front door like he owned the place. "Hello, Turk. A pity we have to meet again. This time it won't go so easily for you." The short white-haired man turned to us. "Thank you for the tip, Barber."

Barber nodded. "Layla's fine?"

"She'd be regardless. She wasn't aware, nor were you." Oh boy, these guys were in trouble. Paddy only loses his brogue when he's royally pissed. "Hex, do you need any help?"

"I have Barber."

Paddy smiled. "Then you are in good hands." Paddy reached up and patted Barber's elbow tenderly. The white-haired bar owner was on the short side of five foot. Barber allowed the touch and actually smiled at Paddy. The leprechaun stepped away and turned his attention back to Turk, who was now in a pink tutu without a leotard; he was apparently cold, scared, or both. Dionysus, god of wine, women, and song (and a pretty good bartender) and Demeter the Earth goddess (and a seven out of five-star chef) were watching the exits as we left. We exchanged pleasant nods all around.

"This Daks knows we're coming now. Mind if I body slide us there?" I asked. The Stormers were being piled naked outside the building and I could hear it rumbling at its foundations.

Barber nodded his assent. As I aimed us, I heard the building crumble, and turned just in time to see the roof settle on the rest of the rubble.

I phased us out of sync with existence for a moment and used the available forces—gravity, momentum from the Earth's rotation, revolution around the sun, and so forth—to shoot us sideways across reality. We ended up in Daks' living room. Alone, I would have landed outside—body sliding always takes me a few moments to recover—but Barber was fine. Norman attacked. Barber laid him out with a single punch.

Unfortunately, I was a little slower. Daks was indeed the mage with the beard. He was holding a containment bottle and chanting. Before I could mount a defense, I was sucked in and my world went black. I barely had enough time to concentrate to keep my body's molecules together. Normally, that particular spell would kill a human, leaving only the spirit trapped in the bottle to do Daks' bidding. Of course, staying trapped forever was also an option.

I couldn't figure a way out. I couldn't feel my body. Or see, or hear. It was total sensory deprivation.

I had no idea how long I had been in there when I heard a blessed pop and my spell to manage my body unwound. Suddenly I was standing back in the room, the containment bottle at my feet.

Barber had obviously opened the bottle, but the trapper managed to catch him in a spell circle, one of many he must have lined the floor of the apartment with.

"*Freeze*," I ordered.

"What do you want, Mr. Hex?" demanded Daks. As his jaw was unable to move, the words came out slow and stunted.

"I'm here for Jake." I focused on the spell circle around the vamp bouncer. It was a basic model, easily broken so I intoned, "*Open*."

Barber was free again and I saw bright lights all around me. A migraine was starting. "Thanks."

"Just returning the favor, big guy," I said. I might never have gotten out of that bottle by myself, which made me wonder, "Why didn't he suck you in?"

"He tried. Didn't work. I don't move unless I want to," Barber said. I was impressed.

Daks apparently less so. "How do you even know about Jake? He's been in a bottle for decades."

"Hex is the homeless guy you wouldn't let me finish off," Norman said bitterly, rubbing his jaw where Barber had slugged him.

Daks did a double take. "Mr. Hex is homeless?"

"I partied too much and was trying to sleep it off," I lied. Had to cover up the curse.

Norman shifted into mist form and headed toward me by way of Barber. He wasn't real bright. Vamps don't need to breathe, so Barber just stopped. The mist named Norman turned and came for me, but this time I was ready. It wasn't even going to take magic. I put on the gas mask I had picked up at the army surplus store.

"Nice try," I said. The cloud pooled above me harmlessly, so Norman solidified into his black cat form, intending to drop on my head. I whipped up my trench coat, slipping out of it as I caught the vampyre cat in it like a sack. I proceeded to smash the cat in the coat against the floor several times, then gave the package to Barber to hold, but not before getting in the last word: "Bad kitty."

Now I turned to the frozen trapper. "Where's Jake?"

"I'm not going to tell you. And even if you do find him, you'll never be able to free him."

"Yada yada yada," I said. Magí are more powerful than the average mage. We can work any kind of magic; it's just a matter of knowing how, which isn't as easy as it sounds. You might know how to open a safe, but without the combination or a way to hear the tumblers it was going to stay shut.

Containment bottles are easy, however. Daks was still ranting about how we could never undo his mighty magics, blah, blah. I wanted him to shut up, but didn't want to waste more magic on it. The immobilization spell was already making me stiff, as if I had worked out for two hours straight. The guy actually had doilies on his coffee table, so I picked up the biggest one, crumpled it into a ball, and shoved it into his mouth. Without the use of his face muscles, he couldn't spit it out.

Now it was just a matter of sniffing out where he had put the bottle. Daks was good. I went over the apartment three times and didn't find a thing. Either Jake's bottle wasn't here, or I was slipping. Asking Daks anything was going to affect my bargaining strength, although I could have Barber beat it out of him. I didn't want to do that either. Believe it or not, Barber was a rather gentle soul.

I was stumped and about to break down, when I saw a single key on a ring in the middle of the kitchen table, the kind used in a bicycle lock. And then it came to me.

"Barber, watch them," I said, and headed out into the hall. I stopped an older woman who was carrying laundry. "Excuse me, where is the building storage area?"

"In the basement, next to the laundry room." She gave me an odd look, probably because I hadn't taken off the gas mask.

"Thanks," I said, running down the hall and taking the mask off. I passed the stairs and had to backtrack, which got me a stare from the woman. I went down the four flights in hopes the exercise would loosen me up a bit. It didn't, so I popped more aspirin.

I found the storage room easily enough. The woman with the laundry came out of the elevator and watched me strangely as I struggled with the outer door. The key didn't fit, so I had to force it. The building supplied a storage area a little bigger than a walk-in closet for each apartment. The woman followed me in and watched as I tried the key in each of the locks. It opened the fifth one.

"You don't live in this building, do you?" she asked.

I opened the door and went in. "Just visiting."

"You're stealing something, aren't you?" she said from outside.

"What makes you think that?" I said and again someone answered my rhetorical question, only this time in great detail about my suspicious behavior. I ignored her because I found the containment bottle. It was on a shelf next to some old porn.

A lot of power goes into making a containment bottle, but it doesn't take a whole lot to undo one. Either opening or smashing it will do the trick. Of course, sometimes they are booby-trapped to discourage that kind of thing. As near as I could tell, this one wasn't.

If I just opened it, it could be reused, so I smashed the thing. Jake came out as smoke, then solidified into a man lying on the floor. He wore baggy pants, white shirt, suspenders, and an old-style cap. He got himself to his feet, looking around.

"How long has it been this time?" he whispered.

"Less than a day, Jake," I said.

"How do you know my name?" he asked.

"Long story. I'm Hex."

"I know you. You were the bum in the alley I asked for help."

"Did I really look that bad?" I had about a week's worth of face stubble. Maybe it was time to shave.

"I don't know how you did it, but thanks," Jake said, shaking my hand.

"My pleasure. And the fun's not over yet," I said.

The woman with laundry was now banging on the storage door. "I have my cell phone out. I have the super on speed dial.

That area belongs to Mr. Daks in 3B. It's a great apartment, one of the nicest in the building, but you don't live there. You better come out, or I'll call the super and the police."

I rolled my eyes. "Jake, I'll explain everything, but first, would you do me a favor?"

"You just freed me. What do you need?"

"Turn into a cat and follow my lead," I said. Jake did as I requested, and I picked him up and stepped out.

"Ah, a kitty!" the woman said reaching out to pet Jake, who cringed back.

"He's shy around new people," I said. "Daks couldn't find him, then realized he must have been locked in here earlier."

The woman gave me a beady-eyed stare. I guessed she was the busybody of the building and knew everyone's business better than they did. "Mr. Daks has a black cat."

"He adopted this one from the shelter last week," I said. "And he's been cooped up for a while. I'm going to take him upstairs and feed him. Bye." I ran into the stairwell, not waiting for a reply.

On the first-floor landing, Jake became a man again and ran alongside me. I explained what I could. When we got to the apartment, I introduced him to Barber. Seems Jake had been trapped during the Kennedy administration by Daks' uncle, who couldn't control him enough to have him kill on command. Norman had turned him into a vamp against his will, as a toy for the adolescent Daks to play with. The family had used bajang for generations, but they couldn't control Jake. Daks had put the bottle away and forgot about it until recently, when he tried to break Jake again. Jake wasn't any more amenable after over four decades in a bottle, but managed to escape briefly.

Jake was angry, and moved to hit Daks. Then he stopped. "He can't move at all?"

"Nope," I said.

"Hitting him doesn't seem right," he said.

"He stole your life, had you turned into a vampyre, and locked you in a bottle," I said.

"When you put it that way..." Jake kneed him in the groin.

Even the doily in his mouth wasn't enough to muffle Daks' scream.

"That's it?" I asked.

"Ain't right to do anymore with him unable to defend himself. Now, if you'd like to free him or wake up Norman…" Jake smiled and cracked his knuckles.

I shook my head at Jake's suggestion. "Not a great idea. But I do have one I think you'll like." I lifted the containment bottle Daks had used on me. Jake took one look and dove behind the couch. "Jake, this isn't for you." I reset the bottle with a chant of my own, paying for it with the migraine going full blown. "It's primed and ready to be used on anybody."

Jake came out smiling. "Even them?"

"Yep," I said. "Mind you, it might kill them."

"Could it have killed me?" he asked.

"Yes," I said. If he hadn't been in mist form or tried to change to escape.

"Seems a fair risk and solution. An eye for an eye, an eternity in darkness for an eternity in darkness. How does it work?" asked Jake.

"Pull the stopper, point the open end, and it'll suck anyone in."

Jake picked up the unconscious black cat and laid it out on Daks' immobile arm, then flicked the cat's ear with his finger. "Wake up, Norman. You don't want to miss this."

The black cat opened one eye. Before the second one was open, Norman was racing away, but Jake had already opened the bottle, and the trapper's own magic pulled them in.

"Put the top on quick," I said.

Jake did. "What do I do with the bottle?"

"Your call," I said. "But if you break it, they'll get out."

"I'll have to think about it. I'm also going to have to figure out a place to stay and some way to make a living. During my short-lived freedom, I figured out that I've been gone for a while."

"I can help with the living arrangements. I own a building, and I have a few empty apartments."

"Really?" he asked, shock and gratitude seeping from his tone.

"Sure. I already have a graveyard angel and the former empress of the world living there. Why not a vampyre? You're probably going to get along well with Peaches. She's the empresses' cat."

"Empress of the world? No more USA?" Jake asked.

"Not exactly. It's a long story."

Barber chimed in. "Think you can bounce?"

"Like at a bar? Sure."

"We'll ask Layla if she'll hire you," said Barber. What he didn't mention was that, if he was recommending someone, they pretty much had the job.

"So, it's your first night as a free man." Or vamp, depending on your viewpoint. "What are you going to do?"

His face got real sad. "I'd like to find my Ma if she's still alive. And look up my girl, but she probably moved on. Might even be a grandma by now."

It might take magic, so I couldn't offer to help without being limited to mundane means. Hopefully, he'd think to ask.

"I'm going to go home and get some sleep. Pack some things and I'll take you to your new place," I said.

"Pack what? All I got is the clothes on my back," said Jake.

"Go through Daks' stuff and take what you want. He won't be needing it, and it's the least he owes you," I said.

Jake packed up a bunch of stuff, then stood in front of the big screen, flat panel TV. "What's this? A way to talk to spaceships?"

"Nope. That's a television." I turned it on, including the sound system. Jake was dumfounded. "Want it?"

"Oh yeah." He was grinning ear to ear.

When we had everything together, Jake looked around. "How are we going to move all this stuff?"

I picked up Daks' keys. "Take his car. I can forge his signature on a bill of sale."

"I think my driver's license is expired."

"Layla can help with that," Barber said.

As we were loading the car, the nosy neighbor watched us the entire time. She finally came downstairs as Barber was finishing tying some furniture on the roof.

"Where's Mr. Daks and his roommate, Norman?" she

demanded.

"Can you keep a secret?" I asked, knowing full well she couldn't.

"Absolutely."

"Turns out they were terrorists. They've been sent down to Guantanamo Bay for questioning," I said.

"They didn't look Arab," she said.

"You think only Arabs are terrorists? These two are the ones that knocked down that building in Jersey City," I said.

"I saw that on the news. They said it was a gas main leak," she said.

I leaned in to whisper. "That's the cover story, of course. Not that I could ever confirm what I'm telling you, you understand, but you look like a loyal and trustworthy American citizen who'd never leak a word of this."

"Of course. I won't tell a soul."

She had called into a talk radio show before we even got Jake to his new home.

HARSH CHORDS

The dance floor was alive, writhing and gyrating with a primal heavy metal beat thrown in for good measure. The band providing the motivation was The Coffin Heads. The group was raw but good. It had the vamp wannabes going wild, an amazing feat in and of itself. Usually somber and sullen, the pale skinned, black wearing Goths didn't really have lives of their own. At least not lives they were happy with or they wouldn't live in a bloody Never-Neverland.

Not that my life is any prize, but at least it's real. Sometimes too much so, especially using tonight as an example. I agreed to do a favor for Layla and fill in for Barber. The two of them needed to take care of some outside business and Layla needed to leave Plasma in the hands of someone she could trust and who could keep the clientele in line. Seems simple enough on the surface, but if surface was all that counted, plastic surgeons would be out of business. Layla's nightclub is a playground for the deadliest of addicts, the blood junkie. Heroin addicts will take your cash or maybe your life. Damn blood junkies might take your soul. Vampyres are like that, grabbing all they can get. They don't share well.

Looked like Ash, the lead singer and guitarist, didn't know that or he wouldn't be egging on Kasha, who happened to be the intimate lady friend of a Lampir gang lieutenant who went by the name of Tanner. Rumor had it he got the name because of what he did with his victim's hides. The Coffin Heads had the regular Thursday night gig here, so Ash had to at least suspect that all the fangs in the place were not of the clip-on variety. Kasha's pale skin and long incisors didn't seem to faze Ash in the least. Neither did Tanner's, which was going to lead to trouble. Most people didn't believe vamps were real and most of the blood suckers were smart enough to keep it that way. Hunting was done in the shadows, away from witnesses. Tanner looked jealous enough to ignore good sense and Layla's rule about no feeding in-house. I moved closer to the stage.

Kasha was poured into a tight and shiny leather number, whose short skirt stopped just long of being a belt. The sleeveless low cut top was holding her shapely breasts in, but I couldn't figure out quite how. Magic I would be able to sense, so I was betting on double sided tape. Her soot black hair was cut neck length and kinky. It flew nicely as she threw her head from side to side. Kasha was a sight to see, even before the vampyre glamor kicked in.

Knocking four competing human groupies to the edge of the crowd, Kasha took to the stage in a leap that a gazelle would have envied. Her wild dancing knocked the bass player into the mash pit, but they caught him. He crowd surfed back to the stage and was plugged back into the amp before the refrain. Kasha swung Ash's guitar from the front of his pelvis, so it hung on his back. Kasha took up the position the guitar had vacated, wrapping her legs around his waist and holding onto Ash's shoulders as she stroked the front of his leather pants with a part of her that Tanner obviously wanted kept exclusively for his personal use.

The vamp lieutenant was moving toward the stage. Kasha, in an ecstasy that was far past the point of caring, had peeled off Ash's shirt and was licking his right nipple ring as she pulled hard on his shoulder long brown mane.

I moved in to intercept. Tanner saw me coming and snapped his fingers twice. That was the signal for his troops to frenzy feed.

"Grab me or save some innocent lives, Hex. Your choice," Tanner said, with a pointy-toothed grin.

Not counting Tanner and his errant girlfriend, there were seven Lampir and they were already moving in on the crowd.

"Call them off," I said in my best tough guy tone. Sometimes it worked. This time it didn't. "You only get one warning." The one warning thing was a habit of mine. If the warnee didn't listen, whatever happened after it was no longer my fault. Tanner wasn't impressed. His mistake.

"No," Tanner replied, pushing past me to get to the stage. He always bragged he was never scared of me. I guess he was telling the truth. I debated about telling him that Kasha wasn't acting under her own free will, but that wouldn't change anything. Tanner had already lost face and to maintain his authority he needed to do something brutal and bloody.

The Goths had begun to realize something was wrong, like so many zebras at the lions' favorite watering hole. More than half decided the game wasn't fun anymore and were moving for cover, but it wasn't fast enough. Someone was going to get hurt. Using my gifts, I learned the gang's signal to halt a frenzy and snapped three times. The Lampir stopped. Five were scared of me, two not.

"That's far enough, ladies and gentlemen," I said.

"Hex, we're only following orders," said Kyle, Tanner's second.

"You know that doesn't carry any weight with me, Kyle. You know you only get one warning." No one gets a second. "Tanner's used up his. He's going to be dead soon. You want to listen to a dead blood sucker? It just means you'll join him. Of course, with him out of the picture, you move up a notch, don't you?"

Might as well use ambition and fear against him. Kyle had been wanting Tanner's spot but was too much of a wimp to challenge him for it. Kyle was too afraid of the gang leader to attempt an assassination.

Kyle nodded to the vamps and four of them moved into protective positions behind him. "We'll stay out of it."

"Good. Now get out," I said. At this, one of the remaining pair, a lady vamp Gabriella, did a double take. "You know Layla's rules, Gabriella. You fight or feed, you don't get to play. Do it and you're banned from Plasma."

The blond vamp ran to catch up to Kyle and his crew. Gabriella was too much of a party girl to give up the best underground club in New York.

Meanwhile, Kasha had stripped down to a thong and was doing her best to convince Ash to party naked. One of the other bouncers, Jake Rathburne, had moved to intercept Tanner. Being a bajang, Jake was a bloodsucking lightweight compared to a Lampir. A bajang's powers include being able to transform into a cat and to mist out and make people sick. Neither was much use in a bar fight, but Jake was holding his own, mainly because he was stubborn as hell and kept coming back no matter how many times he was knocked down. Problem was, he still couldn't hold Tanner. Lampir can fly, so Tanner got smart and simply went over Jake's head, literally.

The remaining Lampir stood unsure. One of the Goths, Tashanna by name, ran up to the vamp and stuck out her neck.

"Take me, dark lord. Make me one of you," Tashanna begged. Girl had a death wish. There is more to being made a vamp than being bitten. The Lampir wasn't about to turn down a free meal and leaned forward to sink his fangs into her jugular. I had only a second to stop it.

"*Dust*," I intoned. Like water changing the color of a sponge, the Lampir turned into a gray powder. It held the shape of a body until Tashanna opened her eyes and screamed. The movement shook the remains and powder collapsed onto the Goth in an ashy cloud.

"How dare you!" Tashanna screamed and slapped me across the face, not bothering to even brush the dust off her body. I rubbed my face stunned, as she stormed out. I turned my attention toward the front of the club, just in time to see Tanner throw Jake fifteen feet into a wall.

Nothing stood between Tanner and Ash. Amazingly, the rest of the band played on without missing a beat.

I sprinted, but I knew I'd be too late. Tanner's own lady friend turned on him, in an attempt to rip out his throat. It never connected. Tanner gave Kasha a side roundhouse kick that knocked her to the ground. As the vamp turned on Ash, his hand transformed into a claw. With a smooth, rhythmic motion, Ash pulled his guitar around and struck a power cord, flipping a switch that popped a blade out of the guitar neck, stiletto style.

Kasha leapt naked on Tanner's back, slashing his face. The vamp lieutenant was distracted long enough to let Ash slash the claw and thrust the blade into Tanner's chest like a bayonet. Each movement was carried out with the rhythm and grace normally seen in the swing of a conductor's baton. It was done in perfect time with the song.

Tanner stood there, staring at the piece of metal sticking out of his chest in shock. Taking a stake to a vampyre's heart is nowhere near as easy as TV slayers make it look. If it were that easy, vampyres would have become extinct ages ago just by accidentally bumping into things. Besides, there are some vamp bloodlines staking won't kill.

The splattering of blood broke the spell Kasha was under and she saw what was really happening. In fear, she backed away. Ash was oblivious, lost in the thrall of the music. He hadn't even stopped playing as the vamp's spilled blood ran down the neck of his guitar. Too late I realized the blood was the last ingredient for a summoning spell.

The air at center stage had begun to glow, the telltale sign of a hellhole forming. I had assumed Tanner to be the greater danger. I was wrong.

Even before the hellhole opened, I knew where in the netherworld it went. I have the gift of knowing, one of many mystic talents. The damned punishments are not always based on their sins, but on passions. Music is a pure passion of many, but there is no music in Hell. Part of its nature. On the other side, there was a gathering of human and demon damned, starved for music. The blood sacrifice would set them free on the Earth and empower Ash by enslaving the damned to his will.

I had doubts that Ash was just planning to form one hell of a band. As the music crescendoed, the hellhole became more solid. Screams of the damned, the only true musical art form of Hell, filled the air, sending chills down my spine. In half a minute, damned and demon were going to come pouring out.

"Hex, I don't like this," Jake screamed. I wasn't crazy about it either. Jake was level headed enough to realize cause and effect and he plugged the plug on the band's amps.

The music faltered for half a second before a yellow glow flowed out of the hellhole and into the instruments, replacing the electricity and amplifying the sound. This had gone far enough.

"*Dead air,*" I intoned, using radio slang for silence. The yellow glow dimmed and faded and even the drums grew silent.

Ash tried to take it acapella, but I hit him in the stomach, knocking the wind out of him. Ash dumped the bloody guitar and Tanner stumbled back. Without the song to sustain it, the hellhole collapsed in on itself.

The remaining Goths in the audience thought they had witnessed the most amazing stage show ever and rushed the stage. Ash made sure he put plenty of them between him and me.

"Hex, you want me to grab him?" screamed Jake, trying to wade through the tides of humanity. Ash had picked up a second guitar and popped a similar blade out of the neck. If we rushed him, he'd slash some clueless Goth.

Unless he was cornered, Ash wasn't an immediate danger. Tanner, punctured, pissed and bloody, was. "No. Let Ash go for now," I rasped. My muffling spell had given me a mild case of laryngitis. Like for like personal suffering was a side effect of my curse.

Ash had left the bayonet guitar sticking out of the vamp's chest. Tanner stumbled to the backstage area, which was basically a tiny portion of the stage with a black curtain in front of it. I followed. Tanner turned and saw me.

"He's insane," Tanner said, referring to Ash.

"Actually, no. Just sadistic," I said. Vamps are always shocked when they find someone more violent than they are. Tanner was trying to pull the blade out of his rib cage.

"Hex, could you give me a hand with this?"

"Nope," I said, twisting the blade. Tanner screamed with agony.

"What are you doing, you stupid fu..."

"I warned you," I said.

"But he's the one who cut me open."

"If he was a normal human, you would have gutted him. Not to mention the damage your flunkies could have done to the crowd."

"Could have?"

"They left. Most of them anyway."

"They disobeyed a direct order? Those little shi..."

"Don't worry about them. They listened to their warnings. You didn't."

I shoved up on the guitar bayonet, forcing Tanner to his toes.

"Hex, can't we talk about this?"

"We did. I told you to leave, you didn't. End of discussion." I pushed the guitar hard, impaling the blade into the wooden stage wall, pinning Tanner like a butterfly.

"Listen, you mother fuc..."

I was done listening. Stakes could take out Lampir, but it was hard, messy work. I opted for an easier way. Fire.

"*Burn, baby, burn,*" I intoned. Flame crackled from the inside of Tanner's chest, consuming his whole body, with him screaming the whole while. I watched until the fire burned out, which seems cold blooded unless you realize that my gifts allowed me to see how he killed each of his victims and could hear their cries for vengeance and justice. Several were still alive when he skinned them. The cries stopped when the flames died.

I turned, right smack into Kasha. Still clothed in only her thong, she had been watching the whole thing. Speechless, her brown eyes stared at me, filled with fear that I would do the same to her. Someday I might, but not tonight.

"Tell your gang what you saw. Tell them Mr. Hex is watching. No more killing, no more violence to feed. Consider yourselves all warned," I said, for all the good it would do. Some vamps were too stupid to take advantage of alternative food sources. Layla ran the place with donated blood. No one needed to die or be turned. Layla used to be a social worker and still believed in redemption. So did I, which is why I let vamps live. That and my curse.

Vampyres are not evil by nature. Problem is, for all intents and purposes they are beyond normal means of punishment, so they generally can get away with whatever they want. Add to that a bloodlust that puts a kill higher than an orgasm on the pleasure charts and you have temptations galore, paving a road to evil. One needs a very advanced moral code to even try to resist. Most vamps never bother. At heart, they are just like the rest of humanity.

"Tell them. Understand?" I said.

Kasha nodded wordlessly.

I bent down and picked up her little leather outfit from where she had thrown it during her striptease. "Good. Now get out." I threw the outfit at her. Kasha caught it and fled.

Jake and the rest of the bouncer crew had managed to regain some sense of order. Some of the crowd had fled, but their numbers were easily replenished from the "B" crowd hopefuls standing in line outside the velvet rope. The sight of most of the "A" crowd fleeing didn't even faze them in the least. This was New York after all. Besides Plasma was in the Village and stranger thing happened here than a bunch of party people making a running exodus. Our Monday DJ was in the crowd. "Lezza, you're up. Get me some music five minutes ago."

"You got it, Mr. Hex."

It took her about twenty seconds to plug her phone into the sound system and get the party back on while she set up her gear.

"Hex, what just happened up there?" Jake asked me.

"Ash is a charmer," I said.

"So, what does his being likable have to do with anything?"

"Not that kind of charmer. A charmer is a mage who uses music to work magic," I explained.

"Did you know Ash was a charmer?"

"Sure. It's not uncommon. Most of your better musicians are, even if they never realize it. Most never do, which is why I wasn't worried about Ash. Actually, everyone in the band is a Charmer, which I'll admit is unusual. Most rock Charmers use their talents to seduce, which is what Ash was doing to Kasha."

"That explains a lot. How'd the Coffin Heads learn how to move to the next stage?" Jake asked.

"I don't know, but I plan to find out."

"Now?"

"No. Tomorrow," I said, sighing. My voice had stopped cracking and now sounded mildly husky. It had already been a long night and sleep seemed a too distant dream.

"Why wait? Won't they just do it again?"

"I'm sure they will, but part of the spell he was weaving drew on the crowd's energy. He won't be able to try again without an audience, which I think leaves us safe. At least until tomorrow night. Besides I have a mess to clean before Layla gets back," I said pointing backstage with my thumb. Jake strolled back to take a look.

When I say mess, I mean mess. Burning flesh, even vamp flesh, stains badly and leaves a lot of ashes, bone, and burned meat.

"Oy. Layla's going to be pissed," Jake said. Layla is a Mora vampyre. Not the strongest vampyre, but near the upper middle echelon. Layla was a night queen, but it was due more to her control of the deathless blood trade than vamp power. Jake knows his place on the vampyre food chain and it's pretty near the bottom. Bajang are easily enslaved by others to do their dirty work but are lucky in one aspect. Their bloodlust is less intense than many of the other breeds.

Jake tried to steer clear of confrontations with other vamps, but he didn't run from a fight. He was a scrapper, and I've seen him take down much stronger vamps. Thing is, jobs for vamps are hard to come by and he wanted to keep his.

"Don't worry. I'll clean it," I said, walking to the kitchen. I grabbed a plastic tarp, a bucket and filled it with water and every cleaner I could find. Then I threw a scrub brush in the soapy mess.

Jake saw me head backstage and followed.

"You're going to clean it with that? Why not just magic it away?" Jake asked.

"I don't use magic for trivial things," I said. Of course, I didn't mention the curse. I never mention the curse.

"You're a better man than me. I'd use it for everything," said Jake.

"Maybe, maybe not," I said with a smile. I might use it more except using magic hurts me. The stronger the magic the worse the pain. I was still hurting from the two spells I used earlier. The three aspirin I dry swallowed in the kitchen hadn't kicked in yet and my head was killing me. Much more magic and I might induce a migraine. I didn't want that. Also, the curse prevents me from using my magic to butt in or help someone unless I'm asked. Luckily, Layla's asking me to watch the club let me interfere in this mess.

It only took a half hour of scrubbing to clean the wall and Layla's bouncers had a system in place to dispose of the remains. The rest of the night at Plasma was relatively uneventful.

About an hour after sunrise, I found Ash and the rest of The Coffin Heads crashed out in a rundown loft, not far from Alphabet City. It wasn't that difficult. I didn't need magic, just looked up the address they had left Layla on their tax forms.

The lock was a joke. Using my Swiss army knife in place of the traditional credit card, I got inside the loft in under ten seconds. From the looks of the place, it was the maid's year off. Clothes were scattered everywhere, except on people. The loft was one big room. The only real furniture were three beds, all filled to overflowing with band members and assorted groupies. The drummer, bass player and even the roadie who sold their homemade CD's at the door, had two women each to their credit. The backup guitarist must have been low man on the totem pole because he had only one lady friend and was forced to sleep on the floor. The roadie got the couch.

In the center of the room, positioned like a throne, was a king-sized bed. It was in front of an old-style cast iron radiator, which seemed to be serving as a headboard. Ash slept, his body entwined with four naked beauties. Three of them were on the wrong side of sixteen. One of the three was pregnant but didn't know it yet.

Ash snored like a cartoon pig and drooled out of the side of his mouth. He had a dozen tattoos on his arms and legs.

It was time to make an impression.

"*Sleep,*" I intoned, making sure nobody but Ash would be up for our conversation. I popped and downed another two aspirin to deal with the pain. These were the migraine kind with caffeine which helped counteract the curse's backlash that was making me want to take a nap.

There was no kitchen, so I went into the bathroom and filled a mold-encrusted glass with cold water. The freezer was in serious need of defrosting, so I used the cup to scrape some ice into the water to make slush. Returning to the king-sized bed, I took a seat on the cold radiator so I was looking down on Ash's upside down head. I raised the glass and poured the icy cold liquid onto Ash's face. He sat up spewing obscenities.

"Morning," I said with a smile. It did nothing to brighten Ash's disposition.

Realizing what had happened, Ash jumped up and rushed me, with a plan of pounding my face. It wasn't a bad plan, but it had no hope of succeeding. As Ash leapt I moved, so he smashed his head into the wall and his knees into the radiator. There was a yelp of pain. When he turned, he saw me at the side of the bed, pulling a sheet up over the naked pregnant girl, whose name was Katie.

"You've got no class," I said. I didn't mention the girls' ages. Ash knew and couldn't care less.

"I got everything I need. I don't need class."

"That's debatable, but my class is in. You're treading on dangerous ground."

"Like I care," said Ash, stepping over the girls onto the floor, in an attempt to intimidate me. He stood six-foot-two to my five-eleven and he had thirty pounds on me. I had faced down bigger and badder. "I think you better leave." Ash lunged, grabbing at my leather jacket, missing by inches because I wasn't where he was grabbing any longer.

"I'll leave when I'm done. I'm here to get you to stop."

"Or what? Layla'll fire me and the band? You'll call the cops?" Ash laughed. So, he did know Tanner was a vamp and that Layla would never involve police.

"Cops? You should be so lucky; and by the way, consider yourself fired," I said.

"Plasma ain't your club. Only Layla can fire me."

"Wrong. When Layla leaves me in charge, what I say goes," I said. It was part of our deal.

"We'll see what Layla has to say about that. She knows a good thing. We pack in the crowds."

"You ever been to Plasma on a night you weren't playing?"

"No."

"Just as packed. Trust me, after that stunt, you're fired." I didn't add that he would probably have a pack of Lampir on his tail for attacking Tanner.

"Fine. We'll find another club."

"You're trying just a little too hard to raise some Hell."

"That's the whole point of the life, isn't it?" Ash said grinning.

"Sex, drugs, and Rock and Roll, huh?"

"Hey! I don't do drugs," said Ash, genuinely offended. That may have been true for him, but there was enough pot, coke, and ecstasy in the room to keep the average drug pusher in business for a holiday weekend.

"Power is the strongest drug of all. Is it worth your soul?"

"I don't believe in souls. What you see here is it."

"Pretty boneheaded position for someone who opened a window into Hell a few hours ago," I said.

"It wasn't Hell."

"It wasn't?" I said incredulously.

"No, it was an alternate dimension. That Hell stuff is just for the fans. Those things were just different life forms. These people in the other dimension are fans too. They talk to me in my dreams." That explains how he learned the ritual. "They don't have music on their world. To get it, they're going to make me their king."

A little knowledge is a dangerous thing. "King? You're no Elvis." Now there was a Charmer. "I underestimated you in the club and I overestimated you here. I figured if you were bright enough to figure out the ritual, you were bright enough to know what you were doing. My mistake. Regardless of what you think, you're not going to be king. If you don't stop, you're either going to be dead or dragged off to the Pit. This is your only chance for redemption and your only warning."

"I got no clue why those freaks at the club are so scared by you," said Ash.

"You're about to find out. *Night, night,*" I intoned and Ash fell into a deep sleep. I wrapped his naked carcass into a blanket and loaded him into an Uber. A fifty-dollar tip was enough that the driver didn't ask any questions.

I took care of Ash in my own unique manner, caught some z's during the daylight hours, then headed back to Plasma after the sun set. Jake was waiting for me. He wanted to know what happened, so I told him.

"So, Ash woke up in the department store window naked?" asked Jake, laughing hard enough to bust a gut.

"Well, naked and a few other things," I said.

"Such as?" asked Layla, who was back at Plasma, sitting in her black wicker throne. Jake and I were at her table. Barber was back, so I was off bouncer duty.

"A reverse Mohawk, for one thing," I said.

"Reverse Mohawk?" asked Jake.

"Hair across the head from ear to ear," I said.

"What else?" Layla asked, sipping a mug of donated blood, still warm from body heat. Jake was having the same. I wasn't drinking, despite the bar's ample supply of more human refreshments. I learned early on that only a fool eats or drinks in a place not his own.

"I found a red permanent marker and made a few doodles."

"Such as?" asked Layla.

"Eyes and a mouth on the back of his head. 'Your Ad Here' on his chest. 'I Love Disco' on his back," I said.

"Ouch," said Jake.

"'Kilroy Was Here' on his butt."

"Traditional," said Jake.

"Topped off with my hex brand on his forehead." It's an H in a circle reminiscent of the anarchy symbol. "Had to sign my work."

"That's my Hex, the artist," said Layla.

"What are you going to do if the kid doesn't stop?" Jake asked.

"Put an end to him," I said.

"You mean…" stammered Jake.

"Yep," I answered.

"But you're one of the good guys." Jake had a highly-exaggerated opinion of me after I saved him from the mage who enslaved him and a touch of hero worship.

"So?"

"I don't get it. You spend all your time helping people, so how could you kill one?" said Jake. The tough guy was acting like a disillusioned kid. I felt like I was kicking a puppy.

"I protect people. Sometimes the only way to do that is to permanently eliminate the threat. I always give the one warning. There is always a choice. If someone listens, they live. If not... Why the concern? You've seen me kill and it never bothered you before."

"It was only monsters," said Jake.

"Like you and Layla? Are you monsters?" I asked. Jake had to think about that.

"No," he finally answered.

"Why not?"

"Because we choose not to kill."

"That's part of it. What about your former master? He was human."

"But he was definitely a monster."

"Yes, he was. If Ash completed that spell correctly, everyone but the band would have been killed by the escaping damned," I explained.

"If he did it incorrectly?" asked Layla.

"Everyone but Ash would have been slain."

"And my club?"

"Toast in either case," I said. Layla had backed my decision to fire the band without batting an eyelash.

"Well, I'm glad you were here. That was a bit beyond Barber's skillset," said Layla.

"I wouldn't underestimate Barber." The vamp was in the League of Shadows alongside Wisp and Mikoli back in the day. Talk about your original mystic gangsters. "Besides, I couldn't have done it without Jake here."

"That's what Jake's been telling me," Layla said, with a grin and both eyebrows raised.

"Well, it's true," Jake said, equal parts embarrassed and defensive. Barber choose that moment to walk over. Barber is a big man, or rather a big vamp. It was as if part of the wall was moving.

"Hex, heard what happened last night. Thought you might be interested in this." Barber handed me a piece of paper and then left. He was never one for small talk.

"What is it?" Jake asked.

I handed him the paper. It was a folded flyer advertising a free underground, aka permitless, concert to be given by the Coffin Heads in Thompson Square Park at midnight on Saturday.

"That's tomorrow night," Jake said.

"Yep," I said.

"Maybe it's just going to be music," Jake said.

"And maybe the sun will be out for the opening number," I said, getting up from the table.

"What are you going to do?" asked Jake.

"Take care of it."

"Now?"

"No. I'll give Ash the benefit of the doubt, until the concert."

"How are you going to take care of it?" Layla asked.

"Fight fire with fire, or this case, music with music."

Layla thought I meant to take on Ash myself in a kind of mystic music duel. She was half right. Being a magí means – unlike most mages who can do one or two types of magic – I can work them all. I play a mean guitar, but I'm not in Ash's league. He'd kick my butt, so I grabbed a cab and headed into Brooklyn to look up an old friend.

Walt Roberson owned a club called Brooklyn Blues and played there most every night, usually the last set. The rumor mill said it was because traditionally the best act goes last and not even the headliners could top him. That part was true, but Walt said it was because he was a night owl. Besides, more often than not, the headliners asked him if they could sit in.

I walked into the club and turned a few customers' heads. Not because they were struck by my beauty. It was more due to the fact that I was a white boy walking into a black blues club with a guitar strapped across my back.

It wasn't so bad that anyone would have made it physical. It wasn't that kind of club. They saw white people in there most nights, even ones with guitars, but usually the ones toting instruments were on the bill. My actions appeared unbelievably cocky.

The hostess was new and didn't recognize me. She looked me up and down like I was something the cat dragged in after a drunken binge.

"We don't do open mike nights," she said, making her dislike plain.

"It's okay. I ain't Mike," I said. "Table by the stage, please."

"I ain't going to seat you by the stage, especially carrying no guitar," she said.

"I think you have your clichés mixed up. Its white men can't jump, not can't play. Tell Walt that Hex is here," I said.

"I won't do any such thing. Just cause you know his name, don't mean Walt knows you," she said.

"Not only does Walt know me, he taught me how to play," I said.

"I doubt that," she said. I got a glimpse inside her head. She had the hots for Walt.

"What you should doubt, Sandra –" Her eyes widened in surprise by my use of her name. "– is the possibility of getting anywhere with Walt. He loves his wife and Betsy would kick your scrawny ass if she even caught you drooling in his direction." Walt was taking the stage for a solo gig. "Now get out of my way," I said, taking my guitar out of its soft case. Walt had started his set instrumentally. I howled from the back. He recognized the sound. Still in the audience, I joined in and my notes came out of the house speakers. No magic there. Walt uses wireless hookups to the amps and I had my own. Sandra was still running after me, in an attempt to somehow stop me.

"Ladies and gentlemen, Mr. Hex is in the house," Walt said, pointing to me with his eyes. "Let's give him some love."

The audience listened to Walt and clapped. Once he got playing, they'd do anything he wanted. Luckily, he usually wanted to make them feel to the utmost of their soul's capacity. He mostly succeeded. I turned and stuck my tongue out at Sandra. She turned and stomped back to her post by the door to pout.

We launched into a rendition of Smokestack Lightning and I

sat in for the rest of the set. Pleasure before business.

Just the act of making music is magical. While I play, I get transformed, taken to another place that resembles paradise. I've heard some musicians claim it's better than sex. I would disagree. Sex and music are two different things, but each done right can leave you feeling fantastic.

By the time we finished, the sun was threatening to rise and the club was almost empty. We sat over two cups of coffee, mine untouched as always, talking about old times and exchanging pleasantries.

"So, Mr. Hex, what do you need?" Walt asked.

"What makes you think I need something?" I asked, with a sly grin.

"Because when you come here just to hang out, you drop by earlier and see Betsy and the kids. When you need something, you show up during the last set." Sandra walked in to say goodnight to Walt. She ignored me and left. "I don't think Sandra likes you," Walt said smiling. Earlier, I told him what happened and he had set Sandra straight, instructing her to do whatever I asked when I came in.

"She definitely likes you," I said.

"You noticed that too, huh?"

"Yep. What's Betsy think about it?"

"Thinks it's cute. She's not worried. Betsy trusts me. However, it might do my ego a little more good if she didn't trust me so much and was at least a little jealous."

"Never happen. She knows you," I said. "You put your soul on the line for hers. Can't ask for more love than that."

"Guess not. Even after all these years, I still have trouble believing I beat Nick," said Walt. Nick is what we call Satan, the devil himself. We didn't use his real name or title or he would know we were talking about him. That wouldn't be a good thing.

"But you did, fair and square."

Back when I was a snot nose kid starting to grow my first couple of chest hairs, I met Walt. He was a few years older. Turns out he heard an old legend about bluesmen selling their souls at the crossroads for the ability to be the best. Depending on the story, it was either the Devil or Legba. Walt gambled on it being Legba. He gambled wrong. Legba might not have demanded his soul, but the Devil did.

Walt didn't want the ability to play without the work it took to earn it. What he wanted was lessons and who knew the blues better than the Devil? Not that I have a high opinion of Nick, but think about it. He was God's favorite, sat at his right hand in heaven and all that. Gets into a fight and gets kicked out of Paradise and sent to the Pit for eternity. Hard to beat that story by complaining your wife ran off with your best friend the day after you got fired down at the plant. Don't feel sorry for Nick. It's not like he's ever even apologized.

Anyway, I met Walt when he was trying to get out of the contract. Managed to do it on a technicality. Nick had claimed to be Legba and misrepresented himself. The story didn't end there. Walt had met Betsy and they fell in love. Turns out she had sold her soul to Hell, although not to Nick directly. She had asked to find true love. By finding Walt, she forfeited her soul. Walt couldn't stand by and see Betsy carried off to the Pit. He challenged Nick to a guitar duel, ended up kicking the Devil's butt and saved his love. I may have helped a little.

"Now I have someone else I want you to beat," I said.

"Who and what are the stakes?"

"A charmer by the name of Ash, backed by a rock band of lesser charmers. You win, you save a lot of lives and stop a little bit of Hell on Earth. You lose, you, me and the rest of the audience die or get dragged down to the Pit."

"Why don't you do it?"

"Simple. He's better than me."

"That wouldn't be true if you practiced more," Walt lectured. It was a sore point with him. "You could be better than me."

"In about a decade."

"That decade is going to come and go, whether you do it or not."

"My time is better spent on other pursuits," I said.

Walt grinned. He knew what I did. "Is this Ash guy better than me?"

"He's a bit more powerful, but you're better."

"How can you be sure?" asked Walt.

"Simple. Music is his means to an end. It's your end," I said. "You up for it?"

"When?" he asked. I looked at my watch. The sun would be up soon.

"Midnight tonight."

"I'm in, but you're telling Betsy," he said with a smile.

"I'd rather face the horde from the hellhole alone," I shot back, but I was smiling.

There were probably over a thousand people in Thompson Square Park by five of midnight. The Coffin Heads were popular with the locals and free is free. Thursday night at Plasma there were maybe six hundred fifty. Ash could get that hellhole open faster and make it bigger with this crowd behind him.

They had popped a plate off the side of a lamppost and plugged their equipment in the electric socket beneath. I could have ended it then, but I couldn't kill Ash until I was sure what he intended to do. I had to wait until the hellhole actually started to open. If he wasn't going to try, I'd be slaying an innocent, which would pretty well damn my soul. I had made too many enemies in Hell to let them get their claws into me.

Guitars in hand, Walt and I waited at the rear of the crowd. I had planted mini amps around the park and we had our wireless hookups. We wouldn't be able to match the Coffin Heads on sheer volume, but we would win in terms of clarity. All their amps were piled up on the sides of the stage.

Ash was ready to start the show, so he and the rest of the band took the stage. Ash was wearing a long sleeve shirt and I realized he had shaved his head bald. Guess he didn't like the hairdo or my drawings. He wore a red bandanna tied like a pirate to cover my hex mark on his forehead. It took me a minute to check out the rest of the band. Something was wrong with their umbras, what most people would call auras.

"Oh crap. Ash called in ringers," I said.

"What do you mean?" asked Walt.

"The other guitarist, bass player and drummer are possessed."

"As in demon?"

"Yep. Must have offered up his band members as a sacrifice."

"What does this mean?"

"I don't need to wait. I can stop it now," I said, as I noticed Kyle and a pack of three Lampir mixing with the crowd. "It looks like I may not have time. We have trouble." I explained to Walt what was going on. "Get up in front, but stay away from him. Ash is a killer. If you see a groupie get on stage, he'll probably try to kill her. Start playing if that happens. Hopefully, it'll be enough of a distraction to save her life. I'll head off the vamps."

I moved on Kyle. If I controlled him, he'd control the rest. I came up behind him in sheath mode and tapped him on the shoulder. Kyle jumped.

"Hex!"

"Kyle, don't."

"I have to. The boss didn't like how we left Tanner. We have to redeem ourselves by killing Ash."

The band was starting.

"Sit back a half hour and it'll be taken care of for you."

"That's not the way it's going to work this time, Hex," Kyle said. He started to snap, but I was faster and broke his fingers, mystically enhancing my strength. He tried to use the other hand so I crushed that one too. By way of thanks, Kyle head-butted and knocked me to the ground. It took a few seconds for the stars in front of my eyes to fade, but I still sensed his lunge and got my arm up in time to save my jugular. Instead, Kyle bit my arm. Luckily, my leather jacket was tough enough that he didn't even leave teeth marks. I rammed my elbow into his ear and his jaws went slack. By the time he hit the ground, I was back on my feet.

The other Lampir were all ones that I warned at the club Thursday. They saw Kyle and me getting into it and decided to join in the fun, which was good. If they were worried about me, they wouldn't have time to go after the crowd. On stage, the roadie was bringing Ash another guitar. The roadie was still human. He held out the new guitar. Ash popped the blade from the one he was holding and did the bayonet thing into the roadie's beer gut. As soon as the blood hit the guitar, the hellhole glow appeared.

The smell of blood distracted the Lampir for a split second. I made a mad dash for the stage. Predators, human or otherwise, react to prey running the same way. They chase it.

I wove in and out of the crowd, while the vamps tried to push their way through, so I made better time. I jumped on the stage, just as the Lampir realized it would be quicker to fly.

The hellhole was solid enough for damned to start coming out. Or vampyres to start going in. At Kyle's signal, the three dive-bombed me. Like a matador facing down three bulls, I zigged and zagged so they flew close enough to the hellhole for hungry claws to grab. Vamps know blood and killing. They didn't know demons and hellholes. All three were caught and struggled to get away, but the grip of the damned was too strong. Kyle flew down to try to pull his fellows free. Part of me started to feel compassion at his act of bravery until I got a flash of his real motivations. He didn't want to face me alone and was terrified to explain to his boss how he had lost his men.

After a few seconds, Kyle was caught. The vamps struggled for freedom in what was obviously a losing battle, but the longer they held out, the longer the wormhole was plugged up.

At that moment, a blues riff rang out from all corners of the park. Then another, each note composed with such beauty that the demon-possessed musicians stopped playing to listen. Even Ash paused a second. The hellhole stopped growing. Walt had everyone's attention and he wasn't about to let go. The bluesman launched into a song he had written for his kids. The possessed drummer started banging his head and playing along. The bass player and the other guitarist did the same.

Ash froze. His music was part of the ritual and Walt had turned his musicians away from the spell. It wasn't their fault. These demons were starved for music. They'd follow whoever gave them the best song. If Ash didn't regain them soon, the ritual would blow up in his face.

Ash pulled the bayonet guitar out of the roadie's gut and fired off some power cords. It got the demon band's attention and they stopped again. Walt kept playing and the battle was joined.

I rushed to the roadie's side and stabilized his condition. All those years of medical school didn't go to waste, even if I did use them to become a shrink. The roadie wasn't dead, but he was going to wish he was with all the pain he would have come morning.

Music is part emotion, but it wasn't just one. The best songs run the gambit. Ash's song was filled with anger, rebellion, and self-righteousness. Walt's song had sorrow, happiness, pride and the topper, love. It had more appeal, even to demons. They abandoned Ash and musically followed Walt.

"Nooo!" Ash screamed, using the bayonet to open his own veins to pour more blood on the guitar. The fresh blood distracted one of the Lampir long enough that the damned pulled him in. The other vamps quickly followed. Ash's gesture had otherwise been futile. The hellhole neither grew or shrunk. Time to pull the plug.

Someone beat me to the lamppost and pulled it. No gold glow from the wormhole this time. I froze in my tracks when I realized who it was.

"Hello, Hex."

"Hello, Nick," I said calmly to the devil himself. "Enjoying the concert?"

"Very much, thank you," Nick said, taking to the stage. At the sight, the demon band not only stopped but dropped their instruments. When Walt turned to look, he strummed a bad cord and dropped his pick. "But as much as I enjoyed it, I'm afraid I'm going to have to end the music."

Nick walked over to the demons in the band. "This is unsanctioned. You know the rules." They all looked guiltily at their shoes. "All of you, head home now."

Like chastised children, they obediently walked to the wormhole. I barely got in front of them in time.

"Nice try, Nick. They aren't willing participants. The demons can go, but the bodies stay," I said. Nick and I stared each other down. Whenever we did this without something on the line, he wins hands down. When it counts, I win more often than not. Even the Devil has rules to follow. The key is to learn the rules. I knew most of them.

"Very well. Out, boys," Nick ordered. The demons vacated their human hosts, who immediately collapsed to the stage. Nick turned toward Ash.

"Who the frick are you?" Ash demanded.

"I'm the Devil you don't believe exists. Time to visit that alternate dimension of yours that didn't have music. The natives have a name for it," said Nick.

"What's that?" asked Ash.

"They call it Hell," Nick said, and with a gesture tossed Ash into the hellhole. Before it closed behind him, you could hear Ash start to scream.

Nick strolled over to Walt.

"So, Walter, how have you been? How's that lovely wife of yours? And those darling children I keep hearing about?"

"Leave my family out of this, Nick," growled Walt. Nick was unflustered.

"Or?" asked Nick coolly.

"We'll have to have us a rematch," said Walt, through clenched teeth.

"Oh, count on it, although to be honest, I was planning on waiting a few decades until your hands were crippled with arthritis first. I look forward to our rematch. Bye, Hex," Nick said as he climbed down from the stage and lost himself in the crowd, who stood watching as if it had been a show. They figured Nick's exit to be the end because some started clapping.

Walt quoted some Charlie Daniels as Nick left. "Well, Devil come on back if you ever want to try again. I told you once, you son of a bitch, I'm the best there's ever been." He then broke into *Devil Went Down To Georgia.* Before he could finish, sirens were heard in the distance. The police were coming to shut us down, signaling the end of the underground concert.

I grabbed Walt and started moving him out of the park.

"What about your speakers?" Walt asked.

"I'll lift them out of police lock-up tomorrow," I said. "You did great up there. Thanks."

"My pleasure," said Walt. He paused a minute. "You think Nick meant what he said about waiting?"

"Yes," I said. "But we'll worry about that when it comes. Our real worry is to get you back to Betsy before your curfew or we're both in real trouble."

CHANNELING XIPE TOTEC

I'm cursed. A lot of people say that when things don't go their way, but with me it's the truth. I'd like to say it wasn't my fault, but the guy who did it would disagree.

I often have to do things that end up making me feel lousy on a good day. I don't even like to think about the bad ones. Of course, I usually only get this way by helping other people. If I minded my own business, I'd feel fine. Of course, the people who ask for my help would usually die, so I figure it's best to work through the pain. The only remedies that seem to do any good are aspirin, caffeine, and sleep. Mostly sleep. It might sound like a hangover, but a curseover is nowhere near as pleasant. A hangover won't kill you or make you pass out while fighting for your life or someone else's.

I was at the tail end of my curse-induced pain. A few more hours of sleep and I'd be golden. At least as golden as I get.

Unfortunately, the noise level in my apartment wasn't about to allow that to happen. On days like this, I almost wished I lived alone.

Mind you, my roommates don't exactly keep a normal schedule. When I opened one eye to look at my alarm clock, I realized I'd been passed out for almost twenty hours. Still, the clock was claiming it was three in the morning. A man deserves a little peace and quiet in his own home at that hour. What I got instead was more along the lines of the cruise cabin scene from that old Marx Brothers movie. More chaos, but fewer people. Although technically, I was the only person present; my brood were family, but far from human.

At times like this I considered ruining the open space of my two thousand square foot studio by putting up sound proof walls. There was a chase scene minus the cars going on: a fox and wolf were chasing a coyote through the air in my apartment. And they were all glowing. No, I wasn't drunk or seeing things. I live with five spirit animals, three of which are wolves. The other two were a fox and a coyote. They sort of followed me home from the spirit world where something bad had been going down. I let them stay, although nights like this made me wonder why. As spirit animals, they were able to exist in a state of semi-solidness. Not only could they run, they could fly or selectively pass through solid objects. It was the last part that was really aggravating me, because they were crashing into things and knocking them over instead of phasing through them.

The food processor was going full blast as a pixie tried to make chocolate cake. Don't know if you have ever seen children after having large amounts of chocolate, but it is nothing compared to when a pixie gets a chocolate fix. Bollywog had already been sampling the batter. I didn't know why she was using the food processor instead of the mixer and I didn't much care. Splattering sounds made it clear plenty of the batter was ending up on the floor, counter, ceiling and walls. Hummingbird-esque buzzing meant the pixie was darting about the room, probably trying to catch the flying batter in her mouth. It was a game to her.

Last and far from least, so far as sheer size was concerned, Jeeves was sitting on the floor watching television. The reason he sat on the floor was because he was big. Huge really, topping out at over seven feet tall and several hundred pounds. The golem was too large for most furniture. Jeeves can't talk, so he couldn't tell the others to be quiet unless he used American Sign Language, and the others weren't exactly stopping to look at his hands. I think he was trying to ignore them in favor of his program. To do that, the clay man had the volume on the flat screen turned up to a hundred, blasting through all the surround sound speakers in the apartment.

Jeeves has had limited human contact, except for the mage who created him. (A real evil bastard, but not someone Jeeves has to worry about anymore. Neither does anyone else.)

The clay man literally stands out in a crowd. His appearance, combined with being mute, makes in-person socialization challenging, but doesn't stop him from being fascinated by people. Which is probably the reason he loves public access television. By law, they have to put anyone that can produce a program on the air – and in New York, you get just about the most varied collection of shows anywhere. This particular program was shouting about being some sort of game show and how it was going to change the world.

I pulled the covers over my head and tried to put the pillow over my ears. Then a lamp hit the floor and smashed into pieces.

That was enough. "Quiet!" I shouted.

Sorry. said Mordi the papa wolf.

Sorry. said Sly the fox.

Sorry. said Trickster the coyote.

The spirit canines communicate telepathically. Bollywog considered speaking anything beside her native pixie tongue beneath her, so she rarely uses English, although she understands it perfectly. She didn't say a word but the processor turned off. Jeeves lowered the volume. I could still hear the show, but it was low enough that I couldn't make out the words. I could sleep with that.

A moment later I could feel Jeeves's hard index finger poking me in the back.

"Go away, big man. Trying to sleep here," I said.

Jeeves put his hand on my back and shook my body side to side.

"Leave me alone!" I said a little louder than I needed to. The golem ripped the blankets and pillows off me, then lifted me up with both hands and carried me to the TV set.

"Jeeves, just hit record and I'll watch it later," I said.

The golem held me out at arm's length in front of him so my feet dangled off the floor, pointing my face at the big screen TV. There was a host sitting in a circle set up to look like some bizarre 70's game show, maybe the one Dick Clark hosted. There was a logo on the wall behind him that read *The Deadly Aztec Pyramid*. But there were no celebrity guests and he was the only one who looked like he was having fun. Next to him, a woman was tied to an office chair. The host was making like he was playing a game with her, but there was a huge knife in his hand.

"Missy, you still haven't answered my question. How much do the ashes of a cremated adult weigh on average?"

"Ten pounds?" she said, her voice squeaking.

"Oh, I'm sorry, Missy! That's the wrong answer. The correct answer is nine pounds," he said.

"I was close," Missy pleaded, tears streaming down her cheeks. She was almost hyperventilating between sobs.

The host put his hand on her shoulder as if to comfort the woman. "Yes, you were. It was an excellent guess, but on DAP, close isn't good enough. I'm afraid you lose your chance for freedom. Instead, you win the wonderful consolation prize!" He paused to clap awkwardly as he didn't put down the knife, his tone the fake happy of old game shows. "You are going to have your life sacrificed to Xipe Totec and I'm going to wear your skin like a wet suit."

The Evil Game Show Host stood and plunged the knife deep into the woman's chest. She screamed as it went between ribs and right into her heart, which he then cut out and held in front of the camera.

"No!" I shouted, but of course the man on television couldn't hear me. In the corner of the screen the word *LIVE* was spelled out. Jeeves put me down. "Did they say where they are broadcasting from?"

Jeeves shook his head no.

The Flayer is bad news Trickster the coyote projected. That was one of the Aztec god Xipe Totec's titles. Best not to say a god's name directly. It lets them know you are discussing them, maybe even listen in. Or if you're dumb enough to say their name three times under the right conditions, they might actually show up to say hi or kill you. Often both.

Not good. If I remembered Darked correctly, Xipe Totec demanded human sacrifices, which his priests skinned. They wore the human hides for ceremonial purposes. The Aztecs and their gods were a bunch of sick bastards.

The host continued to prove me right by skinning the poor woman's corpse. Apparently, the act helped focus the sacrifice's power, because behind the host, a ghostly image of Xipe Totec appeared. It was a golden mix of man, monster and eagle. The Aztec god wore what looked like a human skin, but not well. The hands and feet flopped to the side and strips ran from his forehead to jaw.

May need to get out of town, agreed Sly the fox.

"Nobody is leaving town. We need to find this sicko and stop him," I said. The host sliced the poor woman's skin off her body and put it on like a leotard. My cynical side was already thinking this was going to be the highest rated show in public access history. Also not good, as some of the viewers might start to believe in Xipe Totec and that would only add to his power.

There are different ways to bring a god to the physical world besides saying their name three times. They can be summoned, called or brought over by sacrifice. This bozo had gone for the latter, using people instead of animals. And he was smart enough to figure a way to get a crowd watching to feed the blood magic. He might be psychotic, but he wasn't dumb. "We're going to go on the assumption they are somewhere in the city. I want the five of you to spread out and see if you can sense them anywhere."

Will do, said Mordi, the father spirit wolf, who took his wife Maydo and his son Rocky as I lowered some wards in the apartment which let them go out the windows.

This won't end well, Trickster said.

I looked back to the TV. The host was rolling the chair the skinned woman had sat in off to the side of the stage and rolled a man back into her spot.

"It didn't start well either."

I still had a problem: My curse. I was only able to use magic in self-defense or if someone asked me to help. So far, nobody had. I couldn't ask someone to ask me – the curse didn't work that way. And even if I used magic when asked, it hurt like hell.

The host stared into the camera and spoke like he was advertising tortoise wax. "Unfortunate for poor little Missy, but we have a new contestant. I want our home viewers to put their hands together and welcome Darren to our show. As a matter of fact, I want to take this time out to thank those at home for tuning in and watching as we work toward our goal of bringing Xipe Totec to New York City. Unlike other churches, we don't want your money, but my god could use your prayers. Think about it – what could be more exciting than an Aztec god running amok in The Big Apple? Think of the glorious death and destruction. Think of the fun! I want those of you at home to do whatever you can to help."

I grinned. The idiot didn't say to help do what! His little statement was enough for the curse to let me kick in the magic.

I reached out with my power, tying to sense where this bozo was. A god materializing on the mortal plane should make a lot of mystic noise. Unfortunately, New York City already had several gods living here, not to mention a lot of other mystic interference. I couldn't get anything.

The Evil Game Show Host asked Darren a question. "Archimedes was killed because of what kind of pi?"

"Apple?" Darren said, not understanding it was a trick question.

I had Jeeves get on the Internet for the address to the cable station. There are plenty of ways to travel mystically, but the one that got me the most bang for the least magic was body sliding. It's an incredibly fast way to travel. Over short distances it seems almost as fast as teleportation, but it's not. You don't suddenly appear at your destination. You actually go through the space in between. No matter where you are on Earth there are forces acting upon you, not the least of which are gravity and the velocity of the Earth rotating and moving through space. It's possible to phase the body out of sync with the rest of the world so it's briefly immaterial and to negate some of these forces while amplifying others. It's akin to surfing using a variety of towropes that are attached to a shark, a jet aircraft and a passing comet. It's incredibly dangerous, but because it used mostly external forces, it had minimal effect on my curse trying to kick my butt.

I used a tiny bit of magic to locate the place and body slid to the broadcast control room of the cable company. It was tiny, just enough space for equipment and a few chairs, one of which was occupied by an overweight man who had his head down and was snoring.

On the screen, the evil game show host was telling Darren he was wrong and that the answer was not food pie, but the numerical pi.

"Wake up," I shouted. The irony of waking someone else who wanted to sleep did not escape my attention.

He woke with a start. "What are you doing in here?"

I pointed to the screen. "What are you doing broadcasting a man murdering people?" I said, just as the host plunged a knife into Darren.

The tech shouted something about blessed feces as the host took out Darren's beating heart and showed it to the home audience. That little bit of butchery would be right up the alley of a different Aztec god known as the filth eater.

"Where is the live broadcast coming from?" I asked as the vision of Xipe Totec became less blurry, as if the ritual murders were bringing a mystic antenna into focus. No telling how many more it would take to let him physically cross over into our world. He sliced off Darren's hide, then put it on over Missy's.

"I don't know. We are connected to him through an Internet feed that he's streaming to us." The tech started playing with the control board. "It's not letting me stop the broadcast."

Magic can do things like that. Suddenly the audio became very loud. "Afraid we'll just have to stop for a moment until the train is gone," the Evil Game Show Host said.

It was loud. He must have been in a subway station or somewhere along the tracks. That narrowed down the search.

Guys, check the subway system starting with Manhattan, I broadcast to the spirit pack.

"I want you to rewind the broadcast to the beginning. Maybe we can see where he's transmitting from," I said.

I reached out to try and trace the signal back to its source, but quickly hit a mystical ward. I had the power to punch through it, but didn't know what kind of shape I would be in afterwards. Like I said: Cursed.

Meanwhile, the technician had gotten the show back to its opening credits.

"Fast forward through it and look for any clues as to where he might be," I said.

It opened with the Evil Game Show Host introducing the show in front of a graffiti version of a Central American pyramid. It turns out his name was Glenn Tetz and he didn't seem to have a cameraman, so he turned the camera on a tripod himself. The camera panned past a bunch of graffiti-style art on the walls of the subway. It was too nice to be just gang tags, so I racked my brain for a subway station that had an art show of some sort. Also, the platform seemed deserted, which pointed to one that was closed. The Second Avenue subway line had been closed and uncompleted for ages. The city was planning to finish it someday, but there wouldn't be any trains on that line yet.

Just then, Trickster came through the walls and floated next to us. As far as regular folks go, spirit animals are fairly close to invisible, but Trickster likes to make the effort to be seen. As to why, it was in his nature. Case in point, the tech screamed and jumped backwards as soon as he saw Trickster appear out of nowhere.

Found it – the old City Hall Station, projected Trickster.

They built the City Hall Station back in 1904 and closed it in 1945 because the tracks curved and the trains had a dangerous gap. It's at the end of the 6 Line and had some pretty old school construction. Some street artists have put up work on the walls, which explained the high-end graffiti. The place is also used occasionally in films and movies, so anyone with a search engine could find out about it.

"Thanks. You want to come with?" I teased.

Suicide? No thanks. I'm not going. However, if you need a quick getaway, you know who to ask, sent the Trickster.

"Mordi," I said, referring to the spirit wolf.

Exactly, said Trickster with a grin.

I body slid to the closed subway station, making sure I ended up on the tracks. Tetz was so intent on playing on his little murderous game show that he didn't notice my arrival. I should have been able to sense this big a surge of magic. Summoning a god by ritual sacrifice was the mystic noise equivalent to setting up a heavy metal concert in a library, which meant the area had to be pretty well warded. Body sliding through said ward could turn me into the consistency of strained meatloaf. I reached out and felt the ward. Nothing fancy, but strong. Xipe Totec's power was supplementing Tetz's.

I could punch through it, but the amount of power it would take might make me useless afterwards. One thing the curse has taught me is that it's not always about power or brute force. Finesse and cleverness can be far more effective weapons. I crawled onto the subway platform. It appeared that the Evil Game Show Host had brought more office chairs than he needed, maybe hoping he would have more contestants. There were also some precut lengths of rope next to the chairs. I sat down on one and used the ropes to make it look as if my arms were tied. The victims in the chairs also had their legs tied, but for this to work I didn't need to do that. As soon as I was ready, I knocked one of the empty chairs over and used my legs to start walking the wheeled chair towards the exit sign.

The host turned away from his current victim and the players' circle and screamed, "Hey, you! Stop!"

Without thinking or wondering what had happened, Tetz ran out, breaking his own ward. He grabbed hold of my chair and pulled me back inside with him. Goal achieved without using magic. Take that, curse.

"Let go of me," I said, trying frantically with my legs to pull away from him. Of course, he had the leverage and I was supposedly tied up. It wasn't much of a contest.

"How did you get your legs untied?" he asked looking over to where he had at least two dozen other people tied in office chairs.

"None of your damn business, you sick psycho," I said. "Untie me and we'll see how tough you are."

The Evil Game Show Host smiled. "So, you're a tough guy, huh? Want to take me on? Okay, then. You're our next contestant." He walked over to the woman who was already in the players' circle. "Sorry, my dear, you just lost your turn. But don't worry, you'll go next." Tetz slid the woman in the chair back into the crowd and rolled me into the players' circle. It was basically a chalk spell circle over a drain. The blood had to go somewhere. Tetz's feet were sticky and covered in crimson.

There was a flat screen on a stand. Tetz had programmed it to show the questions from a tablet computer. He was using a hand held remote to move to the next question.

"So, are you ready to play *Deadly Aztec Pyramid*?" he said.

It was time for me to do my thing. "What you're doing here is evil and wrong. I'm going to give you one warning and this is it. Stop now or there will be severe consequences for you."

I always try to give a warning. I'm a gray walker, which means I do a lot of bad things for good causes. That doesn't absolve my soul of my actions, only mitigates it. However, telling someone else what will happen if they do said evil action is another matter. If they ignore the warning, that means they choose the consequences and that keeps my soul mostly clean. That's important. There are a lot of evil people in the afterworlds who would like to get a hold of me. Best to make sure that doesn't happen. Not that I'm planning on dying by any means, but it will happen someday, hopefully later rather than sooner.

Like so many others, the evil game show host ignored the warning. In fact, he laughed at it. "Thank you. I'll keep that under consideration. It's time for your first question. True or false – Queen Cleopatra had better looking eyebrows than King Rameses?"

"False. Egyptian royalty shaved all hair including their eyebrows," I said.

The evil game show host raised his eyebrows. "Impressive. And correct. Fill in the blank – snails can sleep up to _____ without food."

"Three years," I said.

Tetz frowned. "Correct. In Thomas Jefferson's Monticello home in Virginia he had an entire room dedicated to an illegal activity. What was it?"

"Billiards," I said. The game was against the law in Virginia back then.

Tetz almost growled. "Right again. What capital city of what county, is constructed on nine different islands joined together by bridges."

"That would be Stockholm, the capital of Sweden," I said.

It went on like that for a long time. I answered over two dozen questions correctly. I had excellent recall and read a lot. The Evil Game Show Host was infuriated because by his own rules he wasn't allowed to kill me unless I got a question wrong. It was making him nuts. The ghostly image of Xipe didn't seem too happy either, but as long as my knowledge of trivia held up, there was nothing he could do about it except remain stuck between the two realms.

"Time for the bonus round – what's my middle name?" he asked holding the sacrificial knife up, ready to plunge it into the chest.

Fortunately for me, I can tap into all magic, even the psychic variety. I knew the answer as soon as he thought it. "Harold."

The knife started to plunge down to my chest and stopped half way. "That's … correct. How the hell could you know that?"

Tetz had stepped close enough to me that I was able to answer him with a kick straight to the groin, doubling him over. Since my hands weren't really tied, I reached out and grabbed the knife out of his hand, then brought my knee up into his jaw to knock him to the floor. I raced to the woman whom I had replaced in the players' circle and used the sacrificial blade to cut her ropes, then handed her the knife. "Free the others, but be careful not to cut them. Don't give this thing any more blood. We don't want it coming over the rest of the way."

The woman nodded and to her credit got right to work cutting ropes.

I turned back toward Tetz and the sight wasn't pretty. Literally. He had called upon his god and his god had answered. Xipe Totec granted his priest power, which transformed him into a reptilian-looking eagle man with scales that looked a lot like feathers or maybe they were feathers that looked a lot like scales. Poor dead Darren and Missy's skin had morphed along with him.

The new and enhanced Tetz rushed at me like a linebacker, slamming me into the concrete wall. It hurt and I regretted giving away the knife. As it was part of his power circuit, it would hurt him. In magic, like could be used to damage like. On the plus side, he had no real fighting skills against an opponent who wasn't tied up. I managed to knee him in the groin again. That can hurt even gods. At least the male ones. Yes, I know it's fighting dirty, but if I fell, those two-dozen people behind me would die next, followed by a significant portion of the population of Manhattan when Xipe went to town gathering more sacrifices. He would offer power to every murderous psychopath willing to kill others in his name, which in turn would make him even more powerful. He'd use the extra power to get more psychos to kill, and so on, in an old but deadly pyramid scheme. Then, once firmly entrenched in our world, the Aztec flayer would start killing others himself, just for fun.

I managed to wiggle free and moved to the edge of the platform, stopping to smash his camera. Cut off from the home viewers, Xipe Totec would lose some belief manna. Tetz's body began to elongate. He now had a seven-foot-long serpent-like tail as thick as his torso, and his arms morphed into wings. His face grew a giant beak. Tetz leapt through the air at me. His would-be victims probably thought he was flying, but it was really more a form of levitation. He didn't have enough power for flight yet.

Either way, I didn't want him getting his razor-sharp beak on any part of me. I waited until he was almost on top of me, grabbed hold of his ear and jumped down onto the platform. My body weight pulled him down with me and his momentum carried him right onto the third rail. I rolled away an instant before the electricity tore through him.

Sadly, Xipe Totec was not a forgotten god. Plenty of human lives were sacrificed to him back in the day, more than almost any other deity in the last five hundred years, with the exception of his brother Quetzalcoatl and a couple of other relations. A lot of people knew about him, especially around his old stomping grounds, which made for a powerful combination. His priest was down, but not out.

I stood up and brushed myself off, trying to figure out my next move when I heard the horn. A subway train was bearing down on us. I ran to the platform to drag myself up and found I didn't have to do it alone. Several of the people had already been cut free and they grabbed hold of my arms and pulled me up just in time. Who says New Yorkers aren't helpful?

The train hit Tetz head-on. He stopped moving and his eyes closed. The train stopped with only the last car still in the station.

"Help me," I said to the good Samaritans and together we pried the doors open. "Get everybody in quickly."

Those that were freed grabbed those that were still tied to chairs and rolled them through the subway doors. I got a lot of "thank yous" and "God bless yous". I even got a hug from the woman I gave the blade to. I smiled and returned the hug. I held up my hand and she returned the sacrificial knife. The train typically turned around after this station and headed back.

I jumped down, careful to step over the third rail. I walked down the tracks to where the front of the train was. The impact had caused Tetz to revert to human. He was unconscious, but still breathing. I threw him over my shoulder.

The conductor opened the window. "Did I kill that thing?"

"No, but get the train going," I said.

"What, it was a guy? It looked like an animal. If it's a person I can't. Regs state if a person is hit we have to stay here until EMS and cops arrive," he said.

"This guy wasn't human when he hit you. Just say it was a large dog. You have a lot of people on the train that this guy wants to kill. There're two skinned corpses back on the platform. He used them to crack open the doorway for something big and nasty to come through. If he wakes up and I can't stop him, everyone on board this train, including you, could just be another victim for him to kill and then that door will open wide."

"Ain't no such thing as magic," he said. "And...."

Well, at least I tried telling the truth. "Guy's a terrorist and he left something that is going to blow on the platform. Get these people out of here and you'll likely get a commendation from the mayor."

"I'd rather have a raise," he said, but he got the train moving.

I walked back to the platform, trying to come up with the best way to handle things. The curse kicks in more when I use my own power, less when I tap into that of others. So far, I hadn't had to use much, so I was just a little achy. Tetz was unconscious, but had still been granted power. I had the sacrificial knife that was the focus of that power.

I came up with a plan and smiled. If I were on a game show called Beat the Curse, I'd be about to win or at least make the final round.

I dumped Tetz on the platform and removed the coat he had made from his victims' skin. Next, I slit open Tetz's right palm and put some of his blood on the blade. I went to the wall and used the crimson liquid to draw a large doorway.

"*Prison,*" I intoned and the blood transformed into red energy, which oozed into the stone like neon acid and carved out a tiny room. I dragged Tetz and his TV monitor inside, then got some more of his blood on the blade and made what would best be described as a mystic tractor beam with the blade to get the ghostly image of Xipe Totec inside the carved room as well.

I focused on the pair and the TV monitor and intoned, "*Eternal programming loop.*"

Then I took the sacrificial blade and made some modifications to Tetz's face before I woke him. Then I turned the television on.

A show called Aztec Temple Makeover Home Edition flashed on and Xipe Totec's ghostly image was gone from the real world into the television set, right next to a crowd of pixelated pretend people who were about to digitally rebuild one of his temple ruins. I changed channels and a black and white show came on with a giant heart in front of a curtain. Theme music played and an invisible hand wrote *I Love Xipe Totec* on it.

"Ah, let's leave it on this channel," I said, as someone onscreen shouted, "*Xipe, you got some splaining to do.*"

"Xipe Totec has taken over all the broadcasts in the world?" Tetz said, grinning like an idiot. An evil idiot, but an idiot just the same.

"Not so much. Because you used the TV broadcast as part of your ritual, I was able to tap into the power you raised and trap Xipe Totec in a mystic feedback loop. As long as someone is watching him, he will forever be trapped in revamped reruns. That is, as long as there are enough shows to be converted –and trust me, there are tens of millions of hours of them – he will just replace one of the main characters in each show or commercial."

"I'll just turn away," Tetz said.

I shook my head. "You can't. You're paralyzed by the spell and physical restraints. Even if you did manage to move, the spell insures the TV will move to stay in your sights."

"Then I'll blink and in that instant Xipe Totec will be free," Tetz said then laughed.

"You'd think that would work, but you'd be wrong." I held up in my hand two bits of skin with fine hairs all in a row on the end and held them in front of Tetz's face.

"Are those my eyelids?" he said.

"Yup." Because blood magic was used, I did have to cut a part of him off to fuel the final part of the spell and this seemed the most humane. Not that a man who cut out the hearts from two people deserved mercy, but I figured this was worse than killing him. If he had managed to summon Xipe Totec in a city the size of New York, the death toll would have been at least five or six figures, possibly more if the god had figured a way to trap everybody inside the city.

"You can't do this to me," Tetz said.

"You're obviously not familiar with what the word *can't* means."

The TV went to commercial and Xipe Totec was now selling a set of Xipesu sacrificial knives, guaranteed to cut through a tin can or the human chest.

"I used your own ritual and the power he gave you to make sure that you'll never sleep again, not to mention insuring that the two of you will remain trapped here in symbiotic union forever. Enjoy," I said, stepping out the door the magic had carved from the stone. I had just enough blood left on the knife to seal the stone behind me. Unfortunately, all magic has to have an out, a way to break the spell. This one would require many things, including using the sacrificial knife to get the TV out of Tetz's line of sight. I was friends with a leprechaun that owned a bar called Bulfinche's Pub. It was a magical null zone and would be the safest place to keep the knife away from the hands of any other followers who might want to free Tetz or Xipe. I was hurting bad. Trapping a god for all eternity was a lot harder than pulling a hat out of a rabbit, even if the rabbit was flexible and willing to cooperate. I was too spent and exhausted to use any sort of transportation magic – too much risk of passing out during transit. Hell, I was barely able to walk, but I managed to get over to where I had put the flayed skin I removed from Tetz. I brought it to where Darren and Missy's corpses were. I laid each corpse's skin on top of the victim it came from and intoned, "*Suit up.*"

The skin went back unto their bodies. My friend Moni would be proud. She's a graveyard angel who watches over the dead. I didn't do it for her. I did it for Darren and Missy's families and friends. No one needed to see a loved one like that. As least now they'd be able to have an open casket at the wakes.

That last bit cost me. I was seeing spots and my own skin was burning like I had been dipped in acid after getting a sunburn. The cops would be down here as soon as they talked to the people on the train and they'd take care of the bodies. I tried to stay out of the spotlight to make my life easier and I was careful to make sure my face was never pointed toward the camera. The cops would have a hard time tracking me down. And as lousy as I was feeling, I wasn't in any kind of mood for questions, especially when they'd never believe my answers.

I hopped down on the tracks and forced myself to keep walking. My skin felt like it was stuck to my bones. The curse likes to be creative with my pain. Since I put skin back on the dead guy and girl, it was making mine hurt and hard to move.

I stopped at a small alcove tunnel, which was hidden from view on the tracks. I crawled inside and out of sight, wrapped my navy trench coat around me, reached in my pocket and pulled out a piece of chalk from a metal tube, then used it to draw a protective ward. A train whipped by and rattled the place.

Remembering the ruckus in my apartment when I had left, I smiled and whispered, "Peace and quiet at last."

I pretended not to notice Trickster phase in behind me in the alcove. He feigned indifference, but curled up by my legs. It wasn't long before the remainder of the pack arrived and surrounded me, putting their bodies between me and the rest of the world. I passed out after activating the ward, knowing I would be watched over. And probably woken up too early when they ended up getting bored.

THE HAND THAT ROCKS THE GRAVE

"I need your help. I want you to kill my baby."

That was an usual opening line to hear, even for me. It sounded like something someone I'm usually asked to stop would say, but I wasn't getting that kind of a reading off this woman. In fact, her umbra had an unusual property. When I read the shadow of someone's soul, I can pick up superficial emotions easily, helpful while playing poker. With effort, I can see the damage or benefits that that person's actions have done to their soul.

This woman's umbra was not in good alignment with her physical body, extending a good few inches to her left side. That usually means someone or something was trying to take it.

"As I'm not in the habit of killing children, I think you better explain your situation," I said.

"Yes, Mr. Hex." Carla was actually bowing, practically groveling. I work hard to cultivate a tough rep. It sometimes saves me from having to exert myself magically, something which has been very difficult to do ever since the curse. It proves awkward at other times. We sat across from each other at one of the chessboards in Central Park, and people were starting to stare. Not that I much cared. "My baby girl Ashley died twelve weeks ago from SIDS. My husband blamed me and left because of it. I went into a deep depression and I did something I shouldn't have."

"You sold your soul."

Carla's jaw actually dropped. The satisfaction made me want to smile, but it didn't seem appropriate. "How did you know?"

I saw no reason to explain the umbra connection. Better to be mysterious. "I know things."

This was the type of thing Hell thrived on, taking a basically good but grieving person and promising them their heart's desire. It rarely turns out well. The Devil tended to do it better than his underlings. Likes to give the marks less wiggle room to get out of the contract. The lesser demons are so anxious to get any soul that they'll promise the world and deliver Jersey. Of course, beings other than demons buy souls and there was no reason to ruin my mystique at this stage of the game. "What was the name of the buyer?"

"Jaxic. He said he was a demon."

"Hmmm," I responded.

"You've heard of him?"

Actually, I hadn't. "No, but at least it wasn't the Devil himself."

"How do you know that? And why is that a good thing?"

"Nick would never let another take credit for his work. And his contracts are better written than those the help use, which means there might be a loophole. Do you have a copy of the contract?"

"I didn't ask for one. I guess I should have. Pretty dumb, huh?" I refrained from comment. "I was just so happy to have Ashley back that I didn't care about anything else. You must think I'm an awful person."

"No, just heartbroken and desperate." I could have added foolish, but I was pretty sure she already realized that. "Why are you looking to end your child's reanimation?"

"The last few nights I've gotten up to check on Ashley…"

"It's not Ashley. It's most likely the demon you made the deal with, only in her body."

Carla's jaw dropped, then closed. "I guess that makes sense now. Last night when I got up, Ashley…" She caught my glance. "The baby wasn't in her crib. I waited in the nursery and saw Ash… the baby opened the window and crawled in. We're on the sixth floor, and there's no fire escape outside that window. The baby saw me after it closed the window and hissed at me. To see my baby like that, her face distorted, looking like she was ready to kill me…"

She paused, waiting for me to comfort her. In her grief, this woman had let a demon loose on the world. I wasn't in a comforting mood. "Obviously, it didn't follow through."

"No. When she saw it was me, her face became beautiful again. She crawled over into my lap and wrapped her arms around my neck. She kissed my cheek and whispered 'I love you, Mommy' in my ear. That's when I knew it wasn't her. She was too little to talk, and it wasn't the voice of a baby."

"That's when you decided she needed to be killed?" I asked.

"No. That happened this morning. I went into the shower and there were little bloody handprints on my neck and red lip marks on my face. And I hadn't bothered to read the paper in weeks. It turns out there had been five murders in my neighborhood, all at night with tiny bite marks. My neighbor's husband's a cop, and she said they couldn't figure out why it looked like a baby had eaten the dead people's flesh. That's when I knew."

"We need to end this now." There was a handbag under the table which I glanced at, ready to incinerate it. "Did you bring it with you?"

"No."

Great. There was probably some clause that protected the mother, which extended to not killing in her presence and explained the late-night jaunts. "Where is your daughter's body now?"

"I dropped her at daycare."

Not many things shock me anymore. This did. "You left a demon-possessed zombie baby with a taste for human flesh in a place full of helpless children?"

"I didn't think about it that way. I didn't want to leave my baby alone—"

I was probably a little rougher than I needed to be when I grabbed her by the collar. "Where is the daycare?!"

"I don't remember the exact address. It's a couple of blocks from my apartment in Jackson Heights."

Damn it. Without an exact address, I couldn't risk a body slide or wormhole. Even half a mile away, the demon would sense the transport and head for the hills. A human hearing sirens would probably leave the children behind. A demon feeling someone dangerous approaching would kill the kids just because it could.

"Come with me." I grabbed Carla's hand and pulled her with me as I ran through the park, coming out on the Fifth Avenue side. I jumped in front of a speeding cab and it stopped before hitting me, but only barely. I opened the back door and climbed in. There was already another passenger.

"I already got a fare, buddy," said the cabbie.

The fare was a Wall Street type who felt he deserved extra-special treatment in life because he was rich. "Get out before I call a cop."

I did a quick reading. Broker boy was on his way to an extended lunch with a beautiful young woman. Good for him, not so good for his wife and their three kids. "I was going to ask nicely, but I don't have time. You get out or I call Donna and tell her about Debbie. And where that video file of the two of you from last month is hidden. Should make for a nice settlement, don't you think?"

He wasn't moving. I pulled out my cell. "The file is in your computer under *offshore investment plans*. We both know you'll never get to Jersey before she sees it." I reached over and opened his door. "Out or I dial."

He scurried and stood in the street, his calm shattered. He didn't even bother with asking how I knew. "You won't tell my wife now, will you?"

I shut the door and pulled Carla in next to me. Broker boy was knocking on the window, pleading for my discretion. I ignored him, but I didn't feel too bad for the trophy wife. Their second kid wasn't broker boy's.

"Jackson Heights. And go as fast as you can."

"Traffic's kind of tied up, in case you haven't noticed," the cabbie said sarcastically.

"Not for long," I said. "All green lights."

At the corner, the light went from stop to go and kept green all the way to the 59th Street Bridge.

"Wow. I've never hit every light like that before, but it looks like the bridge is tied up," said the cabbie.

"Then you ain't seen nothing yet. Turn the wheel hard right," I said.

"You nuts? That's a cement barrier."

I opened the Plexiglas barrier and yanked on the wheel. The cabbie slapped me and slammed on the brake, but not before I said,

"Over the river and under the bridge."

We became airborne and dropped down fast enough to make the driver and Carla scream. The car slid under the bridge, swerving to avoid the towers, then shot up and dropped in front of traffic.

"How the hell did you do that?" the cabbie asked.

"I could tell you but then…"

"You'd have to kill me?"

"Naw. It would just change your world forever." Most people ignore the magic all around them, letting their brains explain it away.

"If you can make the car fly, why are we driving?" asked Carla.

"It's too difficult to explain." Actually, it was easy, but then I'd have to explain the curse, that I couldn't even have involved myself if she hadn't asked. And that using even that little bit of power was causing me pain. If I flew the car the entire way, I'd be too useless to fight the demon. And it might sense the power. Levitation doesn't make as big a noise as bending the laws of space and distance, but there was still a risk.

I did another spell to help traffic along, but it was still too slow. As we got closer, Carla gave the cabbie directions, and he pulled up in front of the daycare center. It was in a storefront with a black-tinted front window. I could almost taste the demon power at work. I already had money out and threw it at the driver as I raced out of the car. I hit the door at a run and couldn't force it open. Demon magiks had reinforced the lock.

Carla caught up to me. I took out my key ring and handed her a black skeleton key.

"Put this in the lock and turn it," I said.

"It won't fit," she said. The key looked about eighty years too old for the lock, but I had made the key when I was a kid, and it would open most doors.

"It will."

"Then why aren't you doing it?" she asked.

A reasonable question. Using magic hurts me. Using magic objects hurts less than drawing on my own power, but it still pushed me closer to the point where I might pass out. Bad form in the presence of a flesh-eating, demon-possessed zombie baby. In a regular lock, the magic the key used would be minor, but against demon magic, it'd be a major expenditure. I didn't need to take the hit when all Carla would feel is a mild tingle and a little straining of her wrist muscles.

"If you want to take watch in case the demon attacks, be my guest," I said instead.

"Fine," she said, putting the key in, surprised at how it morphed into the keyhole. It took quite a bit of pulling on Carla's part, but the lock finally turned. Luckily, the glass door opened out. I took the key back and slid it into my pocket.

I was facing what looked like a black wall of latex. It covered all surfaces of the inside of the daycare. Anything mortal that touched it would feel agony. I never used my power to become something more, so I still qualified. I would have preferred to put a spell circle around the building to trap the demon inside, but the daycare was physically attached to the two storefronts to either side of it. I needed another option. Drawing a spell circle barely registers on the curse pain meter, maybe half a paper cut's worth of discomfort. This was going to put me in range of getting a migraine, so I chewed and dry swallowed three aspirin that had caffeine mixed in. The aspirin helped the pain, the caffeine the other symptoms.

I pulled out five pieces of chalk and ripped a paper flyer for a lost dog off a lamppost. I wrapped the paper around the chalk and pulverized it by stomping on it with my foot. Next, I pulled out a flask and poured some of the contents over the chalk dust. No booze, just water, but it wasn't for drinking. Holy water isn't that refreshing, but it's great for other things. I sometimes bounced at Plasma, and the stupid vamps had a tendency to try to get a little revenge on me afterward. Holy water is like acid for vamps, and it also works wonders on demons. I picked up the paste in my hands and spit into it.

"What are you doing?" Carla asked.

"Shhh," I replied. This was going to take force of will, which kicked in the pain worse that spoken spells. I held up my upturned hands in front of my mouth and blew. The paste again became dust that flew to the minuscule space between the blackness and the building and snaked its way around like a ring around Saturn, then the spell circle became more of a sphere, enveloping everything black. The powder made like a cake rising or more accurately sinking, into the dark barrier. The barrier was less than a finger-width thick, so as soon as my circle was complete, I directed it to push aside enough of it to make a door that was safe for us to go through.

"Let's go," I said.

Carla had frozen. "I'm not sure I want to go in there."

"You're responsible for setting that thing loose. Those five deaths and whatever's happened in there is on your head."

"But my soul is already lost. If I die, don't they get it immediately?" she asked.

"If you let this happen, they'll have your soul without the contract," I said. "And many other mothers' children will die." She started to move, but too slowly. The quicker we got in, the better chance we'd have the element of surprise. "You asked for my help. There's a price. Helping me is it." I held out my hand and she grabbed onto it like a drowning woman. I went in first and pulled her in behind me.

The place was pitch dark. I had made sure the door was cloaked. We came in, but the light didn't. The dark shielding had cut through all the wires and even the plumbing so that nothing from the world outside could get in. At least nothing that wasn't a magí like yours truly. Magic is a lot like computer operating systems. What works for one won't necessarily work on another. A magí is kind of the mystical universal operating system, although just because I can tap into a certain type of power doesn't mean the mage on the other end isn't stronger or better versed in that particular field. Without the curse, I could match most for power, but there are so many different areas that it's hard to be as skilled as the masters.

Fortunately, demons tend to be heavier on the power than the skill, although this shield took quite a bit of both.

I could hear whimpering throughout the room, which meant at least some of the kids were alive. Time to go on the offensive.

"Let there be light." Okay, I stole the line, but I figured it wouldn't hurt, considering what I was facing. The room became as bright as it would have been had the fluorescent lights been working. A woman had several children huddled under a mat, protecting and comforting them by shielding them with her own body. She was terrified, but still protected those under her care. Bravery like that can't be taught.

There was a scream like a tribe of howler monkeys had been thrown in a blender. From a back room, a baby came in, dragging a woman behind her. The woman was dead, or at least I hoped so. The demon zombie baby had been eating her brain. It wasn't pretty.

"Who dare disturbs the mighty Beltizon?" bellowed the baby.

"Funny, I thought your name was Jaxic," I said, leaning against the wall.

"It looks like Mommy's been telling tales." The infant turned its head to Carla and snarled, its face becoming all jaw and teeth. "Naughty Mommy. I'll have to spank you."

"Jaxic, I bind you."

"Nice try," the demon said, using the baby's tiny hand to scoop out part of the dead woman's temporal lobe and put it into her mouth.

It at first you don't succeed, try again. "Beltizon, I bind you."

If at second you don't succeed, take evasive maneuvers. Using Beltizon had been a long shot. Any demon smart enough to figure out a way to get loose on Earth is probably not going to be dumb enough to announce its real name. All I had done was piss it off, and even though the bindings didn't work, they still invoked my curse. My entire body felt like I had gained seventy pounds. Another botched spell and I mightn't be able to move. I needed a minute to recover.

The baby's hands reached down and ripped the woman's right arm off, which proved she was dead. Otherwise, blood would have spurted everywhere. The tiny zombie leapt at me, brandishing the limb as a club aimed right at my head. I ducked and spun, but it was faster than me. The scapula clipped my ear, but I managed to reach out and grab it right below the deltoid, using the momentum to throw it into a wall. The demon in dead baby form spun and pushed off the wall, ricocheting across the room to land near the huddled children. It leapt at a toddler, and I was too far to get there first. Any spell that could do enough damage would be strong enough to hurt the toddler.

The woman there dove on top of the child. The baby zombie lashed out with a hand at the woman's throat, but she had bought me the second I needed. I grabbed the abomination by the ankle and flung it, smashing its head on the floor.

"*Spellfire!*" I yelled, and the inhabited corpse became a diaper-clad fireball.

Real fire would have burned me and probably not bothered the demon or its host, but as the caster, I was immune to the spellfire. The demon, not so much. Not only was it turning the Baby Ashley's corpse to ash, it was hurting the demon.

"Ready to surrender, demon?" I asked.

"Never!" Which is when I realized that not all of the demon zombie's remains were on fire. The demon motioned to the woman's corpse and a tooth disengaged from the brainpan. The demon had altered the tiny corpse to make it stronger and more durable. Otherwise, ripping and biting through flesh and bone really wasn't an option for it. One of its fangs must have broken off in the bone.

I swung the baby zombie, and the fang went right into the skull and caught fire.

"Now, before I sent you back to the Pit, let's talk about returning outright ownership of Carla's soul to her," I asked.

The zombie's skin was already gone, and the muscle and fat were burning bright, which made the laugh disconcerting. "No, it's mine."

"I'd like to see the contract," I said.

"I'd like to suck the humor out of your eyes. You give me what I want, maybe I'll give you what you want."

"No." I held the zombie at arm's length as it tried to kick and hit me. The spellfire wouldn't let it, but I'd bet fifty bucks I had a fever of a hundred and one. Probably would have been higher if I hadn't taken the aspirin.

"Fine. I'll just take over one of the other children."

Before I could say that I'd never allow it, Carla stepped out of the corner she's been huddled in. "No. Leave them alone. Take me instead."

"Sorry, Mommy, I would if I could, but the truth is I can only possess a dead body."

And there was a corpse across the room, but as long as the spellfire burned, the demon couldn't leave its host.

"So, what will it take for me to take over that luxury model in the corner?" it asked.

"A blizzard at home," I said, knowing full well parts of Hell were more frozen than Antarctica.

"I think you can do better." I sensed the use of power, but couldn't figure out what the demon was doing, and suddenly the woman who was protecting the kids grabbed her throat. Blood poured out from between her fingers.

I couldn't figure out how he had done it until the flaming baby gave me the finger.

"I broke a nail." Which it had sent flying like a spinning tiny buzz saw into the poor woman's neck.

"I got the carotid. Just a hole, but I can still control the nail enough to move it and rip the rest of her throat apart. Is her life worth my freedom?"

"You can heal her?" I asked.

"Nope. I just won't kill her any faster. You get a chance to save her."

Only if she didn't bleed out first. "*Stasis.*" It would freeze her for a brief time, but if the demon made the cut wider there would be nothing I could do. On the plus side, the spell lowered my body temperature to about normal. "You don't kill anyone else then."

"What's the point? I won't kill for at least an hour."

"A week." I'd be able to track and stop him by then.

"Two hours."

"Three days."

"Three hours."

"A day," I countered.

"Four hours. We can barter all night, but she doesn't have long," it said. "How long will that spell work? Three, maybe four minutes?"

I'm better than most, but I wouldn't bet on more than ten. "I won't consider anything less than twelve hours kill-free. And you give up the claim on Carla's soul."

"I'll give in on the twelve hours, but not the soul."

I had already come up with two possible loopholes, so I could try for the soul later. "And everyone in this room is forever off limits to you," I said.

"I assume you'll be coming after me, Mr. Hex. Yes, I know who you are. I'd be foolish to come to New York and not know about you. I can't grant you the same protection."

"But you'll grant it to them?"

"With 'Mommy's' soul obviously not included," the demon said.

"Fine, but you drop the shield and I'll need an oath." I hated to do this because Nick would know exactly what was happening if he didn't already, but my stasis spell was about to wear off. If I didn't get his word, the woman was going to die. "Swear by your lord."

"I swear by Satan to not kill anyone for twelve hours from now and to not harm anyone but you in this room and to not give up my claim on any souls in exchange for your giving me that corpse and allowing me my freedom, at least at this time. Acceptable?"

It wasn't, but I didn't have any other options available. The demon would be bound by that oath, so I literally blew out the baby, and the body crumbled to ash.

The demon was invisible to the others, but I saw it float over to the female corpse.

"Kids, close your eyes now and keep them closed until I tell you to open them," I said. Bad enough they saw me set what looked like a baby on fire, they didn't need to see their daycare provider get up and walk around with her half-eaten brain hanging out.

The corpse rose and the black shielding vanished and daylight rushed it, brighter than the spell I'd cast. The demon zombie rushed to leave but walked into my barrier. It screamed in pain.

The dead woman turned to me, her features morphing into something fanged and grotesque. "You break our bargain already? I'll kill the children and make a coat from their hides."

I debated about setting it aflame again with spellfire, but I couldn't juggle that and surgery on the woman's throat. "You should have waited for me to lower my ward." The demon turned and growled, rushing toward me. "You stop me from helping her and you break your word." My stasis spell was fading. Her neck was starting to bleed out at a snail's pace. I'd seen too many people killed in my lifetime. There was a small chance to save this one. I had to take it. "You want to go before Nick as an oath breaker in his name?" The Devil's power is partially dependent on keeping compacts and contracts. Things wouldn't go well for this demon if he broke his oath. "*Off*," I said, and my spell sphere dissipated.

The demon zombie hesitated, torn between freedom and revenge. Revenge was safe and familiar, freedom an unknown. I figured I'd help it along. "If this woman dies, Nick is going to be the least of your worries. I'll make you pay worse than any soul you've ever tortured. Make your choice and do it now."

The demon in a woman's corpse lumbered off. I had taken a reading so, as long as he stayed in that body, I'd find him, even if he was shielded. I'd make sure it'd be before the twelve hours were up.

I turned back to the wounded woman and examined her wound. I'm technically an MD, even if I specialized in psychiatry. I spent part of my time as a resident in an ER, so I was competent with basic surgery, but mending a torn carotid wasn't. Doing it while a roomful of kids cried for their mothers wouldn't make it any easier.

"Carla, check on the kids," I shouted. She was kneeling over the pile of ashes that had once been her daughter, picking them up and letting them shift through her fingers. She kept doing it, without any change in expression. Poor woman was shell-shocked. "Carla!" She turned like a deer in headlights. "These kids need someone to help them until their mothers get here." And that person wasn't me. I like kids, but I'm not so good with them. I had a rather unusual childhood, and I find it hard to relate to normal kids.

Carla walked over to me with less animation than the demon zombie. "What should I do?"

The wounded woman didn't have time for this. The blood was moving about as fast as a thick maple syrup. "Move them away from here. See if any know their parents' numbers. Use a cell, because the land lines won't be working, and get the parents here. Don't give too many details."

I purposefully didn't mention 911. They'd only interrupt what I was going to try. Carla got the kids behind a partition with mats that looked like it might be used for naptime.

I ended the stasis, and blood spurted up like a hole in a water balloon. The fingernail had demon taint and would poison her blood if left in too long. It had to come out. I pulled to test the size, but the demon bastard had morphed it into a T-shape after it sliced through. If I pulled it out, the gash would get bigger. If I used magic to vaporize it and missed even a speck, it could be carried away and clog an artery in the heart or brain. Even if a heart attack or a stroke didn't kill her, the eventual blood poisoning would.

I'd have to morph it and pray the spell didn't worsen my migraine to the point where I couldn't see. I reached forward to use contact to make the transformation easier when a hand reached over my shoulder.

"Let me," said a familiar voice that sent chills up my spine. A finger touched the fingernail and it burst into flame, which then not only slid out of the artery but also cauterized it on the way out. The bleeding from the carotid stopped, but the rest of the neck was open and still bleeding.

I guess Nick had heard the demon's oath and sent his detective, Negral, Chief of Hell's Secret Police. Negral was the only denizen of Hell I almost respected. He wasn't a demon, but a mostly forgotten god who didn't want to face oblivion, so he took a job working for the Devil.

My first instinct was to turn and defend myself. I was sloppy. The shielding and murder filled this place with such darkness and so much of Hell's magiks that I didn't sense the Chief's approach. If he wanted me dead – and I think there were many times he did

– he could have killed me. He didn't. More confusingly, he helped.

"Thanks, Chief," I said, turning to see him dressed in his beige trench coat and fedora, smoking a cigarette. He's got a bad Jones for all things Bogie. Back in his day, he was a sun and fire god, so it wasn't like smoking was going to hurt him.

"Innocents shouldn't pay for the sins of the guilty," he replied. He tipped the front rim of the hat up with his index finger. "Have a favor to ask, Hex."

"Don't you already owe me one?" I said, pushing pieces of neck back into place. Fortunately, the woman had passed out.

Hell's Detective frowned. "Sadly, but I'll need to up the tally. I want Beltizon."

"Me too."

"Let me get him. This killing was unauthorized."

"The others weren't?" I asked.

Negral shrugged. "The boss gave Beltizon a quota. He exceeded it. And he wasn't supposed to jack another body."

"I would think exceeding quota would be a good thing," I said.

"Attracts too much attention. Upstairs feels they have to interfere, plus proof of Hell also proves the existence of God. The boss doesn't want that."

Made sense. "So why do you want him?"

Negral narrowed his eyes and gritted his teeth. He hated having to explain himself to me. I could tell by the way his cigarette burned up and became ash, crumbling to the ground.

"Because of her," he said pointing with his chin to the wounded woman. He pulled out another smoke and lit it with his thumb, the tip of which had flared up. "Give me the twelve hours and I'll have him for you."

I tapped into fleshsmith magic and knitted the sternocleidomastoid and then the skin over it, which of course made my neck feel like it was on fire.

"He tried to kill this woman in front of me. I'm going after him," I said.

"Then we have a problem," he said, blowing a stream of smoke into the air. It looked just like an old-fashioned Tommy gun. It turned and pointed at my head. A stream of smoke bullets came out of the muzzle.

The woman was stable, so I stood up to face the Chief. "Carla, call 911."

Negral laughed. "So, you finally admit you're afraid of me? Think calling the cops'll help you against me?"

"Hardly. I figure whatever happens next will keep me occupied and these folks will need some help. So, what are we going to do about this problem? Race? Chess?" I was being sarcastic.

"Doesn't matter. You'd lose."

I was hurting, but still functional. Going up against Negral would be risky, but if he won, he'd still go after the demon. "Every minute we waste is one off the window Beltizon can't kill, which is something neither one of us wants." I couldn't believe what I was about to say. "I suggest a truce."

Negral raised an eyebrow. "Once was enough. And we were both beat out by a bartender."

A group of dark mystics were trying to raise an Old One. Hell didn't want it loose any more than we did—they wanted to be the evilest kids on the block and the Devil doesn't like the competition. Nick sent Negral to work with us to stop it. Ironically, a bartender from Bulfinche's Pub named John Murphy beat us to them and saved the world. And jumpstarted an entire new universe in the process.

"He increases his over-quota kills, you're going to get grief from Nick," I said. Truth was I didn't want to be looking over my shoulder for the Chief. Easier if I knew where he was.

Which is when I heard the cries from the back room. I ran with the Chief on my heels. There was a baby inside a black circle. It had a chunk of flesh bitten out of the right shoulder. There were glyphs engraved in the circle. The Chief and I cursed in unison.

"Can you open it?" I said.

Negral's hair caught fire, incinerating his fedora. "Been seeing a lot of this lately. Mid-level demons banded together and created a new language. We call it Darken. I haven't been able to break it. If they just kept using Sumerian..." Negral was part of the ancient

Sumerian pantheon. "You?"

"I'll try." Damn it. It'll take me hours to open it. "I'll give you first crack. One catch."

Negral's hair flared into a blazing 'fro. "Which is?"

"I want to plead the case for the return of Carla's soul."

"She's no innocent."

"She was a grieving mother who made a horrible mistake. It shouldn't be enough to have her spend eternity in the Pit. If the rest of her life damns her, so be it, but I'll not let her be damned out of misplaced love."

"I agree and I get to hunt him without your interference?"

"I'll give you six hours."

Negral nodded. It was the closest I'd get to a thank you.

"But if you don't have him at one second after that, I'm back in," I said.

"I'd expect nothing less," Negral said.

"That was almost a compliment," I said.

"If that's what your delusions tell you, fine."

"You going to get in trouble for helping that woman?" I asked.

Negral shrugged and I had my answer. He was going to catch Hell for it, literally. "I'll bring Beltizon back and make him open the spell circle," Negral said.

"If I don't get it open first," I said.

"I hope you do. Don't let that child die, Hex." Negral met my eyes, and for once I didn't see hate burning there.

"Not happening if I can help it," I said.

It took five hours and thirty-seven minutes to open it. I body slid the baby to Ringvue. The EMTs took the brave woman, whose name is Susan, to Bellevue. It's a better trauma center for gunshots and car accidents, but Ringvue handles things like demon zombie baby bites better. For one thing, there's no attempt to have you take up residence in a padded ward just for describing what happened.

And by the time I was exiting the hospital, Negral had a different corpse in tow, but it was Beltizon inside. Negral wasn't happy, because the flames on his head rose up at least a foot. On Ringvue's grounds, it might even go unnoticed.

"You got him," I said, stating the obvious.

"There was doubt?" he replied.

"Only minor," I said. "But you were cutting it close."

"The baby is okay?" he asked.

"He'll need some reconstructive surgery, but yes." Negral's flames went from red to orange. I was guessing that was relief. He always had a soft spot for kids, why I'm not sure. "Seems your friend was saving him for a snack, so the spell circle kept him alive."

"Don't insult me. There are no friends in Hell," Negral said. I certainly couldn't argue with that. "Beltizon did not keep his bargain with you. He has killed again."

Negral didn't have to share that, and normally wouldn't have. He'd leave it up to me to find out and then demand restitution. The whole baby thing must really have pissed him off.

"Then I'm entitled to seek restitution," I said.

"What would satisfy you?" Negral huffed, and added under his breath, "As if I didn't know."

Respect does not equal trust. I do believe Negral would end me if it suited his purposes, so I had to look inside this gift horse for assassins. "I assume he's being brought back to the Pit for punishment and won't be let out."

"Yes."

"Then I would like the soul of Carla Dwane returned to her," I said.

"That is an excessive restitution," said Negral.

"Perhaps, but he didn't really bring her baby back to life and Beltizon negotiated the contract under a false name—Jaxic."

"Foolish mistake, but as you yourself know, anyone can take many names," Negral said.

"Carla Dwane, with no hope of changing her fate, offered herself up to save others. Noble sacrifice is an automatic get-out-of-the-Pit-free clause in all Hell's contracts," I said.

"Which you may have voided by discussing with her the merits of acting unselfishly to help her soul in the event the contract was made null," said Negral.

"No more so than any priest, minister, rabbi, or religious TV program she may have seen," I said. "Her soul is all I want."

"Transferring a soul to you is too high a restitution for a simple broken oath," Negral countered.

"I don't want ownership." Which was true. Getting into the soul owning business would have too many hazards to even consider. "I just want it to stay with the original owner. I'm made no richer by it." In Hell, souls are the only currency.

"I'll run it by the boss," he said.

"We both know you're empowered to make the deal." Negral just stared at me. "What if I sweetened the pot?"

"I'm listening."

"What if I teach you what the glyphs mean?" I asked.

The blaze on his head went out and became hair again. "You were able to figure it out?"

"Of course. Was there ever any doubt?" I said. Actually, there had been plenty, most of it on my part. It hadn't been as tough as the one the demon Ramos had manipulated a stalker to use to trap the fugitive succubus Ryth and Murphy during the end of her pregnancy, but it had some similarities. I had to use a combination of tapping into the written version of the magic which lets people speak in tongues and use my power to look through a demon's eyes. It wasn't pleasant. Between that and the body slide, I was barely upright. If it wasn't for another triple shot of caffeinated aspirin, I'd be laid out on a cot in Gabe's office. Gabe was better known as the angel Gabriel, but these days he runs an asylum. Ringvue's just what we call it. It's better not to use its real name.

"You'd be willing to share that with me?" he asked.

"There would be the usual catch of you promising not to use it against any humans or innocents," I said. Negral has never broken his word in at least five millennia, and I didn't think he was going to start. He'd lose some of the god aspect of his power, and worse, his own sense of dark honor.

Negral nodded. "I can agree to that."

"And in the interest of full disclosure, I don't know the entire language. Just a little bit more than I needed to break the circle, but it might be the Rosetta Stone you need to figure out the rest."

"It's more than I have now," he said. "Deal. I'll void the contract, but not any hold Hell otherwise has on her soul. And your word not to discuss your teaching me what you know about Darken with anyone."

"Why?" I asked.

"I have my reasons."

"Return this body and the other to where they belong and I can agree to that," I said. "Lunch?"

Negral chuckled. "That's your and the boss's thing. I don't do lunch. Drinks I'll consider. You buy."

"Fine, but we go Dutch. We use Bulfinche's Pub in two days as neutral ground?" Paddy was going to love this, but I'd make it work. I'd suggest Plasma, but even Barber would have problems controlling Negral, despite their having been allies in the League of Shadow days.

And the Chief would have no problem frying any vamps who got in his way. And in two days I should be back to normal.

"Agreed. And I have to say you've been almost civil," he said.

"Don't get used to it, but anytime you save a woman's life, I'll give it a try," I said.

"Normally, I wouldn't bother, but the dame was willing to die to protect those in her care. Makes her an okay broad in my book," he said.

"I'm heading over to Bellevue to check on her now," I said.

"Susan will have some trouble speaking, but she'll be fine," the Chief said.

"How do you know?" I asked.

"We stopped by on our way here. I made this mook apologize to her," he said.

"You made a demon apologize to its victim?" I said.

"The dame deserved better. It was the least Beltizon could do."

"Can't argue there, although I'd use slang that's been popular in the last twenty years," I said.

"Don't fix something that ain't broke," he said.

"As long as you don't start blabbing about this being the start of a beautiful friendship," I said.

"In your dreams," he said.

"More like nightmares," I said.

"Besides, I already told you there aren't any friends in Hell," he said, ripping the demon out of the zombie and putting it in a soul cage. "Although being with you certainly qualifies in the nightmare category."

"You're not to the first to tell me that," I said.

"I'm shocked."

So was I, at least with how things turned out, but a good woman lived, a demon got sent back to Hell, and a grieving mother would finally get a chance to start healing. All in all, not the worst day ever.

DARKLY REFLECTED

"Please Mr. Hex, help me," said the man in an orange jumpsuit. As far as I was concerned those were magic words.

"I don't know how much help I can be. They have you on video robbing the jewelry store. Seems a pretty open and shut case," I said.

"I swear to you, I was at home when the robbery occurred," David said.

"Then how do you explain the video?" I said.

David ran his fingers through his hair, then stopped as if trying to decide whether to pull it out or not. He decided on not, but it looked like a close call. "That's just it – I can't. My wife and five kids will back me up."

"Five kids?" I said, looking at the man standing unseen leaning against the wall.

The angel smiled and nodded. He always has a soft spot for kids. Most guardian angels do. Mine didn't, at least where I was concerned.

Not that David Tork even realized there was an angel standing off to his side as he pulled a folded photo out of his front shirt pocket and showed it to me. Him and the family. Pretty wife, good looking kids. Smiles all.

Az tried not to smirk. I wasn't good with kids and he knew it. Interestingly enough, angels are closer to kids. There are reasons for it. Az likes to stay off the grid and could remain pretty much unseen with the exception of some types of magic users such as myself and certain innocent children.

And even if he was noticed somehow by somebody, they wouldn't pick up right away that he was an angel. They'd just see a guy with long blonde hair and a white trench coat. The wings were tucked under the coat. Magic was funny sometimes. Takes more power to hide the wings than the whole angel. Magic doesn't like splitting a whole that's still connected.

"I believe you," I said. David's face couldn't decide whether to look confused or happy.

"You don't think I'm crazy?" He said.

"Not in my professional opinion." And despite what I told the corrections officers, I wasn't a lawyer, but I did have a license to practice medicine with a specialty in psychiatry.

"Why?"

I looked at the angel in the corner. Aziel was in the rank and file. There are different orders and guardian angel was lowest on the totem pole. They're stuck with the dirty job of watching over us humans. Back in the day, there were lots of angels for each person. Thanks to the population explosion, now each angel has to watch over lots of people. Az was one of the good ones. "Let's just say someone I trust vouched for you."

"What to hear something strange? Usually, I don't remember my dreams, but last night I had one that you were coming to see me, but we've never met. Isn't that weird?"

I shrugged my shoulders. It wasn't where angels are concerned. Most of them don't get to be seen or even speak to their charges, although some people can feel their presence. The easiest way for them to communicate with people is through dreams.

"Who sent you?" he said.

"Your benefactor prefers to remain anonymous," I said. Az wasn't even his guardian angel. He was his youngest son's, who could actually sometimes see the angel. Must be pure of heart, which spoke well of the parents. Kid says his prayers every night. A child's prayers are like reality TV for the guardian angel set. Az happened to be at their apartment at the time of the robbery and knows the father was home in bed like he said. Not that we can bring Az into court and testify, not even in a Department of Mystic Affairs sanctioned court. It would break too many rules and angels are sticklers for regulations and such.

The next night after his father was arrested, the kid prayed for someone to help his dad. Az decided to intervene and answer that one for his boss.

"Do you know anybody with a grudge against you?"

"Last person with a grudge against me was years ago," he said.

"Who's that? And why did he have a grudge?" I said.

"It was my roommate in college, Eddie Carnasi. He'd gone on a couple of dates with Carol, my wife, but nothing but a good night hug happened between them. As a matter of fact, him going out with her was how we met. It was love at first sight. We got married a year later. Eddie interrupted the wedding when the Reverend asked if anyone objected. The wedding party threw him out and we even called the cops. He got arrested and convicted of disorderly conduct and we got a restraining order, but that was years ago."

"This may sound like an odd question, but was Eddie involved with any kind of magic or odd happenings?" I said.

"He was into the occult, stuff like that. I remember him trying a couple of spells, but nothing worked. I mean it's not like that stuff is real." I refrained from comment. Some people are happier not knowing. "I thought it was like playing the dragons and knights role-playing game, but when I said that it upset him. Eddie claimed he was searching for ultimate power, but he seemed to fall pretty far short of that."

"That may very well be, but have I to start somewhere. What about the rest of your family? Anyone making threats or have any grudges against them?"

David shook his head. "None that I know about."

"I'll poke around, see what I can find out and let you know if anything comes up," I said.

"Thank you so much, Mr. Hex. What do I owe you? Do you have a daily retainer?"

I smiled. "Nothing like that. However, if I'm successful, you owe me a favor, no questions asked. Deal?"

"Absolutely. I didn't do this."

I may have believed him, but that wasn't going to solve this problem.

Az stood over David and placed his hands on his shoulders, then bowed his head. The angel said no words, but it was obvious he was praying over the man. A small glow passed from the angel's hands to the man's shoulders. I'm able to see umbras, what some people might call an aura, and that simple action brightened up David's immensely.

Breaking into a jail is typically easier than breaking out. I didn't have to do either, so I stood and waited. Az didn't have any such restrictions placed on him. He walked by the guards and through the door smiling and waving at me knowing as I had to stay until the corrections officer let me out of the Riker's Island visiting room.

About ten minutes later I made it outside to see the angel lounging with his back against a lamppost.

"Do you think he's innocent?" the angel asked.

"Do you think he is?" I said.

"Why do you always answer a question with a question?" Az said with a smile.

"Do you think it's because you do?" I said. "But yes, if you say he's being set up, that's good enough for me."

"So, you'll help?" the angel said.

I nodded. "I got no mystic clues from talking to him, so I might as well start with the jealous college roommate." True, the idea that someone he knew in college would be plotting against him was far-fetched, but I find that far-fetched strikes closer to home much more than most people realize.

"You waiting for the bus?" Az asked. A visitor bus was supposed to be the only way on and off Riker's Island.

"Are you?" I said.

The angel didn't answer my question directly. Instead, he said, "Thank you. I'll start poking around the college where they went, see if I can pick up any residue impressions to use to track this Carnasi. You'll start with his more current whereabouts?"

I nodded. The Angel would be able to pick up on things that happened there better than I would. Probably start with their dorm.

Az pulled what I like to call the golden glow where his entire body shines and he disappears. Angelic form of teleportation. As a magí, I could technically do the same thing. We magí can to tap into any and all forms of magic, which includes the angelic. However, my curse would punish me as it always does for using magic. The more powerful the magic, the greater the punishment and pain. Instead, I body slid to two blocks away from my apartment and walked the rest of the way.

There are all sorts of mystic ways to track people. For most of those, it's helpful to have an acquaintance with the person or something they once possessed. Even better would be something with DNA – hair, nails, or blood. Of course, there are even simpler ways of doing it. I got my laptop and did a few Internet searches for the man.

It was fairly easy to do since my brood was actually behaving themselves.

Turns out there were few people named Edward Carnasi. I paid subscriptions to services that private investigators used and was able to find the particular Edward Carnasi who had been arrested at the Tork wedding. He had served out his parole and I couldn't find an address more current than two years ago. The man seemed to use credit cards very sparingly. However, he had been ordering takeout almost daily from a Chinese restaurant in Dingmans Ferry, Pennsylvania.

There was a knock at my window. More like something hitting the glass. Az was floating halfway across the street and throwing pebbles at my window pane.

I don't open my window for just anybody. Otherwise, it wouldn't make sense to put wards up around my apartment building. Az was one of the few exceptions, so I popped it open.

"Why, Az, fancy meeting you here. You never call you never write and then suddenly twice in one day. Are you here to serenade me?" I said.

"Hex, it's urgent. I need your help right away," the angel said.

"So, no time then to play a game of *Divine Reckoning III*?" I said. I figured he had something on Carnasi, but it never hurt to tease Az.

"You have to come with me right now," Az said, flying right at me.

Az wasn't one for offering personal transport. When I first met him back when I was a kid, all I wanted was a ride. It rarely happened. The fact that he was offering it now set off all sorts of alarms inside my head.

As he dive bombed me, I noticed his damaged feather – it happened when we first met. It has always been on his right side but now was on the left. I took a step back into my apartment, but since I had let my wards down to speak to him, Az was able to fly in, grab hold of my hand then pull me out and up into the sky. We were far above the Manhattan skyline when the angel let go of me and sent me plummeting down towards the pavement below.

Luckily, my brood was paying attention which includes five spirit animals – three wolves, a fox and a coyote. The father wolf and the coyote came out the open window and caught me, one under each shoulder.

Angel's cranky today Trickster the coyote sent via a form of telepathy.

"Something is wrong. His hurt feather is on the wrong side," I said.

My brood put me down on the sidewalk. I tried not to shiver. It wasn't that it was cold. It was the implications of what was happening.

The angel turned and flew down toward me.

"I think we need to talk," I said to the reflection of an angel.

The blond man in the white trench coat stopped at the growling of the spirit pack, then turned and flew off into the sky.

Should we follow? sent Mordi, the father wolf.

"No. I think someone managed to create a reflection of Az. No telling how good a job they did. Best to let him go," I said. Some reflections have all the power of their original, but not the memories. Angels are incredibly powerful but are bound by the Host-Horde Accord. The reflection of an angel would have the power but no restraints. It would be able to level entire city blocks. And if someone made one copy of the angel, they might have made more. Whoever was controlling it had far too much potential destruction at their disposal. Better for me to go after them alone.

My gut told me it was Eddie Carnasi. A reflection would explain how David could be at home and on video robbing a jewelry store at the same time.

I needed to get to Dingmans Ferry. I loathed the idea of going by bus, train, or some combination thereof. Most people would consider driving, but I've never gotten a driver's license. Don't ask why. There are dozens of ways to magically transport someone or something, but most of them require power. Body sliding takes the least, but it's noisy, the mystic equivalent of arriving by a giant freight train blowing an air raid siren. Anyone mystically attuned would know someone arrived. Best not to announce that to someone that has an imitation angel at their command. Anything else mystic would take a lot of power, which meant I'd be hurting with a migraine or something worse.

Not that body sliding was without danger. The reason I didn't need to use my own power was because it utilized universal forces, which include the momentum of the earth traveling through space, its rotation, gravity and a whole bunch of other stuff. One simply made oneself immaterial and grabbed hold of these forces, kind of like a kid grabbing hold of the back of a truck on an icy road and skating behind. Except instead of a truck, it's a herd of cattle, some of which can fly, others who can burrow under the earth and all of which moved at speeds man was not meant to. One miscalculation and the slider could end up stopping inside of a solid object or maybe even the center of the earth. I've been doing it since I was a kid but I've heard about people who tried it and ended up being thrown off into outer space and never getting back.

I slid to the next town over; a place called Bushkill and stopped in the middle of a field. Made it easier if no one noticed me suddenly appearing from nowhere, holding a bicycle.

I started pedaling, hit an army surplus store for some supplies and made it into town about a half hour later.

Compared to New York City, Dingmans Ferry is a small town, but even a small town has thousands of people. Not exactly easy ground to cover, but I knew where he was getting his food. I had a copy of his mug shot on my phone so I waited until 5 o'clock and went inside the Chinese restaurant. It was a takeout place with a few tables. I ordered some food and sat down at a table near the window. About ten minutes later the guy behind the counter brought the food to my table. I even got a free soda.

He went back behind the counter and proceeded to stare at me as I sat there with plates of food that I didn't touch. It was nothing personal against the food. It smelled decent. I just don't eat anything I didn't prepare with few exceptions. Way too easy for someone to poison you by mundane or magical means. Mundane will just kill you, but magical could make you a slave or worse. Since I figured I'd be there a while, I ordered lots of food. That way the owner couldn't complain about me waiting around.

Still, I could tell it annoyed the guy.

"Something wrong with the food?" he asked.

"Not all. It smells delicious," I said.

"Then why aren't you eating it?" he said.

"I'm waiting for someone," I replied truthfully.

"Might have been smarter to wait for them to get here before you ordered," he said.

"Maybe. I'll keep that in mind for next time," I said. "Will you bring me another order of dumplings please?"

The guy shook his head and put my order in.

I sat there and watched the counter guy pick up the phone and write down orders. People came and picked up their dinner, but none of them were Carnasi. I looked down at my watch. It was 6:55. They closed at eight. Another hour and I'd have to figure out something else. Then Carnasi came in with a woman on each arm. They looked like twins. Worse, they both looked like Carol Tork, David's wife. The man providing the meat in the Carol Tork sandwich had longer black hair than in his mug shot and had added a goatee, but it was definitely Eddie Carnasi.

Looked like he had been duplicating more than angels.

Both reflections of Carol were laughing at everything Carnasi said, but it seemed almost robotic.

"I told you I don't want your fake diamond rings," the guy behind the counter said to Carnasi who was holding up what looked like an engagement ring. "Cash or credit only."

"You're lucky you have the best Moo Shu pork in fifty miles or I'd never come back here," Carnasi said, handing over a credit card. He got the card back, signed a piece of paper and picked up enough bags of food to feed a baseball team.

Carnasi and his female reflections walked by without paying me any mind. I put ten bucks on the table for the counter guy's trouble for cleaning up my untouched food and casually walked out to follow behind the trio.

When he didn't get into a car, I decided to leave the bike behind and follow him on foot.

We had a small parade through the moonlit streets and roads of Dingmans Ferry. None of the trio even once looked behind them. Carnasi handed the women the food so his hands could be free to grab at their buttocks, breasts, and any other parts that apparently needed groping.

Carnasi finally stopped at what looked like it should be an empty field with weeds that had grown to heights that would be impressive on the Serengeti. There was a path where the weeds had been trampled down that led to a house. An odd house at that. It was a mirror image of one of the nicest houses we passed on the way here. It had wires attached to the house, but instead of running to utility poles they lay in a field. My best guess is Carnasi liked the original house, made a reflection of it then made it real in the vacant field. Since it was "impossible" for a house to pop up overnight, people assumed it had always been there and ignored it.

I waited about fifteen minutes then snuck through the tall grass towards the house. It had lights on which meant that there was some source of power. It wasn't hard to find. A generator was running behind the house. There were several large tanks of propane off to one side, each with a sticker of the vender's name reversed. Smart guy. Duplicating fuel as he needed it.

I crept up to the windows and looked in. The living room was in the midst of some sort of bizarre clone party. There were at least twenty Carol Torks running around. Most were naked or scantily clad and they were dancing like they were strippers. The problems for the ones who actually stripped down revealed the flaw in whatever magic Carnasi was using. His reflections had enough magic to create internal organs and bone structures or even propane in the tanks, but the unseen details were glossed over. Most of the Carols had no nipples or belly buttons, although they had skin tone similar to the parts that had been caught in the reflection.

There was one exception. This one was showing all her naughty bits but had a towel wrapped around her head. My guess is her hair must be somewhat lacking or the towel would have been removed. Probably nabbed that shot peaking in her bathroom window.

Even the room was affected. Everything that could be seen from the windows was detailed— painted, had pictures and such— but the rest of the room was barren, the color of the walls and floor was the same as the paint around the pictures, although a strip of room that could be seen from the window had a patch of carpet. There was plenty of high-end furniture, but my guess is it was added later.

I crept in slowly, trying not to be spotted, but considering what the naked reflections of Carol were doing *en masse* to him, Carnasi wasn't exactly concerned with looking out his windows for uninvited guests. Sadly, that may have been because of the one reflection missing from the party. It wasn't as good as the angel because I heard it land behind me.

"I don't think you're invited to the Master's party," the imitation angel said. I was still trying to figure out how Carnasi had captured the angel's image with the wings. My best guess is Carnasi not only could capture reflections but use mirrors as spy glasses and for some reason was checking out his old dorm room when Az went to investigate. The real angel probably took off the trench coat and turned off his cloaking magic so as not to inhibit any of his powers. The angel got sloppy and didn't realize he was being watched. That or Carnasi's figured a way to see cloaked angels using mirrors.

I turned and smiled. "I resent that implication. I got an

invitation. It's right here in my pocket." I reached inside my leather jacket and pulled out one of the metal signal mirrors I'd picked up at the Army surplus store. I'd taken all the reflections out earlier. A simple enough spell, but it made everything seem too bright for a while like when a migraine was starting. Some iced tea in a hip flask helped with that, but not so much with my own reflection disappearing for about an hour.

Pointing the mirror at the imitation angel proved interesting. I angled it so all of the fake Az was caught in the mirror and he coalesced into a beam that got sucked into the mirror's empty surface, trapping the winged reflection inside.

I put the mirror in a jacket pocket on the opposite side so I didn't mix it up with the others and accidentally try to use it again. Each mirror was only good for one capture. I considered using regular mirrors, but breaking the glass would free the reflection. Metal mirrors could be bent, but not shattered so whatever I trapped inside would stay there. I'd only bought two dozen and there were easily that many reflections of his unrequited love.

This wasn't going to be as easy as I thought.

Carnasi's umbra showed no signs of power. He wasn't a mage, which meant that his power was coming from something external. I started looking for mirrors. Although the reflections were impressive, they tended to not be able to duplicate nuances like smell and taste which is probably why he was buying his food and making reflections of material things.

Normally, I like to sneak in through a back door or window. In this house, the back doors and windows didn't exist. The rear of the building was one flat even surface. It would require a chainsaw to make a door which would somewhat ruin the element of surprise.

Same issue with the side windows. There was no way of knowing if they worked or if the hinge mechanism was one solid piece.

Carnasi and two of the Carol reflections had gone through the front door, so I knew that worked. Breaking and entering through the front door would not go unnoticed.

Only one way around it, so I walked up to the door and

knocked. There was no response, so I knocked again. And again. I kept knocking. First I did shave and a haircut two bits and then decided to do the drum solo from *Wipeout.*

Finally, Carnasi threw open the front door and screamed, "What!"

Ignoring his poor manners, I smiled big and did my best imitation of a suburbanite. "Hello, my name is Mr. Hex and I'm here on behalf of the neighborhood homeowners' association. First off, we'd like to welcome you to the neighborhood."

"Thank you," Carnasi said, with some mixture of confusion and trepidation in his voice.

"I trust you got our welcome fruit basket," I said.

"Sure," he lied.

"Excellent. First off, no one remembers seeing any of your building permits and we are all amazed at how quickly you got this put up. You simply have to give me your contractor's phone number. I need some work done. If he could put up your house overnight, he could fix my kitchen in a jiffy," I said.

"I don't have that information handy, but I will try to find it."

"I appreciate it. Now, of course, you know this is a co-op neighborhood. We would have made it a gated community, except we weren't able to get the necessary permits from the town planning board. Still, everyone in the neighborhood has to pay their monthly dues. You get to use the community center, the gym, and the pool. And of course, it covers your school taxes. As you have ignored our request for payment before, I'm here from the board to collect your check for the first three months' dues now."

"And how much exactly is that?" he said.

"Three thousand three hundred dollars and forty-seven cents, based on the size of your house. Which I might add looks amazingly like the Smith house a mile down the road. I guess you must have the same architect," I said.

"Sure, I guess. Look, I'm a little broke after having this place built and I don't have a lot of cash on hand. However, I do have a number of gold items." Reflected money would be backwards and not fool anyone. Reflected jewelry was another matter. "I have a ring that's worth at least that much. Do you think the homeowners' association would be willing to take that in trade?" He said.

"Usually not, but let me be honest with you. My bosses can be real jerks. I have a brother-in-law who owns a pawnshop in town. I'd be happy to see what he would give you for it. I, of course, would get a ten percent commission for helping out."

"Sure, the thing's worth close to five or six grand. Let me go get one," he said, shutting the door, but I caught the knob with my hand and turned it. He never bothered to lock it so I let myself in. Probably didn't have a reflection of the key and could end up locking himself out. Carnasi went up to one of the naked women and grabbed her right hand and took what looked like an engagement ring off her ring finger.

Then he turned and saw me inside his house. "Hey, I never said you could come in here."

"This is a wild rocking party. Unfortunately, due to neighborhood regulations, you need a permit for this." I paused and squinted at one of the women. "Hey, Carol is that you?"

Carnasi eyes twitched and he stammered as he asked, "You know Carol?"

"Sure, she's my mother-in-law's beautician's next door neighbor's dog walker's cousin. We're tight, but she lives in New York City. What is she doing out here? Without her husband and kids? And why are there so many of her?" I said.

"This is obviously a case of mistaken identity. These are all cousins. There's a strong family resemblance. Not that I have to explain myself to you in my own house. Get out now or I'll make you leave," Carnasi said.

"I don't think you have that in you. We both know mirror magic is how you got this house and these reflections of womanhood. Also how you framed David Tork. This is your one warning to set things right or you will have some consequences a magic mirror won't get you out of."

"Who do you think you are to talk to me like that?" Carnasi said.

"Weren't you paying attention when I introduced myself? I'm

Mr. Hex."

"I told you to get out."

"I take it then that you refuse to take heed of my one warning?" I said. The warnings helped keep my soul clean by making what happens after the warnee's fault, not mine.

"Hell, yeah," Carnasi said, stepping over to a secretary style desk. He reached in and out came a mirror that looked like it belonged in a cartoon princess' boudoir. The handle was oblong and the plastic covering it was violet.

I tried to move behind something quickly, but there were only the Carols to use as cover. I was fairly sure the mirror couldn't make a reflection of a reflection or Carnasi would have done it. That or he wasn't smart enough to do it. He'd be able to make money and more exact copies of Carol.

"One question. How'd you get the angel's reflection to find me?" I said.

"I just told him to take care of anyone who might try to stop me," he said.

Made sense. Even without Az's memory, the reflection would still have the angel's powers. It wouldn't take much for him to figure out that I was coming after Carnasi.

"You took out the angel's reflection?" Carnasi said.

"Yep."

"That makes you some kind of wizard or something."

"Or something." This guy was clueless and I wasn't about to explain things to him.

"I'm a bit of a wizard myself. Worked at it for years until I finally found this baby at a garage sale, believe it or not. Now I am the master of all I survey. Beat the crap out of this trespasser," he said to a group of the ladies.

My mother brought me up to be a gentleman and not hit women. I managed to undo most of what my father taught me. I didn't like it, but there are times I needed to defend myself and hit women. Or worse. It was a necessary evil. I was hoping I didn't have to resort to violence this time. I pulled out more signal mirrors. Unfortunately, I had to angle the mirrors to get the entire reflection on the surface and the reflections were moving fast and hit and kicked hard. Ten of them jumped me and pounded on me like I was a piñata. I hit the floor hard and tried to cover my head with one arm and kick out and punch with my other. I felt my foot connect with a knee. I repeated the attack on two more reflections. Three Carols fell to the floor. I rolled over, using the mirrors to suck those three into mirrors. I rolled again and got another two from my angle on the floor. The remaining reflections had some survival instincts and backed away. They'd attack again though if Carnasi ordered them to. Best to distract him and kept that from happening.

The ladies disappearing freaked Carnasi out. Probably figured that once he created a reflection it would always exist in the real world.

"Think you're pretty powerful? I'm even mightier," he said, turning the mirror on me. Foolishly, I'd sucked my only cover into the mirrors. My reflection was caught in the princess mirror, almost like a photograph. Carnasi flipped the mirror toward an empty part of the room and said, *"Be real."*

My reflection turned solid. Boy, I was a handsome devil.

"I command you to destroy the man you were reflected from," Carnasi said.

I was never good with guilt and despite the fact that I neither created my reflection nor ordered him to attack me, the guilt didn't go away. My reflection wasn't exactly alive, but he did have certain aspects of me in him which meant this wasn't going to go well for him. Poor guy had my power, but not my memories.

"You really don't want to try to hurt anybody. Trust me and consider this your one warning. Since you're a reflection of me, I'm guessing you don't want to take orders from anybody." It stood to reason that any reflection of me would have my poor attitude towards authority. Apparently, it was viewing me as an authority because it smiled, then pointed both hands at me with a dramatic flourish.

I rolled my eyes and leapt backward. *"Shields."*

Reflecto-Hex didn't say a word, but even a novice could feel the power pour out of him. Reflecto-Hex was unfocused, untrained, but had the power of a magí. My little shield spell wouldn't have been enough to hold back that level of power except for one other thing Reflecto-Hex got from me – my curse. The schmuck was trying to kill me and that type of magic and the curse don't mix well. It has to be done carefully, gradually, sneakily. My reflection fell to the ground screaming, twitching, convulsing before finally laying still and then dissolving into bits of light. He'd destroyed himself with the backlash from the curse.

From where Carnasi was watching it looked very different. "You killed him!"

Technically, my reflection killed himself by way of the curse, but there was no need to tell Carnasi that. "And it works just as good on real people as it does on the imitation. Give me the mirror before I do the same to you."

Realizing he had run out of options, Carnasi tossed the mirror up in the air and rushed out the front door. I dove onto the floor, catching the mirror before it hit the ground. The thing about broken mirrors bringing seven years' bad luck may not be true with the ordinary variety, but a magic mirror smashing could do a lot more immediate damage. Releasing all the energy stored inside could cause the same devastation as a very tiny tactical nuke.

I caught it. The mirror wasn't even scratched. I ran out the doorway after Carnasi but decided not to chase him. I didn't need to. I had already met him and could magically find him later if I needed to. It wasn't like Carnasi had any kind of real mystic skill to hide with.

I did, however, turn the mirror on his fleeing form to capture his image.

Now that I held the mirror, the reflections had to listen to me. I told them all to sit and be quiet, then searched the house. It was empty except for one upstairs room that had a reflection of David Tork hanging upside down naked, with big spikes rammed through his body. He still had a reflection of life, but not much. I captured him in a signal mirror to put him out of his misery. Then went out to get more metal mirrors. When I came back I got rid of the legion of Carols then did the same to the house and furnishing.

The only thing left was to take care of Carnasi. I've long subscribed to the theory that turnabout is fair play and figured Carnasi had a lot coming.

The next morning a small jewelry exchange in Queens was robbed by a man who looked an awful lot like David Tork. As he ran out the cameras caught him taking off a latex mask, revealing someone who appeared to be Eddie Carnasi. Carnasi's reflection accidentally dropped part of the mask which conveniently had a copy of the Reflecto-Carnasi's hairs in it.

I made a call to Jason Cervantes, a drinking buddy of mine who was a homicide detective on the NYPD and made sure he got all the video evidence. Since the crime was committed while David Tork was locked up in Rikers, a judge ruled he was not guilty of the first crime and David was set free.

Carnasi, however, was arrested thanks to an anonymous tip place by yours truly about where to find him. Carnasi denied having anything to do with the robbery, but the hairs in the partial mask matched his. Fortunately, the DNA testing lab either didn't pick up on the reversed helix issues or ignored it, assuming it was a mistake and flipped it back. Last I heard, he was begging for a plea deal.

A few days later I met Az in the park. The angel sat down on the bench next to me, invisible to everyone else.

"David Tork is back home with his family. All charges have been dropped," said the guardian Angel.

"Never underestimate the power of the child's prayer, right?" I said.

"Absolutely. I'm sorry I was careless enough that he was able to capture my reflection and that it was used against you," Az said.

"I guess even the best can get sloppy. Sometimes. Just don't do it again."

"What did you do with the mirror?"

"Put it into my locker at Bulfinche's Pub," I said. Paddy Moran was nice enough to let me keep some of the more dangerous mystic artifacts I've come across there. Because the bar and the building it's in is a mystic null zone, the mirror is rendered harmless. True, Paddy could give it a dispensation to work, but the leprechaun is about the most trustworthy man I know.

"I assume you took care of my reflection?"

"Of course. I'm saving it for a practical joke later on," I lied. Something with that level power without the restraints of a real angel would be more dangerous than a tactical nuke.

"Actually, I'd like to request custody of my reflection," Az said.

"Why?" I said.

Az looked down and kicked a pebble. "There aren't enough guardian angels to go around. My reflection has the power of one."

"But not the restraint, knowledge or heart," I said. "Or soul."

"Maybe it could be taught. And we both know that something with sentience can eventually gain a soul. I'd like to give it that chance," Az said.

"You think this is part of the divine plan or something?"

Az chuckled and shrugged. "Don't know. Above my pay grade."

"Won't you get in trouble if your bosses find out that it exists?" God is all knowing, the Heavenly Host not so much, fortunately.

"Trouble won't begin to cover it," Az said.

I had to ask, even though I already knew what the angel's answer would be. "Then why do it?"

"Because it's the right thing."

"So, if I hold onto it, you won't get in trouble?" I said.

"Correct."

"And if I give it to you, you might be taken off your earthly duties?"

"Unlikely, but possible," Az admitted.

"We mere mortals are better off with you here," I said.

"Please Daniel." Damn angel is one of the few can use my birth name to make me feel guilty. "I think Gabriel might be willing to mentor him. And if not, he'd be able to lock him up in Ringvue where he won't be able to do any harm."

I sighed and pulled out the mirror. Az tilted his head like a confused puppy. "You didn't leave it with the other mirror at Moran's? Why?"

I smiled and put it in his hand. "How long have we know each other?"

The angel smiled and touched my shoulder. "Not long enough. Thank you."

"Don't mention it. Please." I didn't want to attract the Heavenly Host's attention. Bad enough the Devil was constantly pissed at me.

Az did his golden fade and I decided to enjoy a day in the park.

LUNCH DATE FROM HELL

Sometimes my life doesn't even make sense to me. I had to worry about that time of the month and I was a guy. No, it's not a biological function, but a lunch date. Doesn't sound too bad on the surface, but that's only because I didn't mention that it was lunch with the Devil himself.

We're not friends. Far from it. I think it's pretty safe to say that Nick hates my guts and that's something I'm quite proud of. I beat the Devil when I was a kid in such a way that he still doesn't know I won. The winning was more important than the bragging, so I've kept it that way.

In the process, I found out the Devil's true name. Should I choose to use it, it would give me a great deal of control over him. In fact, I could use it to destroy him entirely, but there's an old saying about the Devil you know being better than the one you don't. Nick has an entire litany of flaws, but there are enough people out there who know how he does things and can figure out ways to stop him to keep him in check. Were the Devil to be taken out, there would be a war in Hell to see who took his spot.

Whoever won would very likely be much worse than Nick and might even focus more attention on attacking the mortal world. There is even some question about whether or not the Host-Horde Accord would still be in effect since he signed it as himself as opposed to the leader of Hell.

Mind you that was pre-curse when I very likely could've taken out the Devil. Post-curse, things might shake out a little different. So instead of ridding the universe of the embodiment of evil, I meet him for lunch.

There's a method to my madness. On several occasions, my magic has kicked in and I've picked up on things the Devil was working on. I've used that info to stop him. Luckily, I have a standing request from multiple sources to try to stop Nick's plans whenever I can. It's one of the few instances where I don't need to be asked to step in to help.

It's mostly a pissing contest between us to see who can tick off the other more by the end of the meal. Not that I actually ever eat. It'd be too easy for the Devil to spike my food with something mystic and nasty. Instead, I sit and watch him devour his food with the most exquisite of manners and do what I can to push his buttons. It can be amusing.

One interesting benefit to knowing the Devil's true name – Nick has put limits on what demons can do to me. Not that it holds much water in the heat of passion. The demons would simply kill me and ask for leniency later.

This particular restaurant was down in the Wall Street area. The food was prepared with a laser and cold concoctions were made using liquid nitrogen to freeze the food.

Nick had arrived first and had two women who looked to be vying for the position of trophy wife fawning all over him. The Devil ate it up. He had the biggest hate on for humans since we were what triggered his fight with the Creator. Nick loved making human lives miserable at every opportunity. When women fawned over him – and fawn they did because the man put movie stars to shame – he enjoyed seeing what hoops he could can make them jump through.

I walked past the maître d' and he moved to stop me. Not a good idea on the best of days, but I could see his point. Most of the patrons were dressed in expensive dresses or pricey suits. I was in sneakers, jeans, a T-shirt with my bandaged Hex moon on it in and a beat-up leather bomber jacket. I wore sunglasses. The curse wasn't really doing much to me today, but the too frequent migraines it gave me made light hurt, so I got in the habit of wearing them when I didn't need to so as not to tip anyone off.

I was already to the table by the time the maître d' caught me. The Devil, himself in a suit that ran upwards of ten grand, raised a hand to the maître d' and waved him off, indicating I was his guest.

"Ladies, I'm afraid my lunch partner has arrived," the Devil said.

The women pouted. One actually said, "Poo."

"Unless Hex here would be interested in a double date?"

The two girls actually cooed and clapped their hands like they'd just won a prize.

"I'd rather try to barbecue a marshmallow on Wisp's head," I said, starting right in with the ticking off. As much as the Devil hated me, he despised Wisp even more. The owner of the Eternity Club long ago won a bet with the Devil, ended up immortal and the sole possessor of soulfire. Wisp's head could actually burst into flame from anger or just for affect. He was a bit of an idol and inspiration of mine.

"Don't you like women?" one asked.

"I prefer substance to flash," I said.

"He's probably gay," the other said.

"What? You didn't tell them about us, Nick? I'm hurt. I may just have to call off our wedding," I said.

"You two are engaged?" the first said, horrified.

"And we've adopted three children and two pugs. Nicky didn't show you pictures of our little family?" I said.

"My companion teases. I will see you both another time."

"Homewreckers," I said.

The Devil rolled his eyes, then stood to kiss each of their hands. As his lips touched their skin, the women shivered. The Devil let them feel just the tiniest fraction of what he was. It flicked a switch in their souls that if it was allowed to remain on would reduce them to quivering puddles. Flipped on for an instant it pumped out adrenaline and made them tingle, which mixed with Nick's pumping out sexual allure made the women shiver. The combination made the Devil seem like the hottest man they'd ever met. Sadly, they had no idea what hot really meant in his case

"A bit of a cheap trick. Can't get by on your looks alone anymore?" I said.

"Even at my worst, I'm still better than you'll ever be at your best," Nick said. He sat back down in his chair without inviting me to join him. Not that I needed an invitation. I plopped down and put my feet up on the table. There were hard rolls on the table with the name of the restaurant etched on top. It was amazing what folks could do with a laser. It was actually pretty cool.

Still it didn't pay to act impressed, so I picked up three of the rolls and started juggling. I could manage more, but sometimes I dropped one when I did. The maître d' was glaring at me from across the room, but he was too intimidated by the Devil's aura of power and wealth to risk coming over and offending him.

"Just because you're not going to eat, doesn't mean I can't. There is no excuse for poor table manners," Nick scolded.

"At these prices, I'm going to do what I want to," I said. The Devil had long ago given up trying to find expensive places to break me. I wasn't rich, but I had more than enough money to get by. Even the most expensive restaurant in Manhattan was within my reach, at least once a month.

"So, what's new with you, Hex?" the Devil asked as he snapped for the waiter to replace his cocktail. He got a fresh drink in record time.

"Looks like they know you here," I said, ignoring his question.

Nick shrugged with a grin. "You'd be surprised what some people would sell their souls for. Or those of other people." That last one was a jab at me. My father had sold my soul to Hell when I was a kid. It may be allowed, but the person who owns said soul has to go along with it. Some do it out of ignorance, assuming they had no choice. I didn't and things did not end well for dear old dad.

"And yet there are those who know enough not to sell for any price. Or let others sell it for them," I said.

"See, I don't believe that. I believe it's just about finding the right price and the right opportunity at the right time. Everyone has a selling point," Nick said.

"Or breaking point," I said.

"You say po-tat-o, I say potato.

"Really, who says po-tat-o? And what's new with you?" I said.

"I shouldn't really answer, now should I? You didn't answer when I asked the same question."

"But unlike me, you love to talk about yourself. What's more, you love to brag."

The Devil grinned. "You know me so well. Should I tell you about the husband who cheated on his pregnant wife with a succubus? Or the good man who stole money from his employer to pay for surgery for his kid because I convinced the employer that getting health insurance for his employees was a sucker move? Or should I regale you about which high ranking person in Congress now works for me?"

"You mean there's a member of Congress who hasn't lost their soul to Hell? Now that's news. The others were old hat. But as long as they haven't sold their soul, there's always a chance for redemption," I said.

"Sure, there's the chance, but so few people bother to even look for it, let alone take it. Redemption's not really much of a blip on my radar."

The Devil looked out the window and stopped smiling. That should have been my first clue. The Devil was trying not to look happy about something. There was a man with a beard wearing a long brown trench coat glaring like he was trying to intimidate Nick.

"Friend of yours?" I said.

"Something like that." Nick stood up from the table and knelt down on the floor, bowing in front of me. "And hopefully soon to be a friend of yours."

The Devil kept bowing at my feet, which made me nervous. It was obviously just a show, but I couldn't figure out why.

That's when the door to the restaurant got kicked open and in walked Scruffy.

"You are the Devil," Scruffy accused, pointing at Nick.

Nick got up on his feet and brushed off the knees of his expensive suit. "Yes."

"Yet you were bowing to him," Scruffy said pointing to me.

"True, I was," Nick said fighting a smile.

"What does that mean?" Scruffy said.

Nick shrugged and stroked his chin. "What do you think it means?"

"The Devil bows to no one; not even God. Yet you bowed to

this man. Therefore, he must be the Devil's master," Scruffy said.

"Interesting assumption. I'll leave you to work things out. Good day, Master," the Devil said sarcastically with a wink, but Scruffy didn't pick up on it.

"The Devil is responsible for all the misery and evil in the world," Scruffy said. That wasn't exactly true. Sure, Nick tried to add to it, but he wasn't the cause of all of it. "That means that all the evil that is in this world is your fault."

"Your logic has more holes than a sieve and the Devil's playing you for a fool," I said.

"There's nothing wrong with my logic and I'm through being played for the fool," Scruffy said, charging at me like a linebacker and knocking me across the room.

As I got to my feet, Scruffy came at me again. I didn't have time for this. I knocked him down with a chair, dropped money on the table for food I didn't even order, let alone eat, before I body slid away. Nick must have a reason for wanting me to fight this wannabe demon hunter. If Nick wanted it, that alone was a good reason not to do it. I didn't care why he wanted it, I just didn't want to be bothered.

I stopped a few blocks away from my home and walked the rest of the way. Layla needed me to bounce at Plasma tonight and I wanted to get some sleep.

I stopped off and bought a new Blu-ray Jeeves and Bollywog wanted to see. Jeeves prefers Blu-rays to streaming, claims the quality is better. I honestly couldn't tell the difference, but figured it would keep two of my brood busy while I napped.

I changed from my vintage bandaged crescent moon T-shirt to one with a more stylish H in a circle, akin to the anarchy symbol. It was my Hex mark. I'd branded it onto more than a few bad guys over the years as part of my first warning policy. Most vamps recognized the mark even if they didn't know me.

On my way down the stairs, I bumped into Moni or more accurately, her black wings. The graveyard angel rented an apartment from me. It really pissed off her parents, although that wasn't my intention. Her mother's Mica, who's a lasa like Moni herself. They were Etruscan goddesses of the grave. The wings and power passed from mother to daughter. Moni was half human. Truth be told, I didn't want to mess with Mica. To most people, she seemed like a typical mom because – unlike her daughter – she had a tendency to hide her wings. Don't let the PTA façade fool you. Mica was one of the League of Shadows back in the depression era and beyond. Was the League tough? The group were the original bad-asses and included Wisp and Barber.

Still, in some way I think Mica appreciated it. My building was warded for protection. Which explained why a lasa was walking down the stairs instead of flying off the roof. Unless I dropped a ward, even the pack had to exit via the stairs.

"Evening, Hex. Where are you off to?" Moni asked, as I followed her down the steps.

"Bouncing at Plasma. How about you?"

"Treasure hunters just opened up a Babylonian tomb. They're not only disturbing the dead, but maybe waking it too," Moni said.

"Be careful going through the Deadlands." It was the only way a graveyard angel was getting halfway around the world in time to help. The trip would take more than a day by plane and would likely take the lasa ten minutes. More dangerous though. Customs might pat her down, but there were things in the realm of the dead that would devour her and her soul.

"Now you sound like my mother," Moni said.

"Since when is Mica a bass? I always thought she was more of an alto. Tenor maybe if she had a sore throat," I said, stepping in front of her to open the outside door and hold it.

Moni gave me a fake smile and walked outside. "I appreciate the concern." Moni leaned in to kiss me on the cheek.

"Saints preserve us! Not only does the Devil bow to him, but angels kiss him!" said the demon hunter from the restaurant. Somehow Scruffy found out where I lived and was waiting just outside the wards.

"Friend of yours?" Moni said, rolling her eyes.

I shook my head. "Somebody Nick sicced on me for some reason."

"Good luck yourself," Moni said as she flapped her dark wings and took off into the night sky. Scruffy dropped to one knee at the sight.

"You don't have to kneel before me," I said. "It is appreciated however."

The demon hunter leapt to his feet scowling. "I'm not kneeling before you. I was paying respect to God's messenger."

I didn't bother to explain to him that although there were physical similarities between lasa and angels, they were different types of folk. It happened to Moni frequently and annoyed her.

"Look I'm impressed that you found me, but I just don't want to be bothered."

"Well you will be bothered, bothered to death. Anyone who consorts with the Devil is evil as he. And anyone the Devil bows to must be the greater evil!"

"First off Nick and I aren't really close enough to consort. He's not my type. Secondly, some of the people Nick associates with don't even know who he is. It's how he operates. How many people would make a deal with the Devil if they knew he was *actually* the Devil?"

"It is my calling to rid the world of demons." To prove his point, he held out a crucifix. I was impressed as it was two-feet long and his pocket didn't look that big. Scruffy moved closer to me as if he expected me to run off screeching. Holy objects only work on demons and vampyres if the person welding them believes they will. Crosses are little bit different as far as vamps go, but that ties back to their origins with Cain and is something entirely different.

This joker seemed harmless enough and nobody had asked me to get involved. I was having trouble getting a good read on him, so he must have had some training in shielding. He obviously had some sort of mystic tracking ability. There were a few mages who could do that.

"Listen, I'm a nice guy. Nick is messing with your mind. He does that. Not that our time together hasn't been special, but I'm going to go now."

I body slid away. Scruffy may only have been able to track

magic use, so I came out on a subway platform and took more mundane means to reach Plasma in hopes that would lose him. With any luck, he wouldn't set up camp outside my building. And if he did, maybe one of my renters would ask me to get rid of him and I could solve the problem.

It looked like a quiet night, but even so there was already a line behind the red velvet rope of eager clubbers hoping to get in.

Layla did her best to make sure vamps didn't need to hunt or feed from humans. Becoming a blood junkie didn't automatically make someone evil, it just gave them more power to get away with things. Plasma helped out the ones who still wanted to be decent people.

A trainee was at the door, but he recognized me. So did a couple of the hopefuls in line.

"Hello Mr. Hex," said Wallace Nickel, a short plump vamp with a goofy grin.

"Hi, Wally."

"Great night, isn't it, Mr. Hex?" said his best bud, a tall, lanky drink of blood by the name of Dagwood Dime.

Nickel and Dime annoyed the heck out of Barber. They were honest to goodness vampyres, with all the viciousness of a couple of daisies.

I liked them. They were Adze, a breed that had more quirks than an OCD convention.

"Evening boys. Spiffy outfits," I said.

"You like?" Nickel said, pointing at himself with his hands and doing a spin.

"They certainly are something," I said. The pair were decked out in leather pants, black boots and leather vests with no shirt. Just because someone becomes a vampyre doesn't automatically give them an amazing physique. Most of the time that's a glamour. These two weren't exactly in the best shape and were true geeks at heart. Put a couple of bowties on them and they'd pass for a pair of Chippendale wannabes.

"You know, sometimes less is more. Maybe just go with a pair of black jeans and a black T-shirt," I whispered.

Their faces flattened like I had told a couple of kids there was no Santa Claus.

"Too much?" Dime said.

I nodded. "But an A for effort. Let's get you inside."

Their faces lit up like I had suddenly produced the real Santa Claus. Barber rarely let them in until later in the evening, if at all, despite the fact that they were real vampyres. I think he found them an embarrassment. I found them refreshing.

"Thank you, Mr. Hex," Dime said.

"Yes, thank you so much," Nickel said, almost bowing.

I lifted up the velvet rope and let them through. Unfortunately, my timing sucked because Barber came out as I replaced the rope. His bulk took up most of the doorway, not leaving any room for the pair to get by.

"Where do you think you two are going?" Barber said.

"Mr. Hex let us in, didn't you, Mr. Hex?" Dime said grinning.

"It's true, I did," I said, also grinning.

Barber was not. He gave me a look that would have terrified most people. He is one of the most powerful vamps on the continent. Fortunately for him, he didn't scare me. Not because he couldn't hurt me. He could. It was because I knew that in his heart he was a good man and he had a very strong loyalty to Layla, who thought the world of me. If Barber did anything to me, he'd have to explain it to her and that likely wouldn't go well.

"Hex, how many times have I told you we have a dress code," the big vamp said.

"Barber, I'm not going to make these guys wear a dress. That would be wrong," I said.

Barber looked over their stripper wear and rolled his eyes. "It would be an improvement."

"Vampyres! Demon spawn!" Scruffy shouted, running toward the door.

I sighed. This was getting ridiculous. Scruffy didn't have his facts straight yet again. Demons and vampyres have some similarities but weren't related to each other in the least.

"I will smite you all!" Scruffy announced and his hands began to glow.

Dammit. His shields were so good he was able to hide that he wasn't a tracker, he was an eradicator, a mage that can find and exploit the weakness of any opponent. They were pretty rare and extremely dangerous. Nickel and Dime didn't stand a chance. Even Barber would be in trouble once this guy got going. Turns out running away was the smartest thing I could have done. He wasn't going after me at the moment, so the self-defense clause in the curse didn't apply. Luckily, Layla had requested that I always use my power to help out her club and its patrons so I could get involved now.

Finding weakness and sensing what an opponent was were two different skills or Scruffy wouldn't be chasing me. He'd have known I was a human with mystic abilities. I might be able to use that against him.

"Vampyres? You gotta be kidding me. You're actually buying into their cosplay?" Scruffy didn't understand. "They are playing dress up." I pointed to Nickel and Dime. "Do these two look like undead monsters to you?"

"Well…" the eradicator said hesitantly, then looked at Barber who lips are drawn back in a threatening grimace showing off his rather large incisors. "…no, but he does."

"Custom molded slips on fangs." I whispered to Barber. "He's got enough juice to kill everybody on line and inside after going through both, so play along."

I reached up and grabbed hold of Barber's left fang and pulled as I intoned, *"Clip-on."* The tooth came off, revealing a flat tooth underneath. I held it up for Scruffy. "See."

The eyes of half the real vamps were bugging out. Bloodsuckers can sense each other's power and Barbers was off the normal charts. I slipped it back on and intoned *"Undo."*

My teeth started to ache and my incisor was wiggly. Damn curse.

I needed a way to get the eradicator away from Plasma without him hurting me or anyone else. Before I could come up with a plan, Scruffy grabbed hold of my wrist and for the first time we had skin to skin contact. His psychic shielding no longer mattered. My power automatically did a reading on him. Because that ability worked on auto-pilot, the curse didn't do much when it kicked in.

I'd dismissed Scruffy as a joke with power, but then I saw what he had done with his magic – destroyed men, women and even children, enjoying each murderous death. The intensity of the vision distracted me long enough for him to shove me into Barber. The big man didn't even budge a centimeter, but it wasn't him who leapt to my defense.

"Leave Mr. Hex alone," Nickel said, the stout vamp stepping in front of me, his hands on his hips like he was posing for a superhero comic cover, but his belly bouncing up and down like a big bowl of jelly.

"That's right," Dime said, the tall, skinny bloodsucker making with a sad looking kung fu stance alongside of his pal. "He's a friend of ours and if you mess with our friends, you mess with us."

"And that's something you can't handle," Nickel said. I was impressed, but not encouraged. Adze turned into fireflies and had some mind control powers, but these two hadn't mastered those skills yet. Not exactly heavy hitters, but they still stuck up for me.

As I separated myself from Barber, I noticed his eyebrows raise. I think Nickel and Dime had finally managed to impress him.

"Now do you see why I like them?" Even as vamps go, they're kind of harmless and incompetent, but their hearts were in the right place. Still I didn't want them to get hurt, which is when the cries of "Help! Help!" rang out from the alley.

I stepped in front of Nickel and Dime and smiled at the eradicator. "Excuse me. Duty calls. Back in a moment."

I hurried around the corner to the alley to see one of the rush breed of vampyre attacking a woman in a dress that had about as much material to it as an old tube sock. It was like waving a hamburger in front of a hungry tiger. It still didn't give the vamp the right to attack her. And it was in clear violation of Plasma's rules – no hunting, feeding or fighting within a three-block radius of the club. It was enforced by Barber and sometimes myself.

I rushed into the alley and kicked the blood junkie in the groin from behind, grabbed hold of his head and smashed his face into the brick wall. I reached for the woman's arm and helped her up. There were holes in her neck and a whole lot of blood missing.

"Did you drink his blood?" I said

She shook her head. It's possible to become a vampyre without drinking, but it has to be done over time or have enough vampyres attack someone at once and then die. She'll be okay.

"Run in front to Barber. He'll protect you."

As she left, I saw that the eradicator had followed me, as had Nickel and Dime.

I looked at the rush and realized we'd met before. His face bore my Hex mark, which meant he'd already been given this one warning and he'd chosen to ignore it and hurt innocents again. By my rules that somewhat absolved me of anything I did to punish him, but I had a better idea.

"Those guys may have been phonies, but this is the real deal. A vampyre preying on an innocent woman. You want evil, there it is."

"Prepare to meet your end, Hellspawn," the eradicator shouted, his glowing hands lighting up the entire alley.

"Hex..." the vamp pleaded.

I shook my head. "You had your one warning. You're on your own. If I were you, I'd run."

The eradicator looked at me a little differently. "Thank you for aiding my battle against evil. I may have misjudged you. I will make sure he is punished for his misdeeds."

Rush can't fly but they can climb walls pretty fast and he was over the top in a blink of an eye. However, the eradicator had his scent and there was no way a vamp was going to get away from him. And it would get Scruffy away from the club.

Scruffy disappeared up over the top, imitating the moves of the vampyre. That was the part of an eradicator's power that made them so dangerous. While hunting, they could duplicate any abilities their prey used. Scruffy probably followed me with an imitation body slide.

"Are you okay, Mr. Hex?" Nickel said.

I put an arm on a shoulder of each of the geeky vampyres. "I am, thanks to you boys. Now come on, we're going to make sure you get in the club."

I got them a table and made sure they drank for free and it made Nickel and Dime's night. Barber forgot to mention the dress code for the rest of the night.

Scruffy had to be stopped but he had the ability to match any magic I used, so this might be the one situation where having the curse was a benefit. It's forced me to minimize magic in fights for years. I had to outthink him. Fortunately, he seemed to be operating more on a need for vengeance than intelligence.

I had the start of a plan, but I needed more information to pull it off. I had several people that might help me, but I also needed to hole up in a place where Scruffy couldn't use his powers to hurt me. I headed up to the East side to a place most people wouldn't find unless they followed a rainbow. The sign on the door said *Sorry, We're Open*, but no one who ever went there was. Unless of course maybe they were a bad guy.

I opened the door to Bulfinche's Pub and walked in.

"Hex!" shouted Murphy from his perpetual station behind the bar. I like Murphy. Once you got past the bad jokes he was a really good guy, willing to put himself at risk help other people. He's taken on many big bads without the benefit of any mystic powers. Murph even saved my bacon once from a rogue Department of Mystic Affairs agent who happened to be a werewolf.

"Evening Murph. How are you?" I said.

"Good. You?" Murph asked, squinting at me. He and some of the others here in the pub know about the curse and Murphy was looking for signs that I was hurting. "Iced Tea?"

"Don't need it, but I might later. Set me up." I took a sip. Yes, I really did. Not only did Bulfinche's Pub make the best iced tea I've ever tasted, but I actually drank it. I trusted the owner Paddy Moran and the rest of the staff that much. It is one of the few places I'll drink or eat something outside of my apartment. They even keep a special batch of iced tea with extra caffeine behind the bar just for me to help with my migraines. It's that kind of place.

The bar was quiet tonight, but the person I was looking for was coming out of the bathroom. There are days that he was passed out, which wasn't much of a surprise considering how much he drank. Mosie was constantly drunk. He had to be. As the greatest psychic there's ever been, he is so good that he can see all of time and space. Being drunk kept some of it out of his line of sight and lets him stay coherent and not babble like a crazy person permanently curled up in the fetal position.

Mosie walked over and handed me an envelope.

"But I didn't even ask you yet," I said with a smile.

Mosie shrugged. "You don't really have time to waste stating the obvious."

"Why? Where am I going?" I was going to ask him if there were any demons visiting NYC, whether authorized or unauthorized. I had a standing request to stop Hell from hurting humanity so the curse wouldn't hold me back in that respect and finding one was the key to my plan for eradicator boy.

"I suggest you open up the envelope and go put on your tux," Mosie said. "And be careful."

"Who…"

Mosie rolled his eyes. "Just look."

I did. Inside were two tickets to the Moscow Ballet Company which was performing at Lincoln Center tonight. There was no note explaining. It took me a second until I realized what demon was going to be there.

"Damn," I said. This is no run-of-the-mill demon. It was a Lord of the Pit.

"Hopefully not."

"What do I owe you for the tickets?"

"Nothing. I've got plenty of money. If I run out, I'll just buy another lottery ticket. Now get moving," the psychic said.

I turned back to the bar and Murphy was already pouring my glass of iced tea into a Styrofoam cup before I could even tell him I needed it to go.

I hopped a cab and had the driver drop me off a few blocks from home. Once in my apartment I said hi to my brood, changed into formal wear, then caught another cab to Lincoln Center.

I drifted off to the far side of the crowd in case Scruffy showed up ready to fight. I doubted the presence of innocents would stop him from blasting me.

Scruffy showed up and walked over to me. No big surprise – he'd been tailing me.

"I don't know what to make of you. Your actions don't seem to be those of someone the lord of evil would obey. And you helped my mission by finding a monstrous vampyre to destroy. Still I can't decide if I should keep following you and destroy the evil that comes near you or if ending you would get rid of that evil."

"Well, I have an opinion on the matter." I handed him a ticket.

"You want me to go to the ballet? Exactly how is that evil?" Scruffy said.

"You'll see."

We went into Lincoln Center to the box seats Mosie had gotten for us. The lights went down which is when the pink demon walked in. Balchain typically masked his true form, especially the horns, but that wasn't enough to fool me or the eradicator.

"That demon is pink!?" Scruffy said.

"That's nothing. Normally that particular lord of Hell wears a pink tutu to match his skin." Tonight, Balchain was wearing a formal black tuxedo. "That's the demon lord of the dance."

Before the Fall, Balchain used to choreograph the legions of angels who danced before the heavenly throne. When the rebellion didn't work out so well for Nick's side, Balchain ended up in Hell, a, place where music is forbidden. He tried to work through his issues by twisting the dancing that he once loved into torture for the damned, but he still had a weakness for those who could do it well.

"You bring me to a demon lord. That is indeed a fine prey. Continue to do this for me and I shall let you live. I go to attack him now," the eradicator said.

I grabbed hold of his shirtsleeve, careful not to touch his skin again. "Not yet."

"Why?"

I whispered part of my plan to him. Scruffy grinned evilly and nodded.

We sat through the entire ballet. It's not necessarily my thing, but I can still appreciate the beauty, skill, and strength needed to do what the dancers did.

As the applause began, the pink demon rose to leave. I guess Balchain wasn't too impressed as he didn't stay to clap. I motioned to the eradicator and we left to follow him. Balchain was noted for sneaking out of the Pit to see ballet and other high forms of dance. That meant he had to go home before Nick realized he was missing.

Right outside of Lincoln Center, he opened up a man-sized hellhole in front of him. The eradicator could track anyone on Earth, but his powers stopped short of letting him go off world without someone specific to hunt. Now that Balchain was his prey, my plan had temporarily given him any ability Balchain used, including opening hellholes. Turns out, he had a quicker option. Scruffy ran silently toward the pink skin demon, leapt onto his back and pushed the pair of them through the hellhole, which closed behind them.

I smiled. Hell wasn't a nice place. I know, I'd been there. But having seen the innocents Scruffy had killed in his depraved mission, it was someplace he belonged. And if he was able to make life more difficult for the likes of Nick and Balchain, so much the better. And even better, Scruffy even thought he owed me one after I pointed out that Hell was where the Devil lived. With his powers, Scruffy should be able to find him and might even survive long enough to make Nick's life more interesting. And without actively hunting someone, he won't be able to get back to Earth on his own

I was actually looking forward to my next lunch with the Devil. It's not often I can rub his nose in something.

STRIVING FOR PERFECTION

There are lots of people who dream of living in a small town. Some even write country songs about a place where everybody knows each other and people can walk the streets at night without fear, while the kids play in the street until they get called for dinner.

Perfection was all this and more. I just wasn't crazy about the place and just like any good country song, Perfection had the potential to make you cry. Guess I'm just a city boy at heart. I'll take sidewalks and streets over grassy fields and dirt roads any day. I couldn't see the appeal. Even so, I kept looking around for Andy, Opie, and Aunt Bea.

Here was the part of the song that'll bring the tears – Perfection was a grand lie, granted form by a town that was cannibalizing itself for the amusement of Hell.

I was asked to come here by Az. The angel had a charge who was in serious danger. The whole town was a mystic protected zone. What it boiled down to was Hell had drawn a line around the place, then put up magic signs that basically said *Mine*. Nobody in the town could use any magic that wasn't aligned with Hell without it coming back at them very painfully. Body sliding into a place like that was also likely to end in death. Same with other mystic transportation, which left me riding on a bus from Port Authority in Manhattan all the way down to Alabama.

It was great, if boredom was your idea of a good time.

Perfection wasn't one of the listed stops on the route, but when I asked the driver to stop, he let me off ten miles away and told me to have a nice walk into town.

A brisk two plus hours later, the people of Perfection stopped what they were doing to stare at me as I walked into town. Being watched happens to me all the time, so I smiled and waved. That got me a few confused looks, a couple smiles back and everyone moving on to leave me alone.

Of course, there were the practical aspects that came with traveling far from home, which is why I hated long trips. I'm uncomfortable anywhere with people I didn't know well. Too dangerous. Then there is the whole matter of eating, which drove me nuts. I had to pack enough food to feed myself. I ate most of it on the way into town and stuffed the rest in my jacket pockets.

Despite my food trust issues, I walked into a place called Mabel's. It was an old-fashioned diner where the waitresses wore white outfits that could place them in any 1950's movie. They actually had egg creams on the menu. A quick glance around showed that they even gave folks who ordered a milkshake the metal mixing cup with the extra shake.

I planted myself at a corner booth then ordered a coffee and a piece of apple pie. Both smelled delicious. I proceeded to sit and watch people as they came in and went or walked by the window. Appearances were not only deceiving, but damn convincing in this town. Everyone looked normal enough, lots of families with kids. If Az hadn't given me the heads up, I honestly think I wouldn't be able to tell something was wrong and that's saying something.

"Something wrong with your pie, honey?" asked the well-padded and matronly Mabel herself.

"Not at all. It smells delicious," I said.

"Pies aren't for smelling. It's for eating and you haven't taken one bite. You're going to hurt my feelings," Mabel said, with a good-natured pout.

I smiled at the woman but wasn't about to explain my food phobia about other mages slipping me a mystic Mickey hidden in a meal. As good as the apple pie smelled, it wasn't enough to change a habit that's kept me alive just so I didn't hurt her feelings.

"I'm waiting to meet somebody..." Hell had to know I was here as soon as I crossed the town line. As an angel sent me, I had some brief and minimal protection under the Host-Horde Accord. The Pit wouldn't attack first. They'll send someone to have a chat first. "...and I don't want to start before they get here. Thank you for your concern."

Mabel gave me a strange look and walked off to take care of another customer.

"You really shouldn't lie to people like that, Hex," the man in the brown trench coat and hat said as he slid into the booth across from me. Of course, they had to send Negral.

I forced myself not to sigh. "Hello, Chief. What brings Hell's Detective to Perfection?"

"I hear they have the best apple pie east of the Mississippi." Negral reached out and pulled my pie and coffee toward him. "You going to eat that?"

The chief knew I wasn't going to and was just trying to get my goat. "Have at it. But you should know I spit in the coffee."

The forgotten sun and fire god smiled and stuck his finger in the cup. The coffee started to boil a second later.

"So now I have the DNA of the magí? The day is looking up after all." Negral took a sip of the boiling liquid which didn't faze him in the least. "That's a good cup of joe." The Chief followed it up by holding his hand over the plate until his palm glowed. A few seconds later steam rose off of the crust and he brought his fork to his mouth.

Negral raised his hand toward the waitress. "Miss, would it be too much to ask to get this delicious pie à la Mode?"

Mabel smiled. "For you, hon, no problem at all."

The waitress brought over two scoops of vanilla ice cream in a small bowl then put it on the pie. "I like you. Don't see a lot of men in hats these days. I miss it."

Hell's Detective tipped his hat, then laid it on the seat next to him. I guess it was a show of manners for whatever reason. "Thank you for the compliment. These kids today got no sense of style." He made a point of turning to look at me when he said it.

The Chief took a bite with the ice cream. "This is wonderful. Could I get a baker's dozen of these delicious pies to go?"

Mabel's eyebrows raised. "I don't have that many made. It would take me until at least tomorrow."

"No problem. Can I pay you now?"

"Pay when you pick them up. Noon okay?"

"Sure."

Mabel ripped the meal check off her pad and put it in front of me. Negral made no move to get it. Our eyes met and all he gave me was a smile.

"I'll cover the ice cream," he said.

"That's mighty big of you," I said. Mabel hadn't actually charged us for it.

Negral shrugged his shoulders and took another bite. "That's the kind of guy I am. You sure you don't want a bite? It's scrumptious."

"I'll pass," I said. That was enough small talk. Might as well get down to business. "What are you doing here?"

"Same as you. This town is about to make a lot of trouble for the boys downstairs. Nick don't like it and doesn't it want to happen," the chief said.

"So, he's willing to make Munrab undo her deal with this town?"

Negral actually looked angry, but not at me. "Nope. The boys downstairs know they got a good thing going here. They aren't about to give it up. They just want Munrab to have them change the *gift* –" Negral seemed to dislike the word. "… in order to make your winged pal happy."

"Changing who the human sacrifice is might take Aziel out of the equation, but me? Not so much," I said.

Negral scraped the remainder of his dessert off the plate with his fork. "I kind of figured."

"Be quicker if you just licked it clean," I said.

"Like I said, you kids got no sense of style," he said, pushing the plate away from him.

"You plan on helping pick out the new sacrificial victim?"

Hell's Detective got angry, shook his head and got up. "You are such a mook. I got no say over this. I had my fill of human sacrifice before Babylon fell."

"I had to ask," I said.

"No, you didn't." The chief was probably right. He worked for Hell, but he wasn't a demon. Back when he was a god in Sumeria, he was a real bad ass, but he always had a code of honor. The better part of a century in Hell hasn't changed that. I don't trust Negral as far as I could throw him. And if I used magic that could be a couple of NYC blocks – but if he gave his word, I'd trust that.

"You are out of your depth. The deal here is within the Accords. That's why Nick doesn't want it messed up. The townies kill one of their own every year, giving Hell an innocent soul and tainting the ones who live to ensure Hell will likely get the rest of them when they die. It's a soul mine. Munrab's deal with these rubes states the gift has to be an adult town citizen. If the victim were changed, would that appease your angel pal?"

"It might."

Negral nodded. "Anyone smart would change it. I'll have a word with Munrab to do that. Problem is, she ain't too bright and since she negotiated this deal has been full of herself. Doesn't like being told what to do, so I can't promise the angel anything, but I'll try."

"I'm still here either way."

"Like I said, I figured. The angel is my problem. You staying is on Munrab," Negral said, turning to leave.

"Wait," I said. "Who is all that pie for?"

Negral straightened his trench coat, then put his Fedora back on. "I've got a lot of cops at the 666th. Recently they all did something I appreciated. Now whenever I can, I try to do something nice for them. I bring these pies back down there, they'll each get a piece. Suddenly I'm the best boss in the Pit. Not that that's saying much. Be seeing you, Hex."

I paid the bill, left a good tip and took a stroll around town for a little bit. I ended up sitting on a bench in the town park. There were senior citizens playing chess while others were feeding pigeons. Kids played baseball and soccer, all of them displaying what had to be some of the best sportsmanship I've ever seen. Even with the kids playing on slides and monkey bars, I didn't see one altercation.

In fact, the only thing Perfection that didn't seem to be perfect was me. I must have stuck out because the town cop moseyed up to me in an attempt to stare me down, his gun belt slung under his beer belly. I've been stared down by the Devil himself, so this cop didn't have much of a shot. Instead of going into defense mode, I smiled.

"How are you this good afternoon, deputy?" I said.

"Not a deputy, long hair." He really called me that. "I'm Sheriff Bernard Taylor."

"Wow, this place really is like Mayberry." I may have chuckled. I couldn't help it. He had Andy's last name and his first name was actually Barney.

"You big city folks think y'all can come to a small town and act like yor better than us," the sheriff said.

"I don't know where'd you get an idea like that," I said.

"Mabel said you ordered her apple pie and coffee and didn't have a bite. That's just not American."

"I gave it to an associate," I said, stopping far short of calling the Chief a friend.

"Yes, Negral. Now there's a fine upstanding gentleman," the sheriff said.

"Really? Deductive reasoning doesn't play a large part of becoming sheriff in these parts, I reckon," I said.

That pissed him off. "Listen, long hair…" I felt like I was in the wrong decade. I wouldn't consider my hair right now to be on the long side. I've had hair down past my shoulders because I was too paranoid to cut it and risk losing the hair. Right now, my locks weren't anywhere near that length, but it was a lot longer than the sheriff's buzz cut. "We got laws in Perfection. We don't allow loitering or vagrancy. So, if you can't show gainful employment or residence, you best be out of here and down the road in time for the seven o'clock bus."

"You gotta be kidding me – you are actually trying to run me out of town? No problem. I'll get a hotel room," I said.

The sheriff smirked. "Ain't got no hotel and the motel's all full."

"Then I'll chat with a real estate agent about buying a condo. Or maybe a little farm," I said.

"Ain't no rooms for rent or houses for sale in Perfection. We've got us a waiting list a mile long. The rest of the country's gone to hell in a handbasket, but we in Perfection stand for good old-fashioned

American values. We got the best place to live in the entire country and therefore by the default the entire world. That's because we keep the riffraff out."

"So, am I riff or raff?"

"Son, you piss me off enough and I'll make you plum disappear," the sheriff said.

"What about due process? There's nothing more American than the Constitution," I said.

"Alright wiseass, you're coming with me," the sheriff said reaching out for my arm.

I stood up and moved behind the bench before he could touch me. "Before you lay a hand on me, you should know I'm in law enforcement and my visit to your town is known." I pulled out a DMA consultant's badge. I've done enough work for Uncle Sam and the Department of Mystic Affairs over the years on a consulting basis that I had insisted on getting a badge. It saved a lot of trouble in situations like these. It wasn't a regular DMA badge. I didn't want any of their charms or embedded tracking devices in mine. Didn't need the government to know where I was every second of every day.

"DMA," the sheriff said with the same enthusiasm among one might say the word cockroach. "I suppose that's as much law enforcement as an animal control officer."

"So, the question is when I don't call in, do you want your town to be crawling with a bunch of feds tonight?" I said. That was a total bluff. I wasn't about to indebt myself to anybody, let alone the government, by arranging for a rescue I'd probably never need. Still, the sheriff didn't need to know that as part of my deal with the DMA anyone who calls to check out my credentials would get confirmation of my status and told that anything else is classified, therefore backing up any story I might cmake up. Of course, I'd later be called in by Uncle Sam himself to be debriefed on whatever I was up to, so I used it sparingly.

"Now all I'm doing is trying to take a little cross country vacation by bus. I like your town quite a bit, but not sure I have any reason to stay. But I will tell you this – I don't like being told what to do. So, I won't be on the seven o'clock bus. If things go well tonight, maybe I'll be on a morning one. Now if you'll excuse me, I've got some pigeons to feed," I said.

"I'll keep that in mind, fed. But just to be neighborly to a fellow law enforcement agent, I'll make a call and get you a room at the motel. Even make sure you receive the military and law enforcement discount."

"Thank you. Sheriff. I appreciate that."

The sheriff left, but he wasn't happy about it. Since he knew I'd be staying the night, he'd wanted me in that motel room when midnight rolled around. The witching hour was when these moral folks gave their gift to Hell by way of human sacrifice. Make them think all was well so they'd go along with their plans, doing the same thing they did every year on this day for the last half-century. Without it, Perfection would just be another town with an ironic name.

I made my way to the very old school motel. No magnetic strips, but actual keys with a twenty-dollar deposit. The bedspreads on two double beds looked about twenty-five years old, but still in good shape. The TV was an old-fashioned nineteen-inch model with tubes. Outside the motel room with no windows were a pair of deputies sitting in a squad car. I assumed they weren't there for the donut shop across the street, but instead were told to keep an eye on me and make sure I didn't leave my room.

It was still a couple hours to midnight, so I pulled my homemade meal – a sandwich and an Apple – out of my pocket and had dinner. Then I pulled out a customized Swiss Army knife and slid out a small saw blade. After knocking on the wall to figure out where the studs were, I got busy. It was a lot of work, but it wasn't too long before I had a man-sized doggie door cut in the sheetrock wall. I then repeated the process on the wall of the neighboring room, went in it and did it again on the wall on the opposite side of the room. I was done after making four Hex-doors, thankful that despite the sheriff's assertion that there weren't many guests at the motel.

The room I stopped in had a door that opened around the

corner from the watching deputies.

Then the door opened and I figured I had underestimated the local lawmen. I hadn't. A couple making out fumbled their way through the door and into the motel room. From the looks, I was guessing they were using the places as a no-tell motel, because he had a wedding ring, but she did not. They stopped their amorous actions, a little shocked to see me standing in the middle of their soon-to-be lovefest.

"We've made sure all the sheets and towels are clean. We ran out of mints, so we left a condom on the pillow for you instead," I said, exiting the room and taking off towards the rear of the building.

The lovers were confused and left with a choice of what to do. They could ask questions about who I was and why I was in their room and chase after me, or they could get back to being hot and heavy.

Hot and heavy won the day.

I've seen a lot of different ways people try to perform human sacrifice. Most of the time the killers had the decency to not try to hide how evil an act it was. Not so in Perfection. The setup was at the town park. The mayor stood on a gazebo and everybody was acting like it was a summer picnic. There were even vendors selling food and chachkies.

"I would just like to thank the people of Perfection for their participation in this act of giving which makes us the greatest place to live on Earth," the mayor said.

The crowd clapped and even gave a couple rebel yells, but Emily Hoskins didn't agree. The eighty-year-old woman had been bound to her wheelchair using plastic ties. Someone had put duct tape over her mouth, but still, she struggled. She may have been old and frail, but she had her mind. Emily knew what was coming.

"Human sacrifices is what makes Perfection what it is," I shouted from the back of the crowd. "Is that worth your higher property values? I think not. People know right from wrong. And sacrificing human life doesn't fall on the good side of morality."

"But that one small act brings so much good to our little piece of heaven. There is no crime in Perfection. No one is killed here in car accidents, bar fights or crimes. In a town this size that would be maybe ten people a year. By choosing one person to die, we're saving all those other lives," said the mayor. "We are truly heroes."

"Sounds like you're buying into your own rhetoric. You are sacrificing an innocent life. Someone who has doneno wrong."

"That's not true. We often try to choose evil doers."

"That's right. Last year it was that criminal Jacob Dwight," shouted a man from the crowd.

A vision came to me. "A teenager who smashed mailboxes with a baseball bat? That's what warrants the death penalty in Perfection? And you are not just killing someone. You are giving their soul to Hell. What's your boss say about making deals with demons, Reverend Marcus?" I asked a pious acting man in black with a white collar that stood next to the mayor.

"The Lord does work in mysterious ways that are not mine to question. He created us all and gives us all we need. I believe the Lord sent Munrab to us disguised as a demon, but he is truly an angel sent here to save Perfection and all those who live here. Those we gift him join God in Heaven," the reverend said.

"I knew coming to the country I'd see some manure, but I didn't know I'd need wader boots because it would get so deep," I said. "I have one thing to say to all of you. This is wrong and you will not do it. If you do not stop and reject the deal you have with the demon, if you do not go back to your homes and try to lead normal, human sacrifice free lives, there will be dire consequences. This is your only warning, both from me and a friend of mine." I looked at the Reverend. "He's a real angel and he's pissed."

Sheriff Barney came up behind me with a billy club in his right hand. He swung it at my head, but I stepped aside and twisted it out of his grip.

"Sheriff, it is still illegal to kill a woman."

"Not on this night in Perfection it's not."

"It is if it's Emily."

The Sheriff reached for his gun. "Mrs. Hoskins is a resident of Perfection."

"For only two months. Not long enough to qualify for resident status to vote, let alone under your agreement with the demon. Her family brought her here to a nursing home. She has not benefited from this and as such is exempt from the sacrifice pool."

"We'd much prefer to use undesirables like yourself, but that's against the rules and would break the agreement. That woman lives here, she's old and sick. Better her than someone with decades ahead of them." He drew his weapon and pointed it at my head. "You may be a fed, but you move and I'll shoot you in the head and deal with the consequences later."

The mayor stepped to the center of the gazebo where Emily's own granddaughter had pushed her wheelchair. There was a big red painted circle with an upside-down star drawn in chalk next to them.

The mayor stood above Emily with a large sacrificial knife. He lifted it over his head and said, "Oh great Munrab, we your children of Perfection, bring forth your annual sacrifices."

The mayor cut into Emily's palm, drawing blood. He held the knife out to his side and let the blood drip onto the chalk. The circle flared to life and I felt a hell gate open. A demon in an expensive dress and tiny horns appeared.

"You have my sacrifice for this year?" Munrab said.

"We do, oh great one. Her soul and her life are yours."

I moved toward the sacrifice. Sheriff Barney cocked the hammer and two more of his deputies grabbed my arms.

I had to be careful. Any magic I used here could be turned back against me, which combined with the curse would give the sheriff the perfect opportunity to put a bullet in my head.

I was going to be too late to get Emily. Fortunately, my real job here was to play prophet and deliver the warning that they just ignored. I wasn't the only one who gave just one warning.

"*Aziel, it's begun,*" I whispered.

A thunderclap louder than a sonic boom knocked most of the townspeople in the park to the ground, including the sheriff and his deputies. I knew it was coming and managed to keep upright, but just barely. I grabbed the guns from the three lawmen.

In the night sky above the park, Aziel, Guardian Angel of the Host of Heaven appeared to his full glory. His angel light was so white and pure it was almost blinding.

Munrab the demon screamed in pain, despite being protected by the pentacle.

"By the Host-Horde Accord, this town is claimed for Hell. You are in violation of the Accord!" shouted the demon from her knees.

"No, you are. That woman is not a member of this town. She is one of my charges. The warning was delivered in accordance with the Accord by a chosen prophet…" That job was new even for me. "…and it was ignored. Now you and this place must face my wrath."

The angel pulled out a sword that had a blade of fire.

The reverend looked up and saw Az and realized the gig was up.

He looked at me. "Tell him we are sorry and will repent."

"Even I'm not buying it, Rev. Too little, way too late. I told you he was pissed," I said.

Az pointed his fiery sword at the pentacle and the blaze shot out like a nuclear flamethrower, hotter than a solar flare. It burned through the protections of the pentacle and reduced the mayor and the reverend to ash.

"Hex, get Emily out of there," the angel said.

The sheriff had regained his footing and came at me. I brought my knee up into the lawman's groin and he collapsed into the fetal position.

I raced up the gazebo three steps at a time. The pentacle wasn't down, but it was just a matter of time.

Fire from the angel's sword made a circle around the park. As the townspeople tried to flee they realized they were trapped.

I grabbed the wheelchair and rolled it down the gazebo steps. It wasn't gentle, but Emily was still zip tied so I knew she wouldn't fall out. I stopped between some picnic tables and took a special piece of chalk out of the metal case in my pocket. It was pre-prepped and didn't need me to do more than draw a spell circle and spark it to life. I drew a ward around me and Emily, then took out my Swiss Army knife and cut the ties of her hands and gently pulled the duct tape off her face.

The old woman couldn't take her eyes off the vision in white wings. "I remember him. I saw him a couple of times when I was still a little girl. That's my guardian angel, isn't it?"

"Yes," I said.

"He came to save me?" Emily said, tears in her eyes. "Even as old as I am?"

I nodded and noticed the chief of Hell's secret police walking along the grass to one side of us.

Negral looked at the old woman and tipped his hat. "Ma'am." In a much harsher tone of voice, he added, "Hex."

Hell's Detective pointed his finger at the patch of asphalt next to us and flame shot out of the digit as he spun in a circle, making his own protective ward.

"I think Munrab has broken the Host-Horde Accords. Want to go arrest her?" I said sarcastically.

The forgotten god chuckled. "And get in between her and her angel friend? Do I look suicidal? She had her chance. I told her to switch the sacrifice, but she told me to do things to myself that would make a succubus blush with shame. I'll take what's left of her back to the Pit when your pal is done with her."

Munrab let loose a blast of red energy, fueled by souls in the Pit. She was pretending she had a chance against the angel, but she wasn't fooling anybody.

Under normal circumstances, the pair would have been evenly matched, although more than likely the demon would have the advantage. She rivaled a demon lord's power due to her deal in Perfection. And although both sides signed the Host-Horde Accords, the Host was the side most worried about keeping their end of the bargain. This was the first time I could recall seeing where Az was able to function without being bound by its restrictions. I'd seen a taste of his full power back when I was a kid, but that was nothing compared to this.

This was biblical, Old Testament style vengeance. Az hit the demon with blast after blast of angel fire. Munrab was no stranger to magic battles and was working on making her own wards, but none would survive more than a single blast from the angel's sword.

The townspeople were huddled up, cringing in terror as far away from the fight as they could get without frying themselves on the circle of fire around the park. Honestly, I felt like doing some cringing myself. They were further away from the fight than we were, but I had to stop somewhere where I could draw a smooth chalk line without risking losing the woman the angel came to save. The cement between the tables was the closest thing that fit the bill.

The demon decided to fight fire with fire and began belching out hellfire. Worse, she was aiming it all at my ward. If I had more than a few seconds to prepare it and could have risked using my own power, it would've held against the assault. Unfortunately, it was a rush job with magic chalk. It wasn't sloppy, at least for the amount of time it took, but it wouldn't hold.

I took the chalk to set up a second spell circle inside of the first, then planned on making a third, but I would run out of space before the demon ran out of hellfire.

I'd have to use power to deflect the blast. Perfection was still a mystic protected zone and my power might deflect the blast, but it would rebound on me. When the curse kicked in, I'd be down for the count. This close, the Chief would be the first to end me.

Salvation came from a most unexpected source. A wall of fire positioned itself outside of my wards, blocking the hellfire as if it was being shot from a kid's water pistol. I looked over. Negral had dropped his ward to make a new one that extended around all three of us. I looked at him in confusion.

"Mrs. Hoskins, despite her age, is an innocent. No innocents get hurt on my watch. You just got lucky enough to be standing next door to her," he said.

"Will it hold?" I said.

Negral gave me a smirk. "It's just hellfire. I eat the stuff for breakfast."

"No!!! This is my town, my place of power. I was promised a soul and by Hell I shall have it!"

Munrab grew so that she was bigger than a house. A tremendous burst of crimson energy leapt from her maw and knocked the angel from the sky. The giant demon laughed then jumped from the gazebo and charged at Emily.

I may have soiled myself. I was helpless or dead. If I used enough power to even slow the demon down, the blowback from using magic in the protected zone would kill me before the curse had a chance to try.

My only shot at survival was the Chief of Police of Hell standing up against one of the Pit's most powerful demons.

"Negral…"

Hell's Detective must have seen the terror on my face because he chuckled, shook his head and shot a laser out of his finger.

That was a new one.

The demoness stopped short and grabbed her chest.

"How dare you!"

Negral shrugged. "I warned you, Dollface. You chose not to listen. Now you're getting what's coming to you."

"You think you can take me here? Chief, I'll use up every last soul I've taken to make you burn."

"Dollface, you couldn't even start my pilot light, let alone deliver me to a meat wagon. But I'm not who you have to worry about," Negral said.

The demoness looked at me. "Mr. Hex? Please." There was a laugh and much rolling of her eyes. "He's a joke and will be dead a moment after you are, Chief."

"No doubt you could take him, but neither of us is your main problem, are we? Rule one of a street fight, Dollface. If you are going to bump off a guy, don't stop until you're sure he's had the final kiss off."

Munrab looked confused, then realization dawned the instant before Az's hand grabbed her by the shoulder and spun the demoness to face him. A foolish move, but even in a battle like this, the angel is too much of a goody-goody to stab even a demon in the back. Munrab didn't have long to consider the error of her ways before Az stabbed his flaming sword into her gut and up through her head, cleaving her clean in two.

The forgotten god flinched. "Off to the Big Sleep."

"Don't you mean back to Hell?" I said.

"Nope. Some things even demons don't come back from and that would be one of them. She's off to Oblivion."

Oblivion was where forgotten and powerless gods go. It may have been nothingness or another plain of existence. Nobody knew or if they did, they weren't talking.

The entire town looked like it had been destroyed by tornadoes. With the demon's destruction, the power protecting the town was gone and it had turned into a desolate wasteland.

Az's protective circle had protected those outside of the park and those cowering next to it, somehow allowing them to survive the conflagration.

Negral snapped and lowered his fire wards then I lowered mine.

I got down on one knee in front of the wheelchair. "Emily, are you okay?"

The old woman was staring open mouthed at Aziel. "Yes. I know the angel, don't I?"

I nodded.

"When I was a child, he watched over me."

I smiled and stepped aside as the angel floated down and hovered in front of Emily.

"I have never stopped."

"You saved me."

The angel dropped to his knees in front of the old woman and nodded.

"Thank you. It's been a long life. What will happen to me when I die?"

"Something wonderful."

"Promise?"

"I do."

"Where am I going to go now?" Emily asked.

Az looked at me worried. Worldly matters were way out of his comfort zone.

The answer came from an unexpected quarter. "Chester Coyle just acquired a nursing home in Astoria. Was a nasty place, but he's cleaning it up. I could put in a word for Miss Emily."

Coyle was an old timer who used to be a DMA agent. He and the Chief were in the League together before Negral went to Hell.

"Thank you, Negral. Hex, would you take Emily back to New York?"

"Sure," I said.

Az stood and slipped into his gentle white light mode. The woman in the wheelchair wrapped her arms around his waist and hugged the angel. The angel hugged her back.

"Will I see you again, Aziel?" Emily asked.

"You will, but for now this is goodbye."

"But what about the rest of us?" the sheriff said petulantly. The survivors of Perfection were milling around, most in various stages of shock. The lot's hair had all turned snow white from exposure to seeing the angel's power. The wards portected the three of us. "What do we do now?"

Az turned to face the lawman. "Be thankful God is merciful."

I'm not about to argue with the angel, but the fact that these lives were spared was all Aziel. Plenty of other angels would have let the bastards in this town fry. The angel had to work hard to spare the survivors. Otherwise, they would have burned.

"Thankful? For what? We have nothing left."

"You have your lives and a true gift – a second chance. Do not waste this opportunity, people of Perfection, or the only angel you will see when you die will be a fallen one."

The angel floated up, did his golden glow and vanished.

I made a quick call to the DMA to have them send in a clean up team. The sheriff was going to see firsthand what the Department of Mystic Affairs really does.

Negral nodded at me and tipped his hat to the woman in the wheelchair. "Goodbye, Miss Emily."

Hell's Detective started to walk away and the sheriff ran after him.

"Chief, your people had a good thing here. Maybe you'd like to make a new deal with us? Or introduce us to someone who would?"

Negral stopped and the sheriff took a step back. When the

forgotten Sumerian god turned to face the lawman, fire was pouring out of his eyes.

The sheriff turned and ran away.

I laughed. So did Negral. Our eyes met for one of those awkward moments when you realize that someone you don't like may not be as bad as you thought. Then the Chief of Hell's Police continued on his way.

I made good on what I promised Az and Emily and I left Perfection behind.

CAUGHT RED LEGGED

"I feel like a real life junior executive, taking a meeting on the golf course like this. Makes me feel like I should have worn a tie," I said.

"You hush, Little Mr. Consequences," said Rebecca, an elderly woman dressed in an ensemble that looked like somebody had taken various clothing styles from the last fifty years, run them through a centrifuge and picked which ever ones shot out first. "Just remember, I asked for your help. If I wanted wisecracks, I would've asked Murphy."

"I'm happy to do a favor for the Mother of the Streets. This makes us even of course," I said.

Rebecca chuckled. "You might like to think that, but you owe me a lot more than one."

That was true. Most folks in the mystic world don't do favors for nothing. It is usually tit-for-tat or as much is you can get. Rebecca had saved my life once back when I was a kid and still rather new to how magic and life in the shadows worked. But just because I owed her one, it never stopped her from helping me out if I asked her. Occasionally, even if I didn't. The kind of sense of honor is a rarity in the world.

We'd been standing on a cement platform overlooking what was supposed to pass for a field. The fact that it was all asphalt and concrete sort of ruined the effect even if someone had taken the time to paint the ground green. For being so far beneath the streets, the golf course was surprisingly well lit. It was done with mirrors. Hundreds of specially spelled small and large mirrors were set up reflecting sunlight from the surface down into the underbelly of New York. The magic spread the sunlight, making parts of the Undercity as bright at the streets above ground. They even glowed for hours after the sun went down.

There were two shadowy figures putting in the distance and

where one of them was concerned, I wasn't waxing poetic.

They left us standing at the entrance for a while. If I was on my own, I would've already started walking down the greens, but we were playing this Rebecca's way.

"How much longer are we going to stand here and wait? They know we're here," I said.

"That's the problem with you young people, always in such a hurry. But Hex does have a point, Inky. Don't you think you've had us waiting here long enough? I think you've sufficiently demonstrated that you're the Lord of your realm," Rebecca said.

The more shadowy of the two figures put the club he was swinging back in the golf bag. It looked like he sank or melted into the floor. An instant later, a living shadow rose up from the ground in front of us. To the untrained eye, it looked as if he had teleported, when in reality he had just flowed very swiftly like water down the drain pipe.

"Very well, Mother of the Streets. You've made your point. However, I've told you many times to not call me Inky," said Mikoli.

"Surprised you're not used to it. She has nicknames for everybody, Inky," I said.

"I suppose she does, Little Mr. Consequences," the shadow said with sarcasm and more than a little hint of question.

"I had a rough childhood." That much was true, but wasn't the reason for the nickname. The less people who knew about my curse the better. I never told Rebecca, but she knows.

The other figure had been slowly walking his way over towards the rest of us. He was dressed simply in black from a shirt down to his boots. The exception to the dark ensemble was a sword strapped to his back with a white blade. It fit in a couple of clips as opposed to a sheath. The ivory blade was carved from bone. His leg bone in fact.

The man in black stopped about ten feet away, faced Rebecca and bowed his head slightly. "Mother of the Streets."

"Sir Corpse," Rebecca said.

The deceased former knight of the Round Table turned to me. There was no bow. "Hex."

"Sagramore. How's your golf game going?" I said.

The Dead Knight had been the one who built the underground course.

"Good. I'm four under par. I assume you've come to caddy for me," the dead knight said.

"I can understand why you need a caddy. You look dead on your feet," I said.

Sir Sagramore had been a knight of the Round Table and had died destroying a sabotaged cauldron of life which effectively turned him into an everlasting, self-healing zombie. Legend had it that one time when he was trapped, he sliced his own leg off, took the femur and carved it down into the blade he carries on his back and used it to kill the people who'd captured him.

It took time, but his leg grew back and he kept the blade as the bone was harder than steel. Supposedly he had sliced through the leg at the joint cutting through the fleshy parts, but not the bone.

"Hex, again if I wanted funny I would have asked Murphy. Now you boys go and play nice while Mikoli and I negotiate."

Sagramore started to walk back to where he had left his golf bag. Normally I was welcome in the Undercity, but today was a little different, so I turned and looked at Mikoli.

"I assume I have your permission?" I said to the person who had literally put the shadow into the League of Shadows.

"The Mother of the Street's champion may enter the Undercity of the Shadow Clan." Mikoli focused and his shadow solidified into a form that looked like a man and he placed his hand on my shoulder. "Our friend Hex is always welcome."

"Then I guess I better go play golf. How come you were playing? I thought you hated the game?" I said.

Mikoli had shifted back into his immaterial shadow self with only the barest hint of features and shrugged. "I do it for Sir Sagramore. He has such a love for the game and he is of course the Shadow's Sword. I've done it enough now that I merely dislike the game. I would consider it a personal favor if you didn't get too competitive this time."

I just smiled. "I'll think about it."

"You know this could all be fixed if you just would not get so touchy about me visiting a place in my own city," Rebecca said as I walked away.

"Rebecca, you know the Undercity is not of the city and therefore not your domain, but mine," Mikoli said. "You get too worked up for your advanced years."

Rebecca made a sound somewhere between a snort and a raspberry. "The Undercity is still part of *my* city and therefore under *my* jurisdiction. I only honor your request because you take care of so many of the downtrodden and unwanted. I'm still not as old as you are."

Mikoli sighed and one could just make out that he was smiling. "Rebecca, you have no power in my realm."

Rebecca chuckled. "All your protected wards do is cloud things up a bit." Rebecca furled her brow. "You know, I think I would like to try this game. Would you mind fetching me a ball and club?"

Mikoli melted into the floor and shadow slid to where Sagramore was with his golf bag, beating me there. He picked the driver out of the bag and sped back with the club floating above the ground in one hand and a ball in the other, then coalesced back into an almost transparent, yet somehow freestanding 3D shadow. The shade handed the club and the ball to Rebecca. "Would you like to play an entire game?"

"I don't have time for that. One hole should be sufficient and only take a moment."

It was the shadows turned to laugh. "Rebecca, this hole is a par six. Very difficult. It'll take a little time."

"Nonsense. One swing should do it." Rebecca placed the golf ball on a small tee-shaped piece of broken concrete, then squinted and looked across the concrete green. "That's the hole over there with the flag thingy in it, right?"

"Yes."

Rebecca's brought the club back over her head and swung faster than a woman her age should have been able to. She connected perfectly with the golf ball, but it flew far away from the little cup in the hole. However, it hit a wall and rolled down a slight incline until it was on the green, about 10 feet away from the hole.

"Impressive, but too bad you didn't get your hole-in-one," Mikoli said.

"The ball isn't done moving yet. Right?" Rebecca didn't seem to be talking to the leader of the Shadow Clan so much as the expanse of concrete surrounding us all. The ground suddenly shook and a portion of the concrete green actually broke apart directly under the golf ball with enough force that it pushed the ball directly into the cup before settling back into place.

I don't think I've ever seen a shadow do a double take before.

"So, let's get back to these negotiations with you realizing the courtesy that I have given you and will continue to give you so long as you continue to protect and take care of those in the city who need it."

The dead knight leaned in towards me and whispered, "She caused an earthquake just to do that?"

"I don't think that's exactly how it works. It was more like the city was looking out for her," I said.

"Are you telling me New York City has a consciousness?" Sagramore said.

"There are places in the world that have achieved sentience. And the Mother of the Streets and the city have an unusual relationship," I said.

"If you want to talk unusual, you should have known Rebecca's predecessor. But I thought it was more of an office than the idea of the city being sentient," Sagramore said.

"Why? You're a knight who died defending Camelot, yet you're still here to defend a new realm over a thousand years later."

In the magic world, sometimes numbers matter. People and non-people will often ban together in groups. They have different names but these days most like to call themselves clans. Vampyres have them. So do a lot of other creatures and people. But there are a lot of people, many of them non-human, who are weak and could be easily be preyed upon by the stronger folks. Years ago, Mikoli started gathering these people together under his protection, shielding them from others who would do them harm. Not that he was universally successful, which is why Rebecca and I were here today

Despite the power of living shadows, he couldn't protect his clan alone. That's where the Dead Knight came in. Sir Sagramore had wandered the Earth since the fall of Camelot, himself an outcast. Although he was once human, he definitely did not look normal. In centuries past he would try simply to pass himself off as someone who was ill, but was often shunned for his appearance.

Back in the day Dagonet, another former knight of the Round Table who also served as its comedic entertainment, was in the League of Shadows with Mikoli. The shade needed a champion so the Infinite Jester brought Sagramore and Mikoli together. In the Shadow Clan, everyone was different from each other so a zombie with a sword made from his own leg bone really didn't stand out. The Dead Knight served as the Undercity's top cop and protector and found his first real home, probably since Camelot had fallen.

"As much as I hate to admit it, I don't think I can match that shot. How much do you know about the negotiations?" the dead man asked.

"That we have three children topside that have been killed. Their thumbs were sliced off and taken, presumably by whoever murdered them. Each child was taken three days before the bodies were found. According to the NYPD medical examiner, the children topside were killed near the end of the second day and their bodies dumped later. Rebecca is convinced the killer is in the Undercity, but Mikoli won't allow Rebecca to come and find whoever it is."

"Inky doesn't like allowing any other major power players in the Undercity. He worries about what they could do to our people," Sagramore said.

"I heard that," Mikoli shouted from across the concrete green.

"He sounds really mad. You're probably going to be a dead man. Oops, too late," I said.

"Hex, I heard that too," Rebecca said.

That's the problem when talking near the supernatural. Many people have ways of listening in on conversations that regular humans don't.

"I'm just doing what Dagonet asked me to do whenever I see you," I said.

"Try to make me smile." The dead man did, but it was a sad one. "Dagonet has never quite gotten over the guilt of what happened to me."

"What guilt? I thought he just liked annoying all of his friends with bad jokes," I said.

"Well that may be true, but I'm a rather special case. Mordred had twisted the cauldron of life after we had acquired it from Faerie. It still brought the dead back to life, but in twisted and grotesque form. It had to be destroyed by a normal human, someone with no supernatural abilities which at the time left Dagonet and me the only ones who were willing to die to protect others. He paused for a moment to say his goodbyes and make some last requests before he planned to sacrifice himself. I simply did what needed to be done and was turned into this. Dagonet blames himself, thinking if he hadn't stopped, he would've been the one this happened to. I've told him for centuries I bear no ill will, yet he is constantly trying to do things for me that he doesn't need to. And even if I did harbor a grudge, his finding me a home here in the Undercity would have evened matters up."

"So why did Mikoli have a change of heart?" I said.

"We have a child who went missing yesterday. A grogan."

"A Cousin It?"

"While some of them would find that offensive, others would find it amusing, but yes." Grogan's were short humanoids with long hair that went from their head down to their feet and did resemble the character from the classic TV show, though the grogan's myth predates that program by centuries.

"If the killer doesn't vary his MO…"

"Then we have less than 12 hours to find the child before it's too late. I have tried, as has Mikoli, but we've had no success," Sagramore said.

The Undercity is a realm claimed by Mikoli and its borders enforced by his power, but is not a mystic realm in the traditional sense where the leader and the land were bonded together. That type of union usually gives the person in charge quite a bit of power in seeing things in their own realm, although the degree of the control and accuracy varies a bit. Mikoli with much effort can reach out and sense things in shadow and darkness. The simplest way to block him from finding you would be simply being in a well-lit room.

"He really should just let Rebecca in. When she says that the streets whisper to those that know how to listen, she's not waxing poetic. The city really does communicate with her. It's not an all or nothing thing, but it can lead her in the right direction sometimes."

"Mikoli is too pigheaded to allow that to happen. He feels if he bends the rules once, people will be expecting him to do it time and time again. He allowed her to choose a champion and since you are friends with both of them, they both not only trust you but are hoping you can get the job done. To save face however, he will insist that as the Shadow's Sword I accompany you, so the credit will be divided between both of them. He doesn't really care so much about that but politics are a deadly mistress. With all the people pushing on him from all sides, he can't afford even the illusion of weakness. As far as I'm concerned, I'm your backup. You find this kid and we go in and get him out," Sir Sagramore said.

I nodded. "I think they're about wrapping things up."

Mikoli and Rebecca were shaking hands, so the Dead Knight and I returned to where the pair was standing.

"Go save the boy. But if possible, please allow the Shadow's Sword to be the one to get the credit," Mikoli said.

"Credit Schmidt. Just get this child killing bastard and if possible bring them back to us alive so we can teach him a lesson," Rebecca said.

I was with her on this one. It didn't matter who got the credit, as long as the killer was stopped.

I turned to the zombie. "Bring me up to speed."

Sagramore and Mikoli had done their best to track down whoever it was who'd taken the grogan boy, both by means mystic and more mundane. There were no clues or evidence left behind that they could follow. That didn't mean there wasn't a way.

"Take me to the boy's family," I said.

"The boy's name is Sheen," Sagramore said.

The main part of the Undercity was called Underbelly. In some respects, it resembled a shantytown. Homes were built out of whatever materials were available, sometimes even built into a wall. For the most part they were small and functional, often no bigger than an average hotel room. Still Underbelly was several city blocks long and wide.

Magic has been on the decline on Earth over the last several centuries. There were mystic groups, families, and clans with a lot of power who banded together, but that left an awful lot of just regular magic folks who didn't happen to be human to fend for themselves. Humanity didn't have the greatest track record when dealing with something different, so most of them avoided people as a survival mechanism. They also had to avoid predators like vampyres and werewolves who would see these people is nothing more than the potential for food, servants or worse.

A perfect example was the woman we'd come to meet.

"Hex, this is Fonte, Sheen's mother," Sir Sagramore said. Their home was built into an old brick building that the newer city had been built on top of. Wooden boards had been used to extend the space outwards. The woman in question was about four and a half feet tall. And to be honest I was taking Sir Sagramore's word that she was a woman, because she was covered in long brown hair from the top of her head down to what I assumed were her toes.

A grogan was the perfect example of somebody who really didn't have much of a place in the modern world. They had no powers, just an unusual appearance. There was supposed to be humanoid under all the fur, but not human. Even if they shaved or cut off all their hair, they wouldn't be able to pass in human society as anything other than a freak or worse. While they may not have had any real power, their hair did a little bit more than the human variety. It gave them some measure of protection against the elements, as well as protect them against germs and such. It also acted a lot like cats' whiskers and that gave them sensory input of about the world around them they could send strands out in different directions when hiding so that even when they're asleep they would get some sort of warning if something came close enough to touch one of the hairs

Even though I couldn't see Fonte's face, it was obvious she'd been crying. "Fonte, this is Mr. Hex. He is here to help us find your son."

All at once the tower of fur rushed at me and suddenly I was enveloped in one huge hairball. All of her hair rose up and wrapped around me, almost like a fairy cocoon. It wasn't just the fur, I could feel a set of arms holding on to me, almost for dear life.

"Please Mr. Hex, bring back Sheen. His lowlife father left us right after he was born. He's all I have in the world. I'll do anything you want of me."

I was feeling awkward enough with the hug, but then the hair covered woman got to her knees and began focusing her pressure right below my waist level. As uncomfortable as that kind of unwanted contact was, it let me know a little bit more about her. I got a reading of her past. Before she had found the Shadow Clan, she had been the sex slave of someone stronger and more powerful than her. Her self-esteem was so low that she thought trading on her well-hidden female attributes was the only way she could convince someone of power to do something she wanted.

"That won't be necessary," I said trying to move her hands away from her attempts at opening my pants, but her fur and hair was flying around, making it difficult for me to get a good grip.

Luckily Sagramore stepped up, reached down and back pulled her up and away from me by her shoulders. "Now Fonte, we've been over this. That's not how we do things in the Undercity. Hex is a good man and he is helping to find your son because he cares and tries to do the right thing."

That set the hairy woman off even more. She fell to the floor moving between half kneeling and half laying in what I could only assume meant she was bowing to me. "I'm so ashamed. Please forgive one so ugly and unworthy as myself and don't hold my sins against my boy."

I genuflected down onto one knee and held a hand towards

the grogan woman. "Nonsense, my dear. There is no reason for me to do such a thing and nothing to forgive. In fact, I'm flattered that such a beautiful lady would be so inclined to offer me something so lovely and enticing."

What I took for the head of the mound of hair slowly lifted up from the floor and seemed to be looking at my face, shocked at my words.

I extended my hand further and the hand beneath one side of the hair reached up and took it. I helped the grogan to her feet.

"I may be able to find your son, but I would need something of his to do so. Do you by any chance have any hair from him?" I said.

The grogan was still holding my hand, pulled me inside her home and went to the back room. It appeared to be the bedroom. There are closets in Manhattan that were bigger. Inside there were two old beanbags covered with blankets that must have served as their beds. She led me to the one in the farther corner and handed me a blanket.

"This is Sheen's bed and blanket. There might be some hair here."

Carefully I opened up the blanket and examined it. I did indeed find a three-foot-long light brown hair. The mother had dark brown, so it more than likely belonged to the boy

"May I have this so that I can try and find him?" I said. Anything containing DNA – hair, nails, blood, or skin – can be used in magic because it still has ties to the person it came from. It was not uncommon for hairs and the like to be used in a lot of dark magic meant to harm someone. Think pins and a voodoo doll only worse. I incinerated my hair and nail clippings. In a case like this it was polite to ask.

The top of the tower of hair bobbed forward and back. "Yes, of course, honored one."

I noticed a stuffed frog beside the beanbag bed and I picked it up. "Is this your son's?" The grogan nodded. "Does he have a strong attachment for it?"

"Oh yes, Sheen still sleeps with it, although he is getting old enough to pretend that he doesn't. He puts it behind his bed and waits until he thinks I'm not looking before he pulls it up underneath the covers with him," she said.

"May I borrow this too?" I said.

"Of course. Whatever you need. Just bring Sheen home."

The dead knight and I walked out and along the old brick building.

"Would you mind keeping a careful eye out and watching my back while I put this put together?" I asked.

Sagramore drew his bone sword out and became even more attentive. "Yes. Are you going to set a ward and used your power? Are you worried that the light will draw attention to you?"

"It's a minor spell. No lights," I said.

"I knew the most powerful magí," Sagramore said.

I nodded. "Merlin."

"I've heard some say that you're almost as powerful as him."

If it wasn't for the curse, I would be. "I've heard the same thing."

"You don't claim to be more powerful?"

"I've never met the man so I couldn't give you a definitive yes or no."

"Whenever Merlin did a spell, there were lights and energy flying everywhere. I'm surprised you don't have to do that," Sagramore said.

I smiled. "Merlin was concerned with trying to keep together the kingdom of Camelot. Everything he did likely had more than a hint of show to it, both to inspire respect and maybe a little bit of fear. His great goal was to create the pinnacle of human achievement. I'm not trying to impress anybody." And he wasn't cursed so showing off was no big deal.

Sagramore nodded.

Very carefully I wrapped one end of the hair several times around the stuffed frog's wrist and carefully tied it tight so it would stay anchored there. I'd probably be able to find Sheen with the hair alone but combining it with the frog would work even better. The hair was linked to his body, but the frog was linked to his emotions. The two would combine and make it easier to track him down. And the frog would only work by itself if the grogan boy was still alive.

I put my finger over the hair wrapped around the frog's wrist and whispered, "*Find Sheen.*"

A tiny bit of power jumped from me into the hair and frog. Since it was only a small expenditure of magic, I just got the start of a stiff neck from the curse.

The hair shot up and pointed in front of us and slightly up.

Sagramore had been around enough magic in his time that I didn't have to explain that we were going to follow where the hair pointed us and would hopefully find the grogan boy.

Sagramore lowered his sword to his side and fell in alongside of me. He put on a head lamp and gave me one.

"Is he still alive?" the dead man whispered.

"It looks like it," I said, at least if the strength that the hair was being held up was any indication. Sadly, there was no guarantee, but it looks like he hadn't been killed yet. Of course, we don't know what else might have happened to him, but that went without saying.

"Perhaps we should pick up the pace." The Dead Knight was obviously worried. In a case like this, a few minutes could mean the difference between life and death. I nodded we both started out at a well-paced jog.

I try to keep myself in pretty good shape. It's crucial to using certain aspects of magic and also lessens the effects of the curse. In the simplest terms, I never know who or what I'll be facing off against so while I may not be crazy about regular exercise it's crucial in my line of work. Yet another aspect by which the curse makes my life more difficult. If I didn't have to deal with the side-effects of using magic, I could simply mystically make myself be in peak physical condition at all times instead of working out.

We ran in silence for a couple of hours, with me taking the occasional break to get a sip of water out of a flask I carry. I made it years ago. Kind of like a horn of plenty, only with liquid. With a thought, I can change it from water to ice tea or pretty much anything. I had it in water mode so I stayed hydrated. I offered some to Sagramore but he declined. He didn't appear to get thirsty or tired. I guess being dead had its advantages.

We were nearing the outskirts of Mikoli's realm. These areas were just as much under his protection, but were more sparsely populated and were a haven for those who didn't want to be around other people. The hair had been steadily rising up. When we reached an old water tunnel that hadn't been used in fifty years, it was standing and pointing straight up. The dead knight and I examined the pipe and neither of us found any evidence of any sort of door or opening, but the hair was insistent that the grogan kid was just above us.

"Any more tunnels or passages above us?" I said.

"Not that I know about. That doesn't mean someone couldn't have carved out their own," Sagramore said.

We both started putting our hands on the upper part of the pipe and knocking on it. There was one section that echoed. Sir Sagramore bent to the bottom of the access tunnel.

"The dirt and dust has been disturbed here. There must be an opening," he said.

Sir Sagramore grabbed a handful of dirt and dust, motioned for me to step back and threw it up at the pipe. He cranked up the flashlight on his head and pointed it again at the pipe. The dust stuck revealed the tiniest line of a three-sided square.

"There's not much that could cut through metal with such a fine, almost undetectable line," I said.

"An enchanted blade would do it."

I pointed to his bone sword. "Could yours?"

The dead knight shook his head. "Mine can cut through it, but would leave a mark. Hayden..." Sir Dagonet's invisible and telescoping sword. "... might be able to."

"I feel comfortable that we can eliminate the Infinite Jester as a suspect," I said. There are very few people in this world on whose nature you could depend on absolutely. I count the former jester knight of the Round Table in that number. "But that means we might be dealing with someone with a magic sword or the like."

The dead man nodded. "Seems like a strong possibility. So, we go up, unless you have any better ideas?"

I reached out to try and feel for any presences nearby. Usually a scared child would be easy to pick up on in close range, but something seems to have cleansed the area.

"I'm not getting anything, but I am sensing something that is trying to block any magical pinging. We've got to be ready for an attack moment you open it," I said

"Or a trap. It would be child's play to trigger an earthslide or enough water to drown us." The Dead Knight walked along the rest of the tunnel and examined it for booby-traps satisfied he returned to the trapdoor and pushed up. A two-foot square hunk of metal bent up and in like the top on a can of sardines. He stood back and waited. Nothing came out of the darkness at us. No dirt or rocks fell. No water rushed out.

"I assume you are good in the dark?" Sagramore said, clicking off his head lamp.

I could tap into enough magic to make even the deepest darkness seemed bright. "I am, but I didn't know that the dead could see well in the dark beyond sensing heat. What we're looking for might be able to hide it," I said.

"I do good with heat signatures and Mikoli gifted me with an ability to see in the dark. It helps down here. I'll take point."

The Dead Knight jumped up through the hole, leading with his bone sword.

Several seconds passed and then I heard, "Clear."

I climbed up into another tunnel that seemed like it had literally been sliced out of earth and stone. I put my hands on the walls.

Impressive work, whoever did it. Some crawling later and we entered a chamber about ten feet tall and eight feet high. There was a tunnel that led off of it, but it was small which meant we'd have to crawl through it

"The tunnel is easily defensible from the other side and it is a bit foolish for us to try and go through," Sagramore said.

I went to the tunnel and felt magic of the deadly variety.

"Anyone who tries to go through that the tunnel will die. Heavy duty warding," I said.

Sagramore chuckled. "Then it's a good thing I'm already dead then, isn't it? Is it a standard ward using stored mystic energy that blasts out when contact is made?"

I studied it some more. "Yes, but you're not thinking about setting off the ward yourself, are you? It would probably disintegrate you and who knows how long it would take you to reform," I said.

"Or maybe it would finally do the job and kill me. Wouldn't that be nice? But no, you must have me confused with the Phoenixian. I have no desire to endure any more pain than I have to. I long ago learned another way to trip the trigger on a ward."

"Once the ward is down, we need to get in there fast."

"Then you need to figure out a way to get me through that tunnel very quickly," Sagramore said.

"What makes you think you're going first?" I said.

"Simple. You may be a magí, but you're still mostly human. Whatever's in there is not going to be able to kill me," the dead knight said.

"But it could hurt you or trap you," I said.

The living zombie shrugged. "Again, I've been hurt before. I always reform and heal. And if I'm trapped, you're just have to free me now, won't you?" Sagramore said. "They'll be expecting me, but hopefully not you. Now do you have anything in your bag of tricks that can get me, then you, through there quickly?

I thought about it. "I can shoot you through there like an old-fashioned pneumatic tube."

"Not like a bullet?" Sagramore said smiling.

I shook my head. "Be too fast, and anything on the other side of you is going to get hurt. It's a bad guy, that's fine, but whoever did this is pretty crafty. I wouldn't put it past them have the grogan kid at the mouth of the hole to be a human shield for any attacks."

Sagramore took the tip of his sword and pointed it down by his side. "Then I better not go through point first I guess."

Sagramore started unscrewing the end of the hilt of his bone sword and when he took the metal off, the ball end of a ball and socket joint was revealed. The Dead Knight walked over to the mouth of the tunnel and rammed the pointy end of his blade into the stone beneath it then moved it back and forth making a bigger hole. He carefully balanced the sword upright so it was inches away from the mouth of the tunnel. He motioned me to follow him and told me to get down and back into the metal pipe. I looked up and watched as he took a large set of keys out of his pocket and tossed them at the sword, then leaped down towards me. I heard the keys hit the bone blade, knocking it over into the ward. There was a flash of light and a large discharge of sizzling energy.

The Dead Knight grinned. "Can't do that with metal. Has to be organic. We best assume whoever's on the other end of that knows we're here so shoot me through already," Sagramore said, grabbing his unhilted sword, tucked it besides him with one arm and put the other over his eyes as he crawled in the mouth of the tunnel. Although the eyes would heal, they'd be rather crucial to finding the kid. Best if he had them to try and save Sheen.

"*Pneumatic tube*," I intoned. There was a whoosh as the air in the room around us gathered together and shot the zombie through the tube.

Luckily, I was smart enough to take a deep breath as soon as I cast the spell, but the curse made it hard for me to breathe. I leapt in the tunnel after him and commando crawled as fast as I could.

By the time I made it through, I was in the middle of a hostage standoff. Sagramore was crouched down, his sword pointed in front of him. The grogan kid may have been covered from head to foot in long hair, but even his follicles were trembling and some of it looked like it was covered with blood. There was a man behind him with his arm locked around where I imagined the grogan's head was and he had a number of blades pressed against his young body. And I used the term man loosely. Others might go with the term creature. The kidnapper stood a little over six feet tall and was naked. Otherwise he might have passed for human.

The first thing that popped out at me were his legs. They were red and covered in something that was a cross between hair and scales. The index finger and thumb of his right hand had fingernails that were long enough to resemble short sword blades. The left hand wasn't showing any, but it was only a matter of the kidnapper thinking about it to make them pop out on the other hand.

This guy was a bogeyman that was prevalent in Europe, particularly Germanic areas, a few hundred years ago. He was a red-legged scissors man. People weren't always clever on how they named monsters, but this was certainly an apt description. His kind were cowards, noted for going after children, especially naughty ones. Bastards cut off kids' thumbs by way of punishment. This guy had a necklace that wrapped all the way around his throat that was filled with thumbs. Most were old, but six thumbs were fresh. Two of them were still dripping blood.

"Give me the child," Sir Sagramore demanded.

The red-legged scissors man laughed. "And what? You'll let me live?"

"Don't put words in my mouth," the dead knight said. "But I swear to you if you harm the child any further, I will end your existence."

"What doesn't really give me much motivation to do as you ask, now does it? I hand over this little one and you will try to run me through with your sword, which really doesn't work for me. How about instead you let me head out my tunnel and I'll let go of the grogan brat when I get to the end," the red-legged scissors man said.

"I don't believe you," the knight said.

"And you're wise not to, for who in this situation wouldn't lie to get what they want?"

"If I gave my word, I would keep it," the zombie said.

"That's what anyone would say. Why would I believe you?" the bogeyman asked.

"Because I am Sir Sagramore of the Round Table of Camelot and the Shadow's Sword. A Knight of the Round Table does not break his word."

"I've heard that. And I've heard of you. That is if you are who you say you are. You could be lying about your identity to low me into a false sense of trust in order to save the child and then murder me."

"Then how about we add me into the mix. I am Mr. Hex."

I watched as the red-legged scissors man's eyes went wide.

Sometimes having a reputation is a very good thing indeed. "No one would be foolish enough to try impersonate me because of what I would do to them. You've already taken the child's thumbs. I will not let you do anything else. I would be willing to give you my word that if you let go of young Sheen that you will live long enough to have a trial."

The red-legged scissors man laughed. "You mean you're going to take me up to the surface world to their legal system? They wouldn't know what to do with me."

"Kidnapping is a federal crime and the Department of Mystic Affairs has their own court system. However, I was thinking more of giving you to the Shadow Lord for trial since this crime was committed in his realm."

"Trial by the Shadow Lord. Hmm." The bogeyman stroked his chin. "They say Mikoli had no problem issuing the death penalty. Why would I agree to that?"

"Because you get to live until the trial and maybe, just maybe, figure out a way not get the death penalty. Because if you don't let go of that child in exactly ten seconds, I will kill you where you stand. And if even one hair is harmed, your death will take days and will involve pain the likes of which you've never dreamed up," I said.

Then I wiggled my fingers in a way I'd seen Wisp do and my hands burst into magical flames that looked just like soulfire, which was quite possibly the scariest thing I could think of. Wisp had managed to win it away from the Devil on a bet. One touch of the flames made a person experience all the good and evil they had done in their life. And it wasn't just what they did to other people, but the effects their actions had on those who loved the people they either helped or hurt. Under the restrictions of the curse I'd have to experience part of the soulfire. No way did I want to risk that, but this bogeyman didn't know I was bluffing.

The red-legged scissors man started to tremble just a little bit. "You couldn't hit me without hitting the child."

"Sheen is a child. I doubt he's done much bad and the joy he brought his mother will offset anything else. Can you think of anyone who you brought so much joy that would balance out what you did to get all those thumbs?" I said.

"Both of you give me your words that you will not kill me if I give you the child?"

"Provided you give yourself up and do nothing to try to harm anyone or attempt to escape, I give you my word I will not kill you on the way to Mikoli," Sagramore said.

"As do I," I said.

The red-legged scissors man shoved the grogan boy away. Sagramore put his sword out to the side and opened his arms and the little boy ran into them weeping. The dead knight held him until he stopped.

I stepped closer to the bogeyman. "Retract them."

The red-legged scissors man gave me a warm smile that made me want to smash the side of his head in with a cinderblock. He was acting like he was in charge, like he'd gotten away with something.

From behind me I heard, "He cut off my thumbs."

Out of the corner of my eye, I saw the grogan boy stick out what could've been two human hands out from under his pelt. There were two bloody stumps where his thumbs should've been. The blood had already clotted. Some predators exuded an enzyme on their fangs and claws that encouraged clotting so they could play with their food. The kidnappers smile grew even wider.

I tore the necklace of thumbs off of him. And it looked like he was ready getting ready to attack me as both his thumbs and index fingers suddenly sprouted nail blades.

Now was my turn to smile. "Please, give me an excuse. Do something that makes sure my word will no longer bind me."

The nail blades disappeared as quickly as they had appeared.

"Sagramore, watch the prisoner."

The Dead Knight nodded and put the boy down, then screwed his hilt back on his bone blade and pressed the tip against the bogeyman's sternum.

The morbid necklace had a clasp in the front where the sharp needles points were attached to a leather strap. The needles were rammed through the fleshy bits of thumbs in order to hold them on. With great care, I pulled the grogan's thumbs off. They were still warm.

"Those are mine," the red-legged scissor man shouted. Sir Sagramore pushed the point of his blade ever so slightly into the kidnapper's chest and he shut up.

I had a medical license, even if I rarely practiced. I had a specialty in psychiatry, but I had done six months of my time as a resident in an emergency room. I wasn't a great surgeon and I doubted than any normal surgeon would be able to successfully reattach these thumbs. However, I had advantages my colleagues didn't. There was a type of magic called fleshsmithing which allowed a mage to mold and change a person's body.

I'm not really good with kids. I'm told I tend to treat them like adults and lose my sense of humor around them. Considering my own childhood, I may have reasons for that. That didn't matter because I wasn't going to treat this grogan like a kid. I needed him to be braver than most men could.

"Sheen, I'm going to try and reattach your thumbs." Normally I wouldn't be able to muster magic for this without being asked, but since Rebecca knew about the curse she made sure her request for help included telling me to do whatever I needed to do to help people.

Sheen nodded. "I'm going to use magic and it's going to hurt, but I need you to remain perfectly still. Can you do that for me?"

"Yes." The word came out clear, without a hint of fighting back a whimper. "Will it hurt a lot?"

No sense lying to the kid. "More than anything else you ever felt before."

"Even more than when he cut them off?"

I nodded. "When he cut them off, it was quick. This is going to take a while and hurt that whole time."

Most fleshsmiths as part of their magic were able to exude a form of anesthetic if they wanted to, so the people they worked on didn't feel it. The curse wouldn't let me use two forms of magic at once without paying a heavy price and the last thing I needed to do was pass out in front of a bad guy.

"Hold out your hands like this," I said. Sheen did. I held up the two amputated thumbs to examine them and then showed them to the boy. "Do you know which was your left and which was your right?"

The massive hair that was the top of the Grogan shook side to side. "No."

"No problem. I got it figured out," I lied. I was guessing using a combination of where the bones fit together and my psych background. The fact that someone saved and wore trophies like this indicated much importance being placed on them and great care putting them on the necklace. Red Legs here would likely want them on the original sides.

There was some deterioration of the tissue but it should still work. I held the thumbs nail out, between my pinky ring and index fingers. I touched the stump with my index fingers, letting the magic pour out of me and into the hand and severed thumbs. When I felt it start to take effect, I moved the thumbs forward and intoned "*Mend.*"

Bone, tendon, muscle, skin, blood vessels, and fascia all started to grow towards each other. The kid was good. He gave a little scream when it started to hurt but his hands didn't even twitch. Fleshsmithing took a lot of mental control. Like most magic power that was only one component. The more important component was knowledge. One needed to know how the parts of the body worked in order to put them back together. Luckily thanks to med school, I had that knowledge, but I still had to focus on the bone first and then work my way outward to the tendons, muscles, fat pads, fascia, and skin, then went back for the arteries, veins and capillaries. Last were the nerves.

I lost track of time but finally managed to get the nerves to grow back and reconnect with each other. That was the hardest part. Nerves normally grow very slowly and you have to make sure that not only do you get the nerves but the myelin sheaths that go on top of them. Not to get into a physiology lecture, but nerves don't work like wires conducting electricity. Think of myelin like insulation. The electric impulses jump between the exposed parts of the nerves instead of going through the nerve wiring. If the myelin sheaths go away, the nerves are mostly useless.

I pulled my hands back but didn't let go. I'd done all I could do but it was still possible to fine tune it some more so long as I didn't break the connection.

"Sheen, move your thumbs," I said.

The hair covered boy did as I said.

His thumbs moved! They were choppy movements, not very graceful, but the thumbs worked.

"Thank you, Mr. Hex." The grogan kid threw himself at me and wrapped his arms and hair around me in a hug. I stood there awkwardly patting him on the back, trying not to make it look like I was petting him. After a moment, I just stepped back and pulled away. The contact had given me a little flash into his future. The kid was going to lead a good and extraordinary life. He was going to dedicate himself to protecting others from the things in the dark, and one day in the future when New York City is destroyed by a mad sea god, Sheen was going to take up the mantle of something wonderful called a Startender and somehow Paddy Moran and Murphy would be involved with the whole thing.

"Nice work," said Sagramore.

"All part of the service," I said.

The rest of us may have been happy, but the kidnapper sure wasn't. His face turned as dark a red as his legs.

"How dare you undo my work! I will see you dead for that."

"If you're still around tomorrow, I'll put that on my list of things to consider worrying about,"

Now that we were both there and paying attention to the kidnapper Sagramore said, "Turn against the wall and put your hands behind your back."

The Dead Knight pulled out a pair of enchanted manacles out of a pouch on his belt that didn't look big enough to hold them and clasped them on the bogeyman's wrists

I went back out the tunnel first with Sheen following me. Sagramore pulled out a length of rope and tied the kidnapper's feet and left a leash attached. He placed the kidnapper feet first in his own tunnel and tossed me the rope and I pulled him out with the Dead Knight following behind him, blade first this time.

On our way back, Sagramore whispered into a shadow that we were coming. It must've worked, because Mikoli and Rebecca, along with a crowd which included Sheen's mother, were waiting near the Shadow's Throne, the name for his throne room and governing area. Interestingly enough it was a few hundred feet below Gracie mansion.

Sheen and his mother had a tear-filled reunion.

"I'm glad to see you back safely, Sheen," Mikoli said from his alabaster throne. The shade had willed and solidified himself so that he took on the outline of a man, but one that was made of ever shifting darkness. "Tell me what happened."

Sheen gave a blow-by-blow. Red Legs had approached Sheen in an outer tunnel and claimed to have lost his own child and said he needed Sheen's help to find them. It was a variation on the old "Help me find my puppy" trick.

Unfortunately, the children in the Undercity didn't always get public service announcements about the tricks predators use on children. Sheen then talked about the torture that ensued including the taking of his thumbs. Things had been about to get much worse before we arrived in the literal nick of time.

Mikoli turned towards Red Legs, who stood alone with his hands still chained behind his back. "In my realm, all have the right to speak in their own defense or have another speak for them. Do you want to speak or have another do it for you?"

"I'll speak for myself," the kidnapper said.

"Then what you have to say about what the child said?" Rebecca said, standing at the side of the throne. The Shadow turned and gave her a dirty look.

"The Mother of the Streets speaks out of turn, but asks the correct questions. Do you deny the child's allegations?"

"No." There was a startled murmur from the Undercity folks in attendance. Like in any trial, the accused will tend to lie about being innocent, especially when knowing that death could be the result. "In fact, what he stated is all true."

"Then you make this very easy. I shall now pronounce sentence..."

"I'm not done speaking yet. My name is Tagone and what I did was in devotion to my duties as a member of the Disseelie Court and as such I am immune from punishment in this court or any other."

The Disseelie Court were a clan of bogey monsters and otherwise bad creatures who banned together centuries ago, not unlike the Seelie and Unseelie Courts.

"You committed this crime in my realm. In fact, you are also suspected in abduction and murder of three other children from Rebecca's city."

"If you mean Ezra Rogers, Franklin Paxton, and Georgia Pines, I will admit that they too incurred my punishment in the carrying out of my duties. I am a bogey and it is my job to punish wicked children. Which in fact all four of these were."

"My son is a good boy," Sheen's mother said.

Tagone again had that smug, swarmy smile on his face. "Of course, all mothers will say that, but in my experience a mother is the one who really knows her child the least. Your so-called good child snuck out into the surface city above, a detail he conveniently left out of his testimony," Tagone said.

"Sheen!" Fonte screamed.

"Sheen, you know you leave my protection when if you go into the city above. Is what he says true?" Mikoli's voice said, seemingly coming from everywhere around us, which made sense. The shadow had no true physical form was able to speak only through magic so there was no reason why he couldn't throw his voice if he wished.

Sheen nodded.

"Why would you go to the city above?" the living shadow said.

"I wanted to try a cronut. I'd seen it on TV," Sheen said.

Although it certainly wasn't a household item, people in the Undercity had learned years ago how to tap in to cable lines and there were parts of the Undercity where they were able to watch television. The cronut had been a bit of a craze a while back, a combination between a croissant and a doughnut. People would wait in line hours to get them.

"And he did indeed get a cronut. The problem was he did not have any money to pay. And even if he did, his appearance would alarm those who live above. No, he did not buy this pastry. He stole it," Tagone said.

"Sheen, is this true?" Mikoli said.

The bob of hair that was the Grogan boy bobbed up and down. "Yes. I hid in a sewer grating near a crosswalk near the restaurant. I waited until someone walked by and I reached out and grabbed the bag and disappeared back down below. It was every bit as delicious as I'd heard. I'm sorry, I know it was wrong and I'll never do it again," Sheen said.

Tagone shook his head dramatically. "And if I'd been allowed to complete my duty, he never would have. Now we only have the word of a wicked child, a meaningless promise."

"Sheen, you're done wrong and will have to make this right. You endangered all of the Shadow Clan by risking exposure in the city above. This is not something to be taken lightly. We also have rules against theft. Just because someone is not a member of the Shadow Clan does not mean that our laws do not apply to them. We will deal with your punishment later. But Tagone, it will be nowhere near as severe as the penalty for the dismembering and attempted murder of a child. I reject the notion that you can eliminate blame simply by claiming to be doing your job. This is something I know quite intimately." That much was at least true. Mikoli had once been a shade assassin.

"I'm afraid I don't really care what you think or don't think. As a member of the Disseelie Court, I hereby invoke the protection of the Pantheon Accords."

The room was filled with even more gasps, but this time Rebecca, Sagramore, and I were among the ones doing the gasping. The Pantheon Accords went back thousands of years. Back in the days when the ancient gods were at the height of their power, pantheons would sometimes cross over and clash, especially when worshipers were switching who they prayed to. The price of gods fighting is usually very dear, both in terms of the mortals hurt in the crossfire and – more importantly from the god's point of view – the loss of power. In order to keep the peace, ages ago someone got the bright idea of a peace treaty governing how the gods behaved with one another. Other groups got in on the act too.

"I invoke immunity on account of the fulfilling of duties," Tagone said. The Pantheon Accords are a good idea in theory, but the immunity clause ruined it for anyone who wasn't protected by it. And that included most people. You had to be part of a group that signed the Accords to invoke its protections. The signers of the Accords met once every century to allow new groups to sign on. Every Pantheon you've probably ever heard of signed, not to mention a bunch of smaller groups, kingdoms, courts and clans.

The immunity clause was their get out of jail free card. The short version basically means that if you're doing your duty by your nature – take for instance a fire god who starts a fire which happens to burn down a forest and homes. He or she was just doing their duties to their nature and therefore the people affected were blocked from taking revenge on you. Of course, those powerful enough to sign the Pantheon Accords weren't worried about your average human. They were more worried about other signers coming after them, so people were very careful when they did in someone else's realm of power. Different groups would even trade tasks to avoid direct retaliation.

Even Mikoli looked a little distressed, although the only way you could tell is that the darkness that made up his shadow form had a flicker of stillness. "The Shadow Clan is not a signer of the Pantheon Accords." As a matter of fact, rumor has it that the living shadow did apply, but enough of the signers were upset with Mikoli for taking in strays and protecting them that they blocked him outright. "And this crime occurred in my realm therefore, you will face my justice."

The red-legged scissors man shook his head and made a tsk sound. "One should never dismiss the Pantheon Accords. By doing so you're given me the right to invoke liberty by immunity from the Accord enforcer. I, Tagone, of Disseelie Court, hereby invoke the protection of the Pantheon Accords and I summon Sekhmet. I summon Sekhmet. I summon Sekhmet."

At the third saying of the goddess' name, Rebecca cursed and there was a flash from an influx of mystic power to the right side of the bogeyman. A woman was standing next to him, but again I was using the term loosely. She had the body of a woman, but the fur and head of a lioness. Back in the height of the Egyptian pantheon's power, Sekhmet had gone a little mad and destroyed an entire city. She would've destroyed more if the cat-headed goddess Bast hadn't stepped in to stop her. There was some punishment after which she broke from her pantheon. When the Pantheon Accords' former enforcer was no longer able to fulfill the duties, Sekhmet took up the position.

A typical goddess is dangerous all on her own, but Sekhmet was probably the single most dangerous being on the planet. And it wasn't because of her powers as a goddess. Each signed member of the Pantheon Accords has to give a portion of their power to the Accords. It both binds them and strengthens the Accords. The enforcer is able to channel those powers. Each one is a fraction of the person who donated them, but there are a great many of them. I doubt even Nemesis could take her in a fair fight and from what I've heard they've bumped heads a few times.

Just because she was Egyptian didn't mean she stuck with the fashions from centuries before. Sekhmet dressed something like a biker, with black leather pants and a black leather vest with no shirt. She had bracers on her wrists and Egyptian looking necklaces around her throat and upper chest. There was a sword strapped across her back and a pair of guns in a belt around her waist. There was also a knife strapped to the outside of each of her black boots.

Sekhmet looked around her, as if unsure of where she was. Unlike a normal goddess who can choose whether or not to appear when her name is said three times, Sekhmet had no choice but to appear when she was invoked by a member of a group that signed the Pantheon Accords.

It didn't mean she had to be happy about it though. And she wasn't, at least if her grabbing Tagone around his throat and lifting him up by his neck was any indication

"I was busy. I hate you little pissants who think just because you're a member of a club that signed the Accords that you can summon me anytime you like. The Accords are very specific. You can't summon without reason. And if you don't have the right reason, you're never going to summon me again."

Tagone tried to speak but it came out garbled because of the hand squeezing his throat. The woman with the lion's head tossed him on the ground. With his arms chained behind his back, he fell hard.

A few attempts later, Tagone said, "I called upon you in full accordance with the Accords. I was being true to my nature and duty and thus claimed immunity from punishment and was denied it. I invoke liberty and a balancing with one who does not recognize the Pantheon Accords."

The shadow stood up from his throne and did the trick with his voice being everywhere again. "This man killed three children and was stopped before he could kill a fourth."

"Child killings are nasty business. Unfortunately, this thing here's a night bogey and punishing children is the nature of their duty."

"I reject…"

The lion-headed woman held up a hand cutting the shadow short. "You're not a signer, so you don't get to speak." Sir Sagramore raised a pale hand. "Nobody gets to speak until I render my verdict." The Dead Knight frowned and lowered his hand. "I'll investigate what happened. If the bogey is telling the truth, he goes free." She turned to glare at Tagone. The ferocity of the look made him use his feet to crawl away. "But if he deviated one iota from his nature, I will kill him myself for interrupting and ruining my spa day."

The goddess closed her eyes. Mikoli started to move forward, but somehow Rebecca caught his wrist and held him back. Despite the living shadow's power, he was no match for the enforcer and the brief second he'd have before she retaliated would not be enough for him to kill her.

Sekhmet probably had more powers than a magi. Several

members had the ability to see the past or future. The goddess with the lion's head could merge those abilities together and watch events unfold as easily as a normal person could watch TV and she was probably doing just that.

Sekhmet opened her eyes. "Tagone here's a nasty piece of work all right, but he did adhere to his nature. The extremes of it, but still within the boundaries. I find his claim of immunity and request for liberty to be valid. I will however out of respect for you, Mikoli, take him far away from your realm and, as a peace offering, I shall put a geas on him to never return."

The lion-headed goddess and the shadow lord locked gazes. This was a fight that Mikoli could not win, but he didn't back down easily.

"There is no shame in conceding to my demand. There are none on this world who could stand against me for long. In fact, many may be impressed that you were able to get a concession from me as a sign of your power," the goddess said. Mikoli nodded. "So, if you do not move to bar me from taking him from your realm, we shall leave with my promise that he will never return. And if he does defy that, I shall kill him for you myself."

"Very well, with that concession."

Rebecca jumped off the stage and started marching towards the lion-headed woman. I moved to intercept her. Rebecca didn't have much by way of her own power and although she would undoubtedly be able to inflict a little hurt on Sekhmet, she'd pay for that with her life and the lion-headed goddess would be healed from any wound within moments. I got in front of her.

"Get out of my way, Little Mr. Consequences."

"No, Rebecca. There too many people out there who are depending on you to protect them. We can't win them all," I said.

"That doesn't mean we just stop trying," Rebecca said.

Sir Sagramore saw what was happening and stepped between us and the Egyptian goddess.

"Sekhmet, now that I may speak, I invoke the clauses of duty and loss," Sir Sagramore said.

Sekhmet raised her eyebrows. "You had more to add before I

rendered my verdict, didn't you?"

"Yes, Milady, but I was told not to speak. And now your verdict has been given so it is too late to change, which is why I am left invoking duty and loss."

Tagone managed to get himself to his feet and laughed a scornful and rather forced laugh. "Only one under the umbrella of a group that's signed the Accords can invoke either of those, Dead Knight. Go find yourself a circular bench to sit around."

Sir Sagramore laughed and it was a cold raspy thing. "The Kingdom of Camelot signed the Accords. And I have renewed my vow to Camelot on a regular basis. Therefore, I am still a Knight of the Round Table and thus able to invoke the protections of the Accords. Tagone by his actions have caused loss to one under my protection and three under my servant's. I charge that while he may be immune from Shadow Clan justice for acting by his nature, he exceeded what was required of him by taking lives instead of thumbs and two thumbs for a single pastry was in excess of any duty he may have to one under my protection. As it is my duty and nature to give protection, he must present himself to me for recompense."

"Camelot was destroyed centuries ago. You're spouting nonsense," Tagone said.

"Lady Sekhmet, Tagone is a coward and a blackheart who only invoked the Accords because he did not realize there could be any consequence for doing so. Also, to the grogan and human children of New York City above, his duty and very existence is unknown. Had the children been raised on tales of nursery bogeys, he would have been within the Accords. Where his nature crossed over mine and my servant's, he loses the blanket protection of the Accords and therefore must present himself for recompense."

"That is ridiculous. How was I to know of his nature?" the bogey said.

"How was I to know of yours? You at least knew you were in the Undercity where I serve as the Shadow's Sword, so while I can claim ignorance of your nature, you cannot do the same of mine, bogey creature."

"The dead man's got a point. What's more, I don't like you, Tagone, and Sagramore has always been respectful towards me. Sir Knight, I will consider your request so long as you understand that he must not die from your actions. I've already said I granted him liberty. My fault for stopping you from speaking before my verdict. Sir Knight, if you should forget this, then we shall see if you can finally die. And if you can't, I'll find a place to put what's left of you trapped and immobile for all eternity."

The Dead Knight gave a small bow in response. "I understand. Then in accordance with the Pantheon Accords, I hereby invoke single-blow trial by combat."

Sekhmet snickered. "Your ally the Green Knight always enjoyed invoking that. Very well. Your request is granted. You and your servant are each granted a single blow and Tagone a blow against each of you. The blow is hit or miss. Now who is your servant, Sir Sagramore?"

"I call forward my servant Rebecca," Sir Sagramore said.

"I ain't no one's servant, you worm-infested…"

I took my life in my hands to put my hand over Rebecca's mouth. "Shush. If you say you're his servant you get one free slice at Red Legs. I know it's not the justice you want, but it'd be better than nothing, wouldn't it?"

Rebecca pursed her lips for a moment. "I suppose it might be at that."

Rebecca walked up alongside the Shadow's Sword and curtsied. "Your loyal servant reporting for duty, Sir Dead Knight."

"You'll be working as an extension of me. If you kill him, she will make good on her threat to me," Sir Sagramore whispered.

"Give me some credit. One of you mostly alive in this world is worth a hundred of him dead," Rebecca said.

I walked over and whispered in both their ears. They smiled and nodded.

"What, I'm just supposed to stand here and let them stab me?" Tagone said. "My hands are still chained behind my back. How am I supposed to land my blows?"

The lion-headed enforcer stepped behind the kidnapper and

tore the enchanted manacles off his wrists as if they were tissue paper. "Once each blow is made, even if used for defense, it is done and no further attacks can be make. Should you however wish to ignore that rule and fight back, I will take you from here and kill you myself, thus preserving my verdict that you leave here alive."

"So, if they swing and miss, they can't try to hit me again?" Tagone said.

"That is correct. Or they also will answer to me."

The red-handed scissor man smiled and threw his hands down and to the side and out popped each of his index finger and thumb blades.

He looked at Sir Sagramore's short sword and Rebecca's machete size knife. "All this shouldn't be a problem. My blades are much bigger than yours. I'll take you both out and then I can get on with getting out of this dismal place. When do we start?"

"Now," Sekhmet said.

Tagone held his finger blades in front of him, prepared to swipe away any swing of sword or knife. With her knife down in what seemed like a foolish position at her side, Rebecca rushed forward and Tagone stabbed at her, only to have Sir Sagramore run in front of the Mother of the Streets and impale himself on the fingernail blades of Tagone's left hand. The red-handed scissor man was unable to move his fingers, so Rebecca stepped in with her knife and cut right through the bones and tendons, effectively slicing off all of the bogeyman's fingers. Three fell to the ground, while the two with the nail blades dangled from the dead man's chest. Tagone screamed out in pain, bringing his other hand up to try and grab his stump, his pain dulling his awareness that his finger blades were extended. Those blades plunged into the other side of Sir Sagramore, immobilizing the second hand long enough for him to take his bone blade and slice through the other wrist, completely severing that hand.

Very carefully, Sagramore and Rebecca held their weapons out to the side and backed away as Tagone fell to his knees screaming

"Grant me vengeance! They have broken the rules of the Pantheon Accords!" Tagone screamed.

"Hardly. That was explained to you and you are the one who summoned me in the first place. This is why people don't call upon me lightly. Plus, I've got things to do. Nicely played, Mr. Hex," Sekhmet said. Mystic hearing at work again.

Tagone looked up at me. I smiled and shrugged.

"Yes, it was my idea."

"Then it's you on whom I swear vengeance. Without my scissors, I am half a man. I one day will take away something from you that will make you half a man," Tagone said.

"Most of your magic power was held in those nails. You're not going to make my list of things to even think of worrying about," I said.

I would later learn to my eternal regret that this was incredibility arrogant and foolish of me.

Sekhmet grabbed the bogey by his hair and lifted Tagone up to his feet.

"I'm bleeding. You have to take care of my wounds," Tagone said.

"Not a doctor and don't care," Sekhmet said as a burst of magical energy exploded around them, teleporting them somewhere far away

Rebecca turned to walk back towards the throne. Sheen ran forward towards the dead knight.

"Sir Sagramore, are you okay?" the grogan said.

"It only hurts when I breathe and that is optional for me. I just have to get these things out of me."

"Can I help?" Sheen said.

"Sure. Get the ones in the side first."

The boy reached up and pulled by the fingers and took the nails out of his ribs. Then very carefully Sheen grabbed hold of what was left of the other hand and pulled it straight out quickly without flinching. I was impressed.

"Thank you Sheen," Sagramore said. His wounds were starting to heal, even if it was slow. Even with mystic healing abilities, magic inflicted injuries tend to heal more slowly than the mundane variety.

Sheen looked down at the partial hand and blades he held.

"Can I keep one of these?" Sheen said.

"Why?" Sagramore said.

"To remind me that there are things in the dark that are there to try and hurt me and others. And I'd like to make it into a sword like yours that I could use to stop those things."

"I think that would be a very good idea," Sagramore said.

"I can help with that. I'm thinking that because you were once stabbed by the finger blades, we might be able to rig up something where you can make the nail retract and extend just by willing it," I said.

"That would be cool," Sheen said.

"It would be. Since I was also stabbed, would you be able make me one as well? It would be nice to have it as a backup weapon," Sagramore said.

"Sure. Anyone else want one?" I said.

Rebecca made a raspberry noise. "I'm fine with my blade."

"I will hang the other two as a reminder to those that would cross the Shadow Clan," Mikoli said. "And thanks to the Mother of the Streets and her champion for aiding the Shadow's Sword in his victory over the invader to our realm."

"You're welcome. No need to be making a big deal about it," Rebecca said and started walking. "C'mon Little Mr. Consequences, I want to make it topside. A group of drunks is looking for a homeless person to beat up. I'm going to let them find me instead."

"Sounds rough to take care of all by your lonesome," I said. One of the other side effects of the curse doesn't allow me to ask someone to ask me for help or it invalidates the request.

The Mother of the Streets chuckled. "You can help if you want to."

"And then of course we'll be even."

"Keep dreaming, Hex, but I like it when you're optimistic."

THE SUMMONS

Usually when I'm summoned it's by someone saying my taken name three times and I can choose whether or not to show up. This time was a little different – I'd been summoned to the Bronx by cell phone. There were barely two dozen people in the world that I trust with my number. The lady behind the teacher's desk was one of the first people I ever believed in to stand up for me no matter what, so my not showing up was never really an option.

"Hello, Daniel James Robinson. Or should I say Mr. Hex?" She knew me by both my given and taken names. I've never bothered to learn my true name. Sure, it would up my power levels and maybe help me break my curse, but it also would leave me open to someone else finding out and gaining total control over me. Not worth the risk.

"Sister Rose, the Iron Nun." The nun who had been my fourth and sixth-grade teacher smiled, not insulted in the least by her nickname.

"They still call me that you know."

"I don't doubt it." Sister Rose was one of the toughest women I ever met. She wasn't scared of anyone, be it the principal, the Diocese, or probably even the Pope himself. Back when my powers started to manifest, I got into a lot of trouble in a lot of places. Sister Rose always had my back, even when my own parents didn't. When they locked me up in a psychiatric ward, Sister Rose was the only one besides my mother and my social worker who came to visit me. The only human anyway.

"I assume this isn't a social call. Or that you finally figured out that I shouldn't have graduated fourth or sixth grade."

"I've known that for years, but that's not why I called." The Iron Nun frowned. "Sister Sophia is missing and I believe she has been taken."

"You've told the police?" I said.

Sister Rose nodded. "Unfortunately, our Mother Superior thinks the life of a nun got to Sister Sophia and she simply ran off."

"You don't think so?" I said.

"I don't. Sophia is a postulant so she can still leave the order simply by not taking her final vows. Sister Sophia has had doubts. The life of a nun is not an easy one. We forgo husbands and children of our own to serve a higher cause. I think we all on some level miss what we've given up, but those of us that stick with it believe it's worth the tradeoff. Sophia had talked to me about leaving. In fact, she'd talked to several of us, including Mother. With the exception of the higher ups, no one made her feel bad about it, so I don't think she would run off in the dead of the night without telling anyone. Both the police and Mother Superior point out that she left a note."

The Iron Nun pulled out a piece of paper and pushed it forward on the desk and she put another one next to it. "Any fool can see that the writing on the note does not match the writing on Sophia's lesson plan. I think she was kidnapped. I'm asking you to find her. Please help, Hex," she said using my taken name or the second half of it anyway.

Sister Rose's one of the few I've told about the details of my curse.

"You know I owe you too much to ever turn down a request for a favor, especially since you so rarely ask. If you think she was taken, then we'll assume that's what happened. I'd like to see where you think it took place."

The Iron Nun actually grinned. "There is a small problem with that. It happened in her cell."

It was my turn to grin. "I knew you nuns had it rough, but I wasn't aware that they had to imprison you for the night."

"You know very well that is the term they use for the tiny rooms they give us. Unfortunately, Mother Superior is exceedingly strict on her policy of allowing no men in the living quarters of the convent," she said.

"So how would you suggest I examine her cell?"

The Iron Nun's grin got even wider as she reached behind her, pulling out a nun's habit and holding it up to me. "I'd guess you're about a 16 or 18 women's long?"

"I feel ridiculous," I said, having put on the habit and the veil.

The Iron Nun chuckled under her breath. "And you look quite silly too. But unless you want to use magic to get it done, this is the best option."

Sister Rose knew that even when I could use magic, it caused me pain. Whatever I cast tended to bounce back on me at a lesser degree. At the very least I got headaches that could progress to incapacitating migraines. If I used too much magic I passed out, which could have deadly consequences. Saving the magic for when I needed it was always a prudent thing to do.

"Aren't the other nuns going to notice that one of these things is not like the other?" I asked.

"With the exception of Mother Superior, we are all worried about Sister Sophia. I told those I trust that I was calling in outside help," the Iron Nun said. "Keep your head down and hope no one tries to take a look at your face."

There were times that I sported facial hair. Fortunately, this wasn't one of them.

We were met at the door of the convent by five nervous nuns.

"Mother is in her office," one whispered.

Sister Rose nodded. "Let's get him in and out quickly."

A moment later I was in the center of a convoy of nuns moving toward the staircase. The penguin brigade had to be one of the most interesting camouflages I was ever involved in. My head stuck up a few inches higher than even the tallest nun, so I had to slouch.

The nuns' cells were on the third floor. They kept in formation even in the stairwell.

"Sister Sophia's cell is …" Sister Rose started, however I was already moving toward the room. Among my abilities is to the power to do a reading on people or places and pick up on things that had happened. Usually, it's just recent happenings, although if something particularly powerful went down it could linger for centuries. Something bad had happened in the missing sister's cell.

It was easy to tell. Trauma makes emotions run dark for the victims and leaves powerful psychic residue. The place was covered in it, but the intensity of the emotions actually covered up the specifics.

"Sister Rose, you were right. Sophia was taken. It is hard to get an exact reading, but it appears to have been three men, although men may not be the most accurate term. I'm seeing fangs and a hunger for blood," I said.

"Vampyres," Sister Rose said. I nodded. "Is Sophia okay?"

"When she left here she was scared, but they didn't cause her any lasting physical harm. I'm getting words that seem to be somehow tied into the why. Virgin and a website address." I pulled out my smartphone and typed in the web address. Virgins had many uses in magic, the most common and deadly of which was as a sacrifice to summon something from another realm. Purity had power that things in the dark didn't.

I started to curse when I realized who I was standing next to. I managed to switch to "Crap!"

"What is it?" she asked.

"Some idiot posted a translation of what he claims is a page from the Necronomicon," I said.

"I thought that was just something in some horror stories by Lovecraft," Sister Rose said.

"There is a lot more to it than that. The Necronomicon is not the only book of its kind but is the most famous among the general populace. There have been copies made of it over the years. The only thing that has prevented it from being mass marketed is that the contents have a tendency to drive those that read it – or even typeset it – mad. Unfortunately, the moron that did this wasn't quite so stupid. Posting one portion of it isn't enough to drive the human mind insane. In fact, it's broken up into sections, so the whole thing can't be read without clicking to the next page. Prevents crossing over into rubber room territory." The Iron Nun and I shared a look as we recalled when I lived in that particular territory. She gave me a sad smile. "Smart in an evil kind of way."

"So, you think they're going to sacrifice Sister Sophia in a ritual?" she asked. I nodded. "How long do we have?"

"This wiki of destruction says midnight tonight. It also lists the best place to perform the ritual, which is odd because this is a summoning ritual, not a freeing one. It depends on cosmic alignment. Location doesn't matter."

Sister Mary, the nun on guard duty in the hall rushed in, shutting the door behind her. "Mother is coming."

"Crap." That time it came from Sister Rose. I raised an eyebrow at her, hiding a smile. "Hex, you need to hide. Sisters form a wall."

All six nuns lined up in front of me while I searched desperately for a place to get out of sight. No room under the bed and the tiny closet had only a tiny plastic accordion door. That left the window. We were three stories up. No ledge to speak up, more of a brick molding. I debated about using magic to vanish, but I'd need to be in fighting shape tonight to stop this summoning.

"Damn it," I whispered and got a glare from the Iron Nun. "Sorry."

"Don't be sorry. Disappear," she said.

Rolling my eyes, I climbed out the window and stepped with my toes onto the tiny brick outcropping and fingers gripping onto matching protruding brickwork on the top of the window frame. I moved over so I couldn't be seen from inside.

The door squeaked open. "What are you all doing in here?" Mother Superior asked, her tone scolding.

"We're looking for clues as to what happened to Sister Sophia," the Iron Nun said.

Mother Superior sighed. "Rose, we've discussed this. Sophia simply left the order. There's no foul play involved."

"I respectfully disagree," Sister Rose said. Silence fell, took a look at all the nuns, then stood up rather embarrassed by the whole matter and apologized for the disturbance.

"Why are you all standing like that? Hiding something?"

"We aren't hiding anything in the room," Sister Rose said. Mother waved and there was a parting of the nuns.

Mother Superior searched and found nothing, but checked the closet anyway. "Rose, close that window. The rest of you go downstairs and help get dinner ready."

"Yes, Mother," the nuns said in unison, the rest leaving the Iron Nun behind.

She leaned out the window and looked over at me. "I seem to remember you trying to get out of a math test in a similar fashion once."

"Only you were waiting for me on the ground," I said. The Iron Nun had never been anybody's fool.

"Are you okay out there or do I need to sneak you inside and out the back door?"

I sighed and looked at what I hoped was a sturdy drainpipe. "If I take my time, I should get down fine."

"So, you'll rescue Sister Sophia?" she asked.

"You know I'll do my best," I said.

"That's all I've ever wanted from you. It just took you a while to realize how good your best was. Thank you, Daniel. Leave the habit behind the bush and I'll get it later."

The Iron Nun shut the window. I climbed down to ground level, ditched the habit and headed to the subway to get the PATH train to Hoboken.

Magic can make it easy to walk around undetected, but people who depend too much on it tend to get sloppy. It tricks regular people, but a good mage can often sense a spell or set wards to do it for them. Thanks to the curse, I've learned other ways to sneak around. Checking for both mundane and mystical alarms is crucial. So is seeing if anyone is home. If they are, a distraction is the way to go.

The warehouse had no security system beyond a locked window which didn't take me a minute to get through. I didn't make any noise. Even if I had, I needn't worry about a distraction. It was being supplied for me thanks to a screaming match between a couple of vamps, some gangbangers, and geeks in velour robes.

The argument was all kinds of wrong. The bangers wore Stormer colors. They were still banned from NYC and I was surprised they were brave enough to come to Hoboken. Their numbers gave them a decent chance against the pair of vampyres. However, the high school nerds shouldn't still be standing. Not only did most of them have poor sewing skills – most of the stars and moons on the full-length velour robes they sported were falling off or held on with duct tape or staples, with one exception and I was guessing his mom did it – but none of them showed any significant mystic ability. Stormers or vamps normally kill or feed on the weak who get in their way. Instead, they were arguing with the geeks as equals.

It didn't make sense.

I did some more recon. There was a guy hiding in the corner with a video camera, maybe a reporter in over his head. Or maybe not.

"Cut!" yelled a man with a ponytail who stepped out of another corner, a second cameraman in his wake. "I'm not buying this. You are all competing for the chance to raise Hzthar the Flayer, not a free pizza."

"I'd rather raise Cthulhu," said one of the geeks. "Ph'nglui mglw'nafh wgah'nagl fhtagn."

"Idiot. We'd have to go to the Pacific," said the geek with the decently sewn robe. "We barely made bus fare."

"Then Goser," said geek one.

"Goser isn't even real. That was a movie," said geek two.

"Excuse me, big person talking here. All of you pay attention or none of you will be on *So You Want to Summon Hzthar* or win the prize of one million dollars and world domination," said the man who was obviously a director of the worst reality show ever conceived.

As the director lectured the others on how to be better actors, I snuck into the next room of the warehouse and, after doing a reading, couldn't decide whether to tear the place down on their heads or simply turn the lot of them into puddles of primordial goo.

Three people were tied up in chalk circles. Sister Sophia, stripped naked, was in one. My first instinct was to turn away. After all those years of Catholic school it seemed wrong to look at a nude in that condition. A blond teen girl, who my reading told me was a local spokesperson for chastity, was also bound without clothes. Last and most infuriating was a newborn girl who was crying and with good reason. Not only were her day-old limbs being pulled apart, but the Stormers had carved their gang sign onto her stomach.

There was another camera crew in here. Standing above each of the sacrificial victims was someone with a long blade. A vamp over the nun, a geek in a robe over the teen, and a Stormer over the baby.

There was another director barking instructions. This one was shaved bald with a soul patch. "Now remember, we only get one take. Action."

Damn, it wasn't even midnight. I counted at least a dozen vamps, more than double that in Stormers and a half dozen geeks plus production people. Too many for me to stop magically with anything shy of mass murder. Not that people who would be a part of killing three innocents don't deserve to die, but I'm not about to dirty my soul by slaying them in cold blood. There is a Hell. I've been there and I've pissed them off. There's no way I'm letting them get ahold of me in the afterlife.

Time to try something insane to stop the blades from going down. I put on my sunglasses, pulled up the collar on my leather jacket and walked into the middle of everything like I owned the place.

"Stop! Who authorized this shot? This production value sucks," I said with all the aloof attitude I could muster.

"Cut!" the soul patch director said. "Who the hell are you?"

"You should damn well know who I am. I'm the one who can shut you down," I said.

"You're from the network?" Soulpatch said with a bit less attitude.

I looked down the end of my nose at him. "This is horrible. Where did you learn to direct? On YouTube? Did you even bother to look at the shot? Sure, you have naked women, but besides tying them up, did you give even the slightest thought to their makeup?

A little rouge to enhance the breasts, some shading to enhance the abs. And look at those blades." I walked up to the vamp over Sister Sophia and held out my hand. "Give me that." The vamp actually listened. I turned to the Stormer and the geek. "That goes for the rest of you. Hand them over." They also obeyed. I tucked two in my belt. "Do these knives scream human sacrifice or Crocodile Dundee wannabes? Well?"

"Well, they were big and we got them on sale at the army surplus," Soulpatch stammered.

"So now we are cutting corners on the most important prop in the show?" I said. "And you have them tied up with rope? Anybody could come along and cut them free and then where would you be? Is a chase scene going to help the story along? Chains, the script I saw specified chains. Where the hell are the chains?" I turned on some guy in a dress shirt holding the director's coffee. "Was it your job to get the chains?"

The guy looked like he was about to cry. "No…"

"Well, it is now. Get me my chains. Run!" I shouted and he did. "I'm not letting you shoot one more frame until this is fixed." I bent over and used one of the knives to cut through Sister Sophia's binding. "I want makeup over here now."

I pulled the nun up and she tried to slap me. I caught her hand and whispered, "The Iron Nun sent me. I'm getting you and the others out of here."

I turned around and was almost nose to nose with a half dozen vamps.

"She belongs to us. I know the rules. No sacrifice means we lose. How do we know you aren't a plant for one of the other teams?" said a vamp whose shirt was open to his navel.

"Because I'm not with the network, but you may have heard of me anyway. I'm Mr. Hex."

The vamps took a step back and I heard a Stormer curse. I've put down a lot of killer vamps in my time. Some Stormers and I had a run-in that didn't go so well for them. No one else had any idea who I was. In fact, one of the geeks hadn't even stopped chanting the invocation.

"And the lot of you are going to stop this insanity, let the victims go and walk away. This is your only warning." If they choose to ignore it, the onus for what happens next gets put on them.

"Get this smuck off my set," Soulpatch screamed.

The vamp behind Openshirt rushed me. His mistake.

There are different type of vamps. Can't kill them all the same way. One way that almost always works is decapitation.

"*Super-duper*," I whispered, mystically upping my strength and speed as I swung the huge knife clear through his neck. And unlike TV and movies, vamps don't conveniently turn to dust when you kill them. I caught the head before it hit the ground, which was made even more impressive by the headache the spell had given me.

Which is when the chanting geek stopped speaking and smiled. "Team Wizard is done. Kill the slut and we win!"

I tossed the head at the nearest vamp and dove for the teen victim, cutting through her ropes. Two Stormers rushed me. My blade sliced their Achilles tendons, dropping them to the ground. I yanked the teen to her feet and shoved her toward Sister Sophia.

Unfortunately, the remaining Stormers teamed up with the vamps and got between me and the baby. A Stormer pulled out a switchblade and made for the infant. I wasn't going to get there in time.

But luckily a Calvary of penguins did. The Iron Nun put herself between the baby and the banger, grabbed his wrist and brought her knee up into his groin. Not only had she grown up in the Bronx, but she teaches the self-defense course at the church.

The Stormer doubled over, then passed out from the pain. Two vamps tried to jump her from behind, but Sister Mary lifted up a giant crucifix and smacked them upside the head with it. Funny thing about religious symbols and vamps – the wielder has to believe for it to work. Normally it would make them cringe, but powered by the faith of a nun it became a flamethrower. Where it touched them, their flesh burst into fire. Another nun was already on her knees and untied the baby's ropes before racing away with the infant. The other three nuns had already grabbed hold of

Sister Sophia and the teen girl and were almost to the back exits. Sister Mary backed up the nun with the infant and they joined the getaway parade.

I got between the exit and the would-be summoners. Sister Rose planted herself at my side, her crucifix at the ready. An uzi would have been more practical.

"How'd you find me?" I had purposely not let the Iron Nun see the website or warehouse address because I knew she'd try a stunt like this.

"I have your cell number and a former student works for your carrier. I had him trace your GPS," Sister Rose said.

Normally I'd be angry, but the penguin brigade had just saved the hostages. A bunch of Stormers pulled guns.

"*Water bullets,*" I intoned, turned all the gunpowder in the building to H_2O. I stumbled but caught myself before I went down. Stormers were clicking off useless shots as the getaway brigade cleared the building. "We have to go after them. On foot they don't…"

"We have the church van. And Sister Nancy loves her NASCAR. She grew up racing stock cars. They'll never catch them."

I figured we were out of the woods, but a quick-thinking evil genius Stormer put us back in the foliage by stabbing the chanting geek with a stiletto. Turns out the geek was a virgin and since he had already done the ritual, a small gate of pure darkness formed in front of them.

"Team Stormers win the million bucks and control of the world!" The gangbanger was screaming and pumping his fist in the air.

Unfortunately for him, Hzthar didn't get that particular memo or read the script. The first appendage through the portal – a cross between a tentacle, silly putty, and a thousand hacksaw-shaped stalks – stabbed into the Stormer and pulled him screaming into the portal, along with the body of his victim.

The camera crew seemed to be having the time of their lives filming it. One went in for a close-up and Hzthar turned it into the extreme version by dragging him and his camera to the dark side of the portal.

Fortunately, neither had been a virgin, so the portal didn't get any bigger. Whoever wanted Hzthar to visit Jersey realized at least two things. One, the elder thing would kill everyone present when he came over and, two, that it would take more than one sacrifice to make the portal large enough for this big scary to fit through. One of the vamps figured that out and grabbed the guy who had been holding the coffee, figuring he was the most likely to be a virgin in arms' reach.

The Iron Nun smacked the vamp with her crucifix and he lit up like an inhuman torch.

"Kill the nun! That will open up the portal!" someone shouted.

The Iron Nun laughed. "You don't have to be a virgin to be a nun." And she wasn't. Rose had a troubled childhood of her own.

I was busy calculating options. If I closed the portal, I'd have to ignore the people who were trying to kill us, leaving me open to an attack from behind. If I stopped the people, I might not be able to stop Hzthar from turning Hoboken into its own killing ground.

Then it hit me.

"*Hunger*," I said, my spell hitting everyone in the room, including myself and the Iron Nun. I still had the knives. There was a form of magic that let people hit targets, so with a little focus I threw the three knives in rapid succession, I hit the thighs of the director, a Stormer and the nearest geek. The wounds would hurt, not kill them, but would spill a lot of blood. Every vamp in the building was now ravenous and I had filled the air with their favorite scent. With luck, they'd go into feeding frenzies, attacking anyone. Sister Rose still had her crucifix to stop any vamp that came near her. The rest of the room was not so lucky.

As the reality show cast and crew turned on each other, I moved toward the portal. Normally, closing a portal takes an obscene amount of magic, but as a magí, I might be able to grab hold of the magic that opened the portal and redirect it. I could feel it pulsing, waiting for another surge so the gate could open wider. What I had to do was make it reverse direction, sort of like screwing a soda cap back on a bottle filled with exploding nitro using only my ears. Much harder than it sounds, but much easier than coming up with enough power to close it, especially with the curse. The energy wanted to move, so I coaxed it out into a loop and looped it back around so it was now going in reverse. The portal began to shrink. Hzthar was not a happy elder thing and lashed out with a limb at my head. The attack was blocked by a nun swinging a giant metal crucifix like it was a baseball bat. The religious symbol itself didn't hurt the monster, but the physical blow startled it long enough for me to shut the portal and amputate the appendage.

Problem is, the link was still open at the microscopic level. Any virgin that died in the immediate vicinity could open it up again, whether or not the death was a sacrifice. It had to be sealed off. At the tiny size, it would only take a fraction of the power it would have moments earlier. That much power I could manage, even with the curse.

"*Shut the front door,*" I intoned and the universe sealed off the breach like it was never there.

"It's done?" Sister Rose asked.

I nodded. "Thanks for the save. I owe you."

"I'll add it to the list," she said. "What about the rest of them?"

I smiled. "I don't have to save up power anymore. They are all going to pay, but…" I looked at Rose, a question in my eyes.

The Iron Nun answered with a nod. "I'll get you home."

I turned to the crowd. The only one the vamps had really hurt was the director, but he was alive. Apparently, he wasn't a total fool and had holy water on him. The other groups had closed ranks around their own.

Summoning up power is more than a mental exercise. Emotion makes a great fuel. Most any emotion will work, although some are more effective than others.

All I had to do was remember finding Sister Sophia, the teen girl and the day-old infant stolen from her parents for a hot fury to build up in me and mix it with my power. This time I didn't have to control it. There was enough anger to make me not care about what the curse would do to me.

"*Payback, all bodies locked and bound,*" I intoned.

Every last one of the bastards who had been involved in this atrocity suddenly froze with their limbs outstretched, then fell to the floor.

They were all breathing and those facing in the right direction turned their eyes accusingly at me. I didn't care. In fact, I smiled, despite the fact that my own limbs felt like steel bars.

"You all ignored my warning. Worst mistake ever. The lot of you will forever be trapped in the same position you offered up those women to be killed in," I said.

Sister Rose looked at me with a frown on her face.

"They'll live, but that's as close as I'm going to get to turning the other cheek," I said.

"I understand," the Iron Nun said. And unlike some other people, she truly did. She didn't like it but had witnessed the evil these people did. She knew that left unpunished they would likely commit more heinous acts. And I didn't kill them. In truth, I couldn't. Not in front of *her*.

The amputated squishy, teeth encrusted tentacle was still thrashing around and in fact inch-worming toward Soulpatch, who could only watch in horror as it writhed toward his face.

"Not so fun now, is it?" I asked. Soulpatch couldn't answer, but his pupils seemed to devour his irises. "Hmm, if you could turn the other cheek, it might buy you a few more seconds."

"Hex." The disapproving tone of the Iron Nun stopped me short. "It's one thing to punish them, but another to torment them."

"I wasn't going to let it get to him," I said, suddenly sounding like a nine-year-old trying to get out of a math test.

"I know."

"And he deserves worse," I said.

"That he does. But neither it is your place or mine to make that judgment. They will answer to a higher Authority one day for what they've done here. We all will."

"So why do I have to answer to a lower authority in the meantime?" I said, smiling to cover up my upset at being scolded.

Sister Rose curled her lip. "Don't make me get my ruler out."

I chuckled. The Iron Nun often carried a yardstick, but never once used it on a student.

We walked to the back exit. I turned back and pointed at the still moving limb of Hzthar the Flayer, then said, "*Dust.*"

It disintegrated close enough to Soulpatch that he got some in his eyes and mouth.

Unfortunately, that spell was enough for the curse to finally kick my butt. I fell against the door frame. My limbs weren't in a drawn and quartered position like the others, but it was going to be a while before I was going to be able to move them enough to walk without looking like Frankenstein's monster.

"I'm stuck," I whispered.

The Iron Nun took out her cell and called the other nuns for a ride, after which she simply bent down and put me over her shoulder in a fireman's carry. She exited and walked down the back alley away from the warehouse.

"What an embarrassing development," I said. "I hope nobody sees me like this."

The Iron nun smiled. "I did always warn you about the dangers of letting yourself get carried away."

PATRICK THOMAS is the author of almost 40 books including the beloved fantasy humor Murphy's Lore series, which includes *Tales From Bulfinche's Pub, Fools' Day, Through The Drinking Glass, Shadow Of The Wolf, Redemption Road, Bartender Of The Gods, Nightcaps* and *Empty Graves* — as well as the future space adventures *Startenders* and *Constellation Prize.*

The Murphy's Lore After Hours spin-offs star the half pixie/ogre Terrorbelle (*Fairy With A Gun, Fairy Rides The Lightning);* the former demon-possessed serial killer Agent Karver of the Department of Mystic Affairs *(Dead To Rites, Rites of Passage);* the cursed magí Hex *(By Darkness Cursed and BY Invocation Only);* Vince Argus, the Soul For Hire *(Greatest Hits);* and Negral, a forgotten Sumerian god who works as Hell's Detective *(Lore & Dysorder* and *Bullets & Brimstone).*

Co-Written with John French and Diane Raetz, his Mystic Investigators paranormal mystery series includes *Bullets & Brimstone, From The Shadows* and *Once More Upon A Time. Assassin's Ball,* his first mystery, is also co-written with John French.

He also wrote the steampunk *As The Gears Turn* and the space epic *Exile & Entrance.* He co-edited *New Blood* and *Hear Them Roar* and was an editor for the magazines *Fantastic Stories of the Imagination* and *Pirate Writings.*

Patrick's darkly humorous advice column Dear Cthulhu has been running since 2005 and includes the collections *Have A Dark Day, Good Advice For Bad People, Cthulhu Knows Best* and *What Would Cthulhu Do?*

His short stories have been featured in over fifty anthologies and more than forty-five print magazines.

A number of his books were part of the props department of the CSI television show and have been spotted on the program. Nightcaps was even thrown at a suspect's head. His urban fantasy Fairy With A Gun had been optioned for film and TV by Laurence Fishburne's Cinema Gypsy Productions. Top Men Productions has turned his Soul For Hire Story, *Act of Contrition,* into a short film.

Please drop by www.patthomas.net or follow him at I_PatrickThomas at Twitter or www.facebook.com/ PatrickThomasAuthor to learn more.

No One Is Above The Lore...
Even In Hell
Hell's Detective
IT'S NOT EASY BEING HELL'S CHIEF OF POLICE
LORE & DYSORDER
THE HELL'S DETECTIVE MYSTERIES
PATRICK THOMAS
MYSTIC INVESTIGATORS
BULLETS & BRIMSTONE
Patrick Thomas & John L. French
TERROR
GHOSTMAN AND HELL'S DETECTIVE IN
CASE OF THE MOON MANIAC
PATRICK THOMAS / BLAIR WEBB
GHOSTMAN
HELL'S DETECTIVE
DANTE
"Gritty, snappy, very dark
and very funny."
-J. L. Comeau,
Creature Feature
"Dark... and charming."
-ELLEN DATLOW
The Best Horror of the Year Vol.4

MURPHY'S LORE
STAR TENDERS
FROM BEHIND THE BAR TO ACROSS THE STARS
PATRICK THOMAS

MURPHY'S LORE
CONSTELLATION PRIZE
"HILARIOUSLY INTELLIGENT!" —LUKE REVIEWS
TALES OF THE
STAR TENDERS
FROM BEHIND THE BAR TO ACROSS THE STARS
PATRICK THOMAS

One Last Chance to Save
Happily Ever After

Can a group of heroes including Goldenhair, Red Riding Hood and Rapunzel help General Snow White and her dwarven resistance fighters defeat the tyrannical Queen Cinderella? And will they succeed before a war with Wonderland destroys everything?

Their only hope to stop Cinderella's quest for power lies with a young girl named Patience Muffet who carries the fabled shards of Cinderella's glass slippers.

Roy Mauritsen's fantasy adventure fairy tale epic begins with *Shards Of The Glass Slipper: Queen Cinder.*

"Fantastic... A Magnificent Epic!"
-Sarah Beth Durst author of *Into The Wild & Drink, Slay, Love*

"The Brothers Grimm meets Lord Of The Rings!"
-Patrick Thomas, author of the *Murphy's Lore* series

"Shards is a dark, lush, full-throttle fantasy epic that presents a bold re-imagining of classic characters."
-David Wade, creator of 319 Dark Street

"Roy Mauritsen's enchanting epic comes at a time when fairy tales are back in the forefront of our collective imagination."
-Darin Kennedy, short fiction author

PADWOLF
PUBLISHING

In paperback & e-book
Find out more at:
shardsoftheglassslipper.com
padwolf.com